Flying Solo

ZOE MAY

Copyright © 2020 Zoe May

All rights reserved.

ISBN: 9798646869280

CONTENTS

1	Chapter One	Pg 1
2	Chapter Two	Pg 6
3	Chapter Three	Pg 28
4	Chapter Four	Pg 42
5	Chapter Five	Pg 48
6	Chapter Six	Pg 57
7	Chapter Seven	Pg 69
8	Chapter Eight	Pg 85
9	Chapter Nine	Pg 106
10	Chapter Ten	Pg 113
11	Chapter Eleven	Pg 134
12	Chapter Twelve	Pg 146
13	Chapter Thirteen	Pg 156
14	Chapter Fourteen	Pg 174
15	Chapter Fifteen	Pg 189
16	Chapter Sixteen	Pg 197
17	Chapter Seventeen	Pg 206
18	Chapter Eighteen	Pg 215
19	Chapter Nineteen	Pg 234

1 CHAPTER ONE

Tonight is the night!

Tonight is the night the love of my life is going to propose. He thinks I don't know but I'm not a fool. It would have been impossible to miss the signs.

Paul's been acting shifty for weeks. First, he popped out for a run the other day and left a Google search open on the computer in our living room: 'Cost of diamond ring'. Hardly subtle.

Then, on my lunch break a few weeks ago, I bumped into him.

I work at a law firm just around the corner from Hatton Garden – London's go-to destination for jewelry. I nipped out to a café down the road for lunch, and saw Paul, hanging around outside the jewelers, eyeing a window display of engagement rings. I stopped in my tracks, unsure whether I should say hi or just scurry back the way I'd come. Paul must have sensed me looking because he glanced around and instantly spotted me. His cheeks flushed. He works on the opposite side of town so it's not like he could just dismiss the incident by claiming he was simply 'in the area'. He was clearly checking out rings for a reason.

'Hey!' I approached, smiling, trying to look casual as I walked up to him, despite the feeling of glee blowing up inside me.

Paul and I have been together for six years and I've been dying to get engaged, but I wanted him to propose. Call me a traditionalist, but I like the fairytale ideal of my boyfriend getting down on one knee, asking for my hand in marriage, wanting to spend the rest of his life with me. It's just so romantic.

'Hey,' Paul replied, smiling awkwardly.

I kissed him, raising my eyebrows slightly in a conspiratorial, knowing way, but Paul didn't react, choosing to act blasé instead, as though nothing was out of the ordinary at all. As though it's perfectly normal to make a trip across the city to peruse engagement rings.

'So… what are you up to?' I asked cheekily, resisting the urge to give him a nudge.

I glanced at the display of rings. There were some pretty ones, some *really* pretty ones, but I have to admit, I did find it a bit strange that Paul would have wanted to buy a ring first-hand when his mum gave him her engagement ring a few years ago. She said it no longer fitted, and she'd rather Paul took it to propose when he 'felt the time was right'. She was clearly trying to encourage him to make a move, but that was several years ago now, and he's never quite gotten around to it.

'Err…' Paul hesitated, glancing anxiously at a passing bus as though looking for an escape route.

Then his phone started ringing. He retrieved it from his pocket. Simon, the name of his boss, flashed up on the screen.

'Great. Better take this,' Paul grumbled, pecking me on the cheek, before answering his phone and wandering off towards the tube station.

It was obvious Paul hadn't wanted to be interrupted and I felt a bit bad that I'd spoilt the surprise, but in an effort to make him feel better, I decided not to mention our encounter. I'd pretend like it never happened and let the proposal pan out as intended. Paul seemed to be on board with this unspoken course of action and neither of us referred to having run into each other in Hatton Garden again.

But I knew. I knew he was going to propose and I've been on cloud nine ever since wondering how he's going to go about it. He came home from work a week ago with a fancy bottle of wine and sushi from my favorite Japanese restaurant. He lit candles and I felt on edge the whole evening, wondering if he'd do a cute at-home proposal. I thought I was going to find a ring tucked away in my tuna nigiri, but nothing happened. No proposal. It was just a regular couples evening in. There were no surprises in my salmon rolls.

But then, a few of days ago, Paul told me he'd booked us a table at the Italian restaurant where we shared our first date, and I instantly knew *this was the night*. Of course, it was. It was so perfect – being proposed to in the same restaurant where we'd had our very first date – a nod to how we've come full circle. The little family-run restaurant tucked away underneath a train tunnel near London Bridge may not be the fanciest or most salubrious venue imaginable, but it has sentimental value and that's what counts. Once upon a time, we were nervous wide-eyed singletons drunkenly flirting over tiramisu in that place and now we're fully-fledged adults who share a mortgage and a joint account; that restaurant is part of our *history*.

Tonight's the night and I cannot wait. I'm all warm and fuzzy inside as I get ready. I even flicked the fairy lights on around my dressing table mirror and I feel almost like a Hollywood starlet as I wind my locks around a curling wand, twisting my hair into bouncy curls. I finish styling my hair and reach into my side of the wardrobe for a dress I bought especially for tonight. Paul hasn't seen it yet. I bought it from Selfridges after work the day Paul and I put tonight in the diary. It cost quite a lot, but it's worth it: a figure-hugging black lace number with a flattering cut that enhances my cleavage and nips in at the waist. I felt confident and sexy when I tried it on in the changing room, and I knew Paul would appreciate it. It makes a change from the boring pencil skirt and blazer combinations I wear to work.

I step into the dress, admiring my pearly pink lacquered toenails as I do so. Paul doesn't realize this, but I took the afternoon off today to get ready properly. He probably thinks I'm coming straight from the office like I usually do on the rare occasions that he and I eat out in town, but I wanted to take some extra time getting ready. I spent the afternoon at a beauty salon near the office having a manicure, a pedicure, a spray tan and even a bikini wax and eyelash extensions. I wanted to look my best for the night that's going to change things forever. The night Paul and I officially become engaged. I can't wait!

Actually, I can. I've waited quite a long time. Tonight is two years overdue according to my Life List. It might sound a bit odd but when I left school, I decided I'd create a plan to follow in order to get the life I've always dreamed about. After all, dreaming alone doesn't get you anywhere. You need to take action, you need goals, you need to work for the things you want. That's been my ethos throughout my adult life. I have fun, don't get me wrong, but I know that if I don't take charge of my destiny, things could easily go awry. It happens all the time, even to the nicest people. They coast along, hoping for the best, and then before they know it, they're thirty and in a job they hate, living a place they don't like, feeling unfulfilled and frustrated. I was determined that wasn't going to happen to me so I made a Life List with clear goals and I've stuck to it.

At eighteen, I'd go to a top university to study Law. *Tick.* I'd graduate at twenty-one with a high 2:1 or a 1st. *Tick.* I'd move to London and secure a trainee solicitor position at a decent firm. *Tick.*

I'd get a close-knit group of nice, fun, caring friends. *Tick*. I'd date with the intention of finding a serious boyfriend by the age of twenty-six. *Tick*. We'd be in a stable relationship and move in together by the age of twenty-eight. *Tick*. I'd make partner at my law firm by thirty. *Tick*.

It's all gone swimmingly. All of my goals have worked out. Except one. In between moving in with my boyfriend at twenty-eight and being made partner at my firm by thirty, I was meant to get engaged. My boyfriend and I were meant to get married and that simply hasn't happened. That's the only goal that hasn't worked out, and now I'm approaching my thirty-first birthday and wondering why that one goal has failed to materialize. Neither Paul nor I are particularly religious, but he knows I've always wanted to get hitched. He knows it means something to me, so why has he been holding back? Loads of our friends have been getting married over the past few years and after every wedding, Paul and I end up being awkward and frosty with each other for days – the lack of engagement rings on our fingers an undeniable elephant in the room. But then I get a new case at work or our house needs some renovation and I get distracted. I push it out of my mind and assure myself that it will happen, one day, I just need to be patient.

But I have been patient and finally, it's paid off. Tonight may be a couple of years late according to my Life List, but it's here now and I'm going to embrace it.

I pull the zip up at the back of my dress, arrange my hair over my shoulders, and spritz my neck with my favorite perfume. Then I slip my feet into stilettos, grab my clutch and don my coat, before heading out into the night, butterflies fluttering their wings in my stomach.

2 CHAPTER TWO

I walk down the tunnel towards the restaurant. It's an unremarkable place, self-consciously as Italian as possible. Not only is it called 'La Dolce Vita' but it has a big flag of Italy painted under the sign. And if I remember correctly, framed black and white photos of famous Italian actors are hung on the walls inside. Paul and I hadn't sought it out deliberately back on our first date, we simply stumbled upon it. I hadn't had particularly high hopes for that date. At the time, I was two or three dates into seeing a suave, cool and confident investment banker called Jared, who I thought I'd probably pursue a relationship with, even though he had a slightly annoying habit of laughing uproariously at his own mediocre jokes.

Paul and I went way back, but we hadn't seen each other for years. We both did our degrees in Sheffield, although we went to different universities. Paul was at an arts school, specializing in graphic design, while I pursued my degree in Law. We met because we both did casual waitering work for an events company. Most of the workers were students like us, and we'd don black trousers and crisp white shirts at the weekends and serve canapes or top up glasses of wine at networking events and conferences for people decades older than us. It was decent casual work and paid pretty well, and quite a few of us became friendly, going out for drinks sometimes after our shifts. I'd always quite liked Paul. I liked his thick dark hair, laidback northern charm and dimples, but quite a few of the other waitresses had their eye on him so I never went there. I didn't want drama at a job I depended on to get by and I was too focused on getting a good degree to really prioritize finding a boyfriend. I finished my course, moved to London, and as time passed, I forgot all about Paul. So, when I was standing on the Tube platform at Waterloo and spotted a familiar face that broke into a smile upon clocking me, with familiar dimples, it was a blast from the past.

Paul and I got chatting. We hopped onto the Tube together and swapped numbers, before he jumped off two stops away. We texted for a few days and agreed to meet up for drinks. I wasn't sure if it was a date or just two old acquaintances catching up, and although I quite fancied Paul, I didn't have particularly high expectations, but when we met for a drink in a bar by the river, conversation flowed. We couldn't stop talking, getting through two or three pints, before taking a riverside stroll at sunset. By the time we got to London Bridge, our stomachs were rumbling. We wandered to the nearest restaurant – this quirky Italian joint – and ate pizzas and drank wine until closing time. I broke things off with Jared the very next day, and from that moment forth, Paul and I have been inseparable. I knew he was the one.

I approach the restaurant. It still has the sign I remember, with La Dolce Vita painted in scrolling writing, but the Italian flag has gone, as have the rickety bay windows that used to be there. My heart sinks as I realize the restaurant's been refurbished. I peer through the window, desperate to see the cute little alcoves that used to be there, housing tables adorned with gingham tablecloths and waxy dripping candles stuffed into old wine bottles, but all of that's gone. It's been completely redesigned. The space has been opened up. There are no alcoves anymore. No gingham. No pictures of Italian film stars on the walls. Instead they've been replaced by prints advertising two-for-one offers on cocktails and cut-price dough balls. The restaurant looks like any other pizza franchise now, with tables lined in rows and a depressingly generic, sterile atmosphere. So much for a trip down memory lane.

I push the door open, remembering the portly owner of this place, who greeted me all those years ago like I was his long-lost daughter. He gave me and Paul free glasses of Limoncello at the end of our meal, alongside complementary gelato. He's gone and instead, I'm greeted by a young waitress with a scraped back bun and a polished but cold smile. I smile back and look across the tables, scanning for Paul. I clock him sitting at the back, eyes fixed to his phone. I point across the restaurant, telling the waitress I'm meeting 'the man in the corner'. She hands me a menu and I make my way over to Paul. The restaurant even smells different. It smelt of freshly cooked pizza dough before, but now the air smells scented, bleachy and floral. It must come from an air-freshener or cleaning products.

The tables are so tightly packed that I have to walk sideways to weave through the narrow gaps between them. Waiters zip between diners, and I overhear one upselling olives and side salads, and another telling a couple which key to press on the card reader if they'd like to leave a gratuity. I feel a little sad as I cross the restaurant. Back when Paul and I first came here, it had a convivial, relaxed atmosphere – a hearty Mediterranean vibe that felt warm and welcoming, and yet now it's more like a pizza conveyor belt, a money-making machine. But this is central London after all. Is it any surprise that a restaurant that lets broke twenty-somethings sit around chatting all night and even gave them freebies has failed to survive? Hardly. And it's not like I even mind efficient pizza joints, I love grabbing a quick margherita as much as the next person, I've just never particularly imagined being proposed to in such a place.

A couple of guys check me out as I cross the restaurant, which makes me feel a little better. At least my outfit's a winner. Although, as I near Paul, I can't really say the same about his clothing choices.

He hasn't exactly made an effort. He's wearing an old navy shirt he's had for years that's covered in bobbles. I keep telling him to get rid of it, but he refuses. He loves that shirt. And he hasn't brushed his hair either. I mean, seriously? Paul may work as a graphic designer in an arty coworking space, he may not be subject to the strict grooming and dress codes as my corporate job, but still. He is meant to be proposing today, he could have made a bit more of an effort.

He looks up and waves limply at me. I fix a smile onto my face, but I feel another twinge of disappointment. He hasn't even shaved. He doesn't even look happy. In fact, he looks quite weary and tense. Perhaps he's as deflated as I am about the restaurant's transformation. I wave back and try to be more positive. All is not lost. The restaurant may be a bit rubbish, but we can always go to a nice romantic cocktail bar afterwards and have a laugh at what a bust dinner was. Maybe Paul will propose there? Or perhaps we'll wander over to London Bridge and he'll get down on one knee with the Thames shining under the light of the moon and the city glittering in the darkness around us. That would be perfect! Maybe this has gone wrong for a reason.

By the time I reach the table, I've practically turned my mood around. I feel so confident that I want to be proposed to on London Bridge and that this twist of fate is in fact mine and Paul's destiny – a cute story to tell the grandkids – that I lean in and give Paul an enthusiastic kiss on the lips.

'You alright?' he laughs, raising an eyebrow, as though my enthusiasm has caught him off guard.

'Yes! Of course, I am,' I insist.

I take off my coat and drape it over the back of my chair. I look over at Paul, expecting him to register my dress, hoping for a compliment, but he doesn't appear to notice it at all. He's not even really looking at me. He's already ordered a beer and he swigs from it, while looking at his phone.

I sit down, willing him to put his phone away and be a bit more attentive.

He taps a few keys and then finally places his phone down on the table. He reaches for his beer again and takes another sip. The bottle's almost empty.

'Good day?' he asks in a low bored voice.

In fact, as he asks it, his gaze wanders across the restaurant towards one of the promotions emblazoned on the walls. His gaze bypasses my dress entirely. He doesn't notice my curled hair, my eyelash extensions, my make-up or anything. Instead, he simply narrows his eyes at a deal on cocktails.

'It was pretty good. I, err…' I'm about to tell him about my afternoon of pampering but he doesn't seem at all interested.

He's not making any eye contact. He's barely even registered me. I feel like I need to wave a hand in front of his face to get his attention, because his eyes are roaming from the specials board to the salt and pepper shakers and even to the faces of other diners – anywhere but me. What's he playing at? It must just be nerves but it would be nice if he could at least look me in the eye.

A waiter passes our table and I order a large glass of red. I thought they might do some traditional Italian wines like Valpolicella or Montepulciano, but they only have commonplace choices like Merlot, Shiraz, and Cabernet Sauvignon, which the waiter refers to as 'cab sav'. I order a glass of Merlot before asking Paul, who still seems in a total daze, what he's having.

'Oh!' He looks between me and the waiter, as though startled. As if he hadn't even noticed the waiter was there until now.

I frown at him, wondering what the hell is up. There's

nervousness but this is getting borderline rude now.

'Can I get you another drink, sir?' the waiter – a tall athletic guy who could easily be a model or an actor, asks.

'A drink?' Paul frowns at the waiter as though he's asked him a baffling philosophical question.

I suppress the urge to roll my eyes.

'Yes,' the waiter replies, smiling professionally.

'Oh, yeah...' Paul blinks a few times, as though reality is dawning on him. 'I'll, erm, I'll have another Heineken, please,' he says, a little hesitantly, before nodding more firmly to himself. 'Yeah, a Heineken'

'Great,' the waiter replies. 'Draught or bottle?'

Paul eyes him blankly. 'Umm, draught. No, bottle. Oh, I don't know,' he sighs, 'whatever's biggest.'

'Of course, sir,' the waiter replies politely before rapidly scurrying away from us.

'Whatever's *biggest*?!' I echo once the waiter's out of earshot.

I get that this isn't quite the romantic meal either of us had anticipated but is getting sloshed really the solution? When I pictured Paul down on one knee on London Bridge, it was because he was about to pop the question, not because he was struggling to stand up.

Paul shrugs. 'Sorry,' he grumbles.

His gaze wanders once more, uninterestedly, across the restaurant. I expect him to elaborate, to tell me that something stressful happened at work or that there was an annoying hold-up on the Tube, or *something* that's made him crave a drink, but he doesn't say anything. Silence stretches between us. I wonder whether I should make a joke about how much the restaurant's changed, but I want Paul to ask me how I'm doing or at least look at me, and yet, he doesn't seem bothered. He swigs the last of his beer.

'This place is different now, isn't it?' I venture eventually, giving up hope of him starting conversation.

'What do you mean?' Paul replies, placing his empty bottle of beer back down.

'Since we last came here! It's completely different now,' I remark.

'What? When did we come here?' Paul asks.

I laugh, rolling my eyes at what is obviously a limp effort to wind me up.

'Umm, our first date, remember?'

Paul stares blankly back at me.

'Our first date?!' I repeat, my voice nervous and a little high-pitched.

Paul frowns. 'Huh?'

My stomach does a little flip. Surely, he remembers. Surely, he's just winding me up. How can he have forgotten our first date? That's the whole reason we're here, after all.

'Yes, our first date. It was in this restaurant, but it was completely different back then,' I remind him, feeling surreal.

'Oh, right,' Paul replies, swallowing. 'Sorry, I forgot.'

'You forgot?' I balk. 'Why are we here then?'

'They have good deals on pizzas. I got a two-for-one promo voucher in my inbox the other day,' Paul tells me.

A two-for-one promo? My heart sinks. Paul loves to subscribe to discount websites that send their subscribers emails packed full of coupons and deals and vouchers. I don't bother with them myself, but Paul loves a good bargain. On the rare occasions that we eat out, Paul will often whip out a discount voucher once the bill arrives, and although I find it slightly embarrassing, it does save us money. But I can't believe it. The reason we're here isn't because it's where we had our first date, it's because Paul got a voucher. What's going on?

The waiter comes over with our drinks. He places my glass of wine down first. I thank him and bring it hungrily to my lips, dying to take the edge off what's been a terrible start to the night.

The waiter places Paul's beer down. He immediately starts drinking too.

The wine creates a comforting buzz in my stomach, and I try to relax. So, Paul may not remember that this is where we had our first date, and he may be acting a little odd, but that doesn't mean he's not going to propose. He's clearly on edge about something, and that something could well be popping the question, right? After all, proposing to your partner isn't something you do every day. I should at least try to cut him some slack and relax. I need to stop expecting everything to be perfect and just relax. Just because I've been waiting for this for two years, doesn't mean the stars are going to automatically align and everything's going to be ideal.

I reach across the table and take Paul's hand, showing I'm on his side.

'What's up?' I ask as I trace my thumb over his knuckles.

He smiles sadly.

'I love you, boo boo,' I add in a quiet babyish voice. I don't usually call Paul 'boo boo' in public. It's a pet name we have for each other that we normally use exclusively at home.

It started as 'baby', but then 'baby' became 'babes', sometimes 'bubs', sometimes 'bubby', and then 'boo boo'. At least 'boo boo' is my own personal favorite. Paul secretly likes our pet names, but tonight, it doesn't have the desired effect on him at all and instead causes his mouth to twist into a grimace.

He pulls his hand from mine and looks around at the diners seated at the tables around ours, embarrassed, in case someone overheard, even though no one else is paying us any attention. The restaurant is full of young professionals catching up after work. There's a loud hum of conversation and it's not like anyone would have heard.

'What's up with you, tonight?' I ask, rattled, my engagement fantasy thoroughly fraying at the edges.

'Nothing,' Paul replies curtly, finally meeting my gaze, his expression listless. 'I just… I don't know. What are you ordering?'

He looks down at his menu. 'I think I'll have a pizza, although the pasta dishes do look good,' he says.

'Great,' I comment weakly as I peruse the menu, but none of the dishes particularly jump out.

I take another sip of wine and look back up at Paul.

'Can you please tell me what's wrong?' I implore him.

Paul glances up from his menu. He looks irritable, fraught almost. I don't often see that look in his eyes. He looks even more despondent than he gets when Manchester United lose, which is *extremely* despondent. He even looks more downbeat than when he found out that the last company he worked for was going into administration, meaning he and all his colleagues would be laid off. He definitely doesn't look like a man who's about to pop the question. He looks like a man carrying the weight of the world on his shoulders. Suddenly, I forget about my engagement fantasy and start to feel really nervous. Has something happened? Has Paul been fired? Is he unwell?

'What is it, Paul? Is it work? Are you okay?' I ask anxiously.

Paul's always had a bit of an issue with his boss, Simon. He often refers to him as 'that self-satisfied prick', which is kind of understandable to be honest. I've met Simon a few times at drinks events hosted by the company and I have to admit, I've never exactly warmed to him. He's forty-five but still talks about his Eton days like they were yesterday. He loves rugby – watching, these days, not playing – and he has floppy foppish blond hair and a penchant for pinstripe shirts and chinos. He also has an annoying tendency to be incredibly overfamiliar. He gives everyone nicknames, although the nicknames tend to vary according to his mood. He's referred to Paul as everything from Paulo and Paulina (which he, naturally, despises) to The Paulinator (a lame twist on The Terminator) and McCartney (in reference to Paul McCartney, who neither Paul nor Simon are fans of). He also has a lax attitude to personal boundaries and doesn't think twice about calling Paul in the evenings or during the weekend if something's happened that he believes is an 'emergency' (spoiler: these incidents are never actual emergencies).

Simon's been scoring contracts with multinational corporations recently and Paul's not been particularly happy about it. The high-paying contracts haven't been reflected in Paul's salary and yet his workload has become far more intense and far less creative. Paul insists the clients he's now working for don't represent the agency's original vision, of being a 'forward-thinking, dynamic, cutting-edge design consultancy', which aimed to represent 'innovative, sustainable, game-changing brands'. Instead, Paul insists the company has become 'nothing more than a cash cow'. Those are his exact words from one of his rants last week, when he ended up bringing work back from the office and burning the midnight oil, while complaining about how pissed off he was to be 'losing sleep so Simon can buy a yacht to seduce poor unsuspecting girls off the coast of Marbella'. I get that it's frustrating for him to not be working on the innovative, edgy, exciting projects he usually prefers, but the market is tough. My company's been in the same boat too. We take on work for the highest-paying clients these days, not necessarily pursuing the cases we find the most interesting, but I don't let it get to me. I'm just grateful that my and Paul's companies are doing well. I'm thankful we're in work.

But suddenly, I get it. Paul must have finally had enough of Simon and told him as much. He must have snapped. That's why he's so spaced out and weird. That's it.

'Did you confront Simon?' I ask.

'What?' Paul looks surprised.

'About all the contracts. Did you confront him?'

'No.' Paul shakes his head.

'What is it then? Did you quit?' I ask, secretly hoping he hasn't.

I know Paul doesn't exactly love his job, but we have a mortgage to pay. We were lucky enough to get a run-down terraced house in south London for a bargain price and even though it's been quite an effort to do it up, it's our first real home and I really don't want to default on our mortgage payments and lose it.

'Huh?' Paul looks taken aback. 'How did you know?'.

My heart sinks.

'It was just a guess,' I murmur. 'So, you really quit?'

The butterflies that were in my stomach earlier because I was excited are now beating their wings because I'm just plain nervous and uneasy.

'I, err…' Paul fixes me with a serious look.

He looks as nervous and uncomfortable as I feel. He takes a swig of his beer and before he has a chance to answer, our waiter comes back.

'Ready to order?' he asks.

I order a margherita with olives, even though I couldn't be less fussed about food right now. Paul always used to take the piss out of me for loving margheritas, claiming they were the most 'basic' of pizzas, but you can't go wrong with a margherita. Paul orders a repulsive-sounding pizza with garlic and egg and anchovies, which doesn't exactly bode well for the epic engagement kiss I'd envisaged on London Bridge. Although to be fair, nothing about this evening is boding well for that.

We hand our menus back to the waiter and he heads to the kitchen.

I eagerly take another sip of wine.

'Paul, what's going on?' I ask, urging him to elaborate, while desperately hoping this whole thing is some kind of wind-up.

Paul may not be the biggest fan of his job, but he's not usually an impulsive person. He wouldn't just quit, out of the blue like that. Sure, he talks about it, but don't we all? I've had moments when I'm drowning in work and I've sworn I'm going to throw the towel in and pursue my long-lost childhood passion for pottery. I've daydreamed about starting my own quirky business, selling handmade ceramics at Greenwich market, but that kind of thing is just a fantasy. It's not like I'm ever going to actually do it. The daydream is a pressure valve, providing a nice little escape during hard times. Paul muses about stuff like that too sometimes, but he's been working in graphic design for eleven years now. He's always been steady and reliable, seeing projects through even when they're tough. He's not the kind of person who'd just wake up one day and quit their job.

Paul reaches for his pint and downs a third of it. He places the glass back on the table with a thud and wipes a moustache of foam from his upper lip, before fixing me with a foreboding look that has me hungrily taking another sip of my drink too. My stomach lurches. I can tell from the intensity in his eyes that I'm not going to like whatever it is he's about to tell me.

'I quit. I finally quit,' he states firmly. 'I'm not going back.'

'But why? What do you mean you're not going back? What about your notice period?' I ask, curious, even though talking about his notice period sounds a little pedantic and trite.

I mean, what's a two-month notice period in the grand scheme of things? Why am I concerned about that when my boyfriend is clearly having some kind of meltdown?

Paul rolls his eyes and reaches for his drink.

'In case you hadn't noticed, we haven't taken a holiday for three years, so I don't exactly have to work out my notice period. I've just booked it all off as annual leave,' Paul informs me, taking another swig of his beer. 'Today was my last day. Ever.'

'Right…' I grumble, shifting in my seat, not knowing quite how to react.

There's a lot to unpack, from Paul's dig about us not having gone on holiday to him suddenly letting me know, out of the blue, that he's simply not going back to work. I decide I'll start with the dig and work my way up to the more monumental life-changing stuff. I know I should have moved on from it by now, but underneath all the questions I have and the shock of Paul's big news, there's still a small crushed part of me, a silly hopeful part, that truly wanted to end up getting engaged tonight. I reach for my wine, eager to numb the sinking feeling inside.

'You never complained that we didn't go on holiday,' I point out, taking another sip.

It's true that we haven't gone on holiday for three years, which I know is a long time, but I never realized it was such a big issue. Instead of going on holiday, we've been spending money on doing up our house. I thought Paul and I had a mutual understanding that it was more important to get our house in order than it was to spend a few weeks in Mykonos or wherever. And anyway, it's not like we'll be redecorating forever. Eventually we'll get the house sorted and we can go on loads of holidays. I had no idea our lack of getaways was getting to Paul quite so much. If I did, I'd have suggested a break.

'If I had complained, would you have listened?' Paul huffs.

My heart lurches. Of course, I'd have listened. What is this? What's got into him? Paul literally drives us to IKEA every other weekend. Only a fortnight ago, he was assembling a cabinet for the bedroom while belting along to an Ed Sheeran song on the radio. He even picked up some gorgeous second-hand curtains and a candle holder from Habitat during his lunch break the other week. I thought he was completely on board with our project to transform our home. I didn't think he minded that we were spending our money and our weekends on the house. And yet now he's acting like I'm some kind of controlling tyrant who's forced him into living a miserable holiday-less existence.

'Of course, I'd have listened!' I tut. 'You know, it might actually have been helpful to *speak* to me rather than keeping whatever resentment you've been harboring locked up inside, quitting your job and then getting at me in the middle of a restaurant!'

A few other diners look our way. Damn. I realize I've raised my voice. I dip my head, allowing a curtain of my hair to fall, partly covering my face.

'I wanted to talk to you, but sometimes you can be a bit… overbearing, Rachel,' Paul states, his voice quiet but clear.

'Overbearing,' I scoff. 'Are you kidding me?' I gawp, staring searchingly at him.

I feel half-tempted to just get up and walk out of the restaurant. What on earth has got into Paul? I'm not overbearing. I'm just a normal woman and a normal girlfriend. I go to work, I come home, Paul and I hang out, there's nothing overbearing about me. I've never stopped him from doing anything and I certainly didn't deliberately deny him a holiday. What's overbearing is making life-changing decisions without talking to the people they'll impact. What's overbearing is character assassinating your partner in the middle of a restaurant. I want to say this, but I've already attracted enough attention from fellow diners, and I don't trust myself to voice my thoughts without losing my cool.

'Yes, you are overbearing. You just assume I'm up for doing all the things you want to do all the time, but maybe I don't like spending my weekends being dragged around homeware stores or upcycling dressing tables. I might actually be really bloody bored and unhappy, you know!' Paul barks.

Other diners look our way again. One woman rolls her eyes and shakes her head, before returning her attention to her calzone. This is mortifying. I look towards the exit. I really do want to just get up and leave, and yet I can't. I need to get to the bottom of all of this. I feel so rattled. It feels like the man sitting opposite me isn't the Paul I know, but some other incarnation. Even the slumped way he's sitting is different. His eyes are usually soft and relaxed, sleepy almost, and yet tonight they're cutting and belligerent. In a way, Paul's choice of venue is perfect, because it's almost like we're on a first date all over again. I feel like I don't even know the person sitting opposite me.

I take a sip of my drink and make a deliberate effort to steady myself.

'Paul, if you hate going to IKEA so much and you're so desperately bored and unhappy, how am I meant to know unless you tell me? Or, I don't know, express it in SOME WAY!'

The woman who was rolling her eyes two minutes ago looks over again, giving us yet another disparaging look. I roll my eyes right back at her and she quickly diverts her gaze.

'Okay, well I'm telling you now, alright?' Paul points out. 'I hate IKEA, okay? I HATE it! One trip every now and again is fine, but we've been at least once a month for two years! I hate assembling flat pack furniture. I hate upcycling furniture. I hate spending my Saturday mornings sanding stuff. I hate eating takeaways after a day spend doing odd jobs around the house. I hate being your unpaid handyman. There's only so much a person should care about furnishings and you've pushed me. I reached my limit a long, long time ago. I'm bored. I am so bloody bored!'

I look down at my lap, wishing the ground would swallow me up. I know people are looking, but I don't care anymore. My hurt has eclipsed the embarrassment. How can Paul act like I'm such a bad person and I've done such terrible things, when all I wanted was a nice cozy home for us. Okay, I might have taken my interest in home furnishings a bit too far sometimes. And okay, I might have started an Instagram account dedicated solely to the interior of our house, featuring before and after shots of different rooms and images of old junk furniture we've managed to do up, as well as wallpaper cuttings, color schemes, shots of pretty curtains and stuff like that. I get that it's a bit middle aged and maybe quite uncool, but it's not like I've cheated on Paul or lied to him or been emotionally abusive, and yet from the way he's acting, you'd think I'd done something terrible, truly terrible.

I glance up. His hands are clenched into a ball on the table, his jaw is tight, his eyes burning. He looks like a ball of rage. You'd think I was the worst person on earth looking at him.

'Okay, I'm sorry. You hate DIY, I get it. I'll stop involving you in it. We can stop spending so much time and money on decorating,' I relent. 'But why have you quit your job? I get that you don't like it, but what about….' I trail off.

'What about what, Rachel?' Paul spits.

I don't reply.

'You were about to say, "What about the house?" weren't you?' Paul sneers.

I gulp. I look away. Okay maybe he's right and I was about to say that, but I don't want to lose the house. We've worked so hard on it.

'Seriously,' Paul scoffs, shaking his head.

The waiter comes over and places our meals down. In spite of everything, my margherita looks pretty good. It's piping hot, the cheese bubbling, and yet, I don't feel like eating anymore. The waiter offers us parmesan and we accept, half-heartedly. After grating it on our pizzas as we sit in tense silence, the waiter retreats.

Paul stares at his pizza but doesn't touch it. He shifts in his seat.

'I… I… I need a change,' he says, wrenching his eyes up at me, his expression desperate, almost imploring.

'Okay… What kind of change? What kind of job *do* you want?' I ask, lifting a slice of my pizza and tentatively taking a bite.

It's nothing like the delicious smoky woodfire pizza we had last time we were here, but it's tasty nonetheless. It's a decent margherita, and I need something tasty and familiar amid all this confusion.

'I don't… I…' Paul fingers the crust of his pizza, peeling back a slice.

He looks at it, as though contemplating taking a bite, but drops the slice, sighing. He pushes his plate aside and buries his head in his hands instead.

'I'm not getting another job,' he tells me, eyeing me warily, before nervously looking away again.

'Umm… Okay…' I reply.

I'm trying to keep my composure, aware that other diners are still casting the odd glance in our direction, but this conversation is testing my patience.

'Paul, what are you talking about? If you're not getting another job, what are you going to do? Am I going to support you, because if that's the case, don't you think we should have spoken about this? We should have worked out a budget, decided how it's going to work. You shouldn't just spring stuff on me like this!'

I might have got a bit shrill at the end, but I think I mostly kept my cool.

'A budget,' Paul tuts. 'That's so you.'

I scoff, my reserve of sympathy and understanding running dry.

'Okay. So you're offended that I would have liked to have thought about a budget to support you with this major life decision? Fine,' I sneer, rolling my eyes.

'I don't need your support,' Paul states, regarding me coldly.

'Okay, so how are you going to live then?'

'I won't need much,' Paul insists, finally picking up his slice of pizza and taking a bite.

'Right… I mean, we do live in London, Paul. It's not exactly cheap,' I point out.

Swallowing, Paul places his pizza slice back down. He takes a long deep breath.

'I'm not going to be in London anymore,' he says, meeting my gaze.

His expression is cold and tough, but a flush appears on his neck that he always gets when he's anxious.

Now I have absolutely no idea what's going on.

'So where are you going to live?' I ask imploringly, my voice tremulous with frustration.

'Sorry…' Paul sighs, a note of empathy appearing in his frosty eyes.

He sits up straighter, almost formally, and fixes me with a steady gaze.

'I'm sorry Rachel, but I need a break. I need to get away. I can't do this anymore. I'm going to India,' Paul blurts out, with a sad, apologetic smile.

'*India?*' I echo.

'Yes. I need to get away,' Paul reiterates.

'So, you're going to India?' I laugh.

Surely this is a wind-up? As if he's actually going to India!

'Yes,' Paul confirms flatly, without a trace of humor.

'What?' I utter, a shiver of dread flowing through me, as it dawns on me that he might be serious. 'What the hell are you talking about?'

'I need to get away, like I said. And I'm going to go to India, where it's cheap and I can support myself. I want to clear my head, take some time out,' Paul tells me.

'But India? It's so far…' I stammer, unable to take it in. 'What are you going to do there? Travel around like a hippy? You're having a mid-life crisis,' I conclude.

Paul shrugs. 'Maybe I am, but it is what it is.'

'Oh right, okay. It is what it is, is it?' I parrot back at him.

I'm aware that I probably sound a bit erratic now, but I don't care anymore. My boyfriend of six years has randomly decided to jet off to the opposite side of the world. How am I meant to feel if not a bit erratic?

'I can't believe this,' I balk. 'What are you going to do? Find yourself?!'

'Stop taking the piss, Rachel,' Paul snaps. 'Maybe I am going to find myself. What's wrong with that?'

'You're thirty years old!' I snap. 'You're not an 18-year-old on a gap year. Haven't you found yourself already? I mean, who have you been for the past thirty years if you haven't?'

'I don't know…' Paul admits in an ominously quiet voice, his eyes strained, pricking with tears.

My anger dissipates slightly as I glimpse the sadness in his eyes. Paul rarely gets emotional. Maybe that's why I haven't noticed how unhappy he is. He has this stoic northern mentality that means he's rarely moved by much, seeing emotional outpourings as self-indulgent or weak. Maybe he has been unhappy and felt the need to just carry on like nothing was happening, locking down how he really felt. Perhaps I should have checked in with him more. We probably should have discussed our priorities around DIY and holidays. I shouldn't have automatically assumed we were on the same page. Maybe I have pushed him too hard.

'Okay fine, we'll go to India, have a proper break. We'll sort this out,' I insist, smiling encouragingly.

So tonight hasn't gone exactly as I wanted it to and I'm definitely no closer to getting engaged, but love is about sticking by someone during the good times and the bad. It's about doubling down when things get tough. Going to India isn't exactly at the top of my bucket list, but if that's what it takes for Paul to feel better again, then so be it.

'No, Rachel. This is a holiday for *us*, it's a holiday *from us*. This is something I want to do alone. I don't want to "sort this out",' Paul insists exasperatedly, doing air quotes. 'I want to leave.'

'Leave?' I croak, my head spinning.

'Yes, I'm leaving the country, and I'm leaving you,' Paul states, sadly but firmly, his expression chillingly serious.

He's leaving me. I blink, unable to quite take it in.

'But… but… what about the ring?' I ask, picturing him lingering by the jewelers near my work, checking out engagement rings.

'The ring?' Paul frowns. 'What ring?'

'I thought…' I feel my cheeks start to flush. 'I thought you were buying an engagement ring?' I ask.

'Oh God.' Paul groans, lowering his head into his hands, looking as mortified as I feel.

'What is it?' I utter.

'I wasn't buying a ring,' Paul tells me, looking sheepish. 'I was selling one.'

'What?'

'I sold my mum's engagement ring to fund my trip,' he tells me.

His words hang in the air between us. My dreams cave in. I'm a fool. Ever since I saw Paul outside the jewelers, I've had a spring in my step. I've felt excited to be moving on to the next phase of my life. I've been able to 'like' pictures of friends' weddings on Facebook without feeling that increasingly familiar twinge of sadness that it's not me walking down the aisle. I've felt hopeful for the first time in ages. I even bought the stupidly expensive dress I'm wearing because I was so convinced Paul was going to pop the question and instead, he's ending things. He's ending our entire six-year relationship. He's pawned a family heirloom that his mum wanted him to propose with in order to jet across the world. Alone.

'I'm sorry, Rachel,' Paul says, looking guilty.

'It's okay,' I utter. 'It's fine. I understand. Enjoy India.'

I stand up suddenly, causing my chair to screech back across the floor. I grab my coat and my bag and turn to leave, my pizza uneaten on the table.

'Rachel, don't…' Paul protests, although his tone is half-hearted and the shamefaced look in his eyes tells me he wasn't exactly expecting this to go swimmingly.

I blink back tears as I hurry away.

3 CHAPTER THREE

It's fine. I'm absolutely fine. So my boyfriend's going to India to find himself. It's cool. So, he didn't come home last night. No big deal. So I got home and opened his side of the wardrobe and found that he's removed all his clothes. No problem. He needs something to wear while he's over there, right?

I'm fine, I tell myself for the four hundredth time this morning as I stand in the rattling Tube carriage on my way to work. I'm exhausted from a night of tossing and turning and trying to convince myself this is all just a bad dream, and yet I'm simultaneously wired from having mainlined practically two litres of coffee when I got up. I'm fine, I tell myself again as a Transport for London announcement momentarily pierces my mantra, to inform me that we're at Chancery Lane station. What?

Damn. I barge through the throng of passengers, dodging sweaty armpits and morning breath and papercuts from people holding copies of Metro, before bursting free onto the platform. Great, just great. I was so lost in my own self-pitying, yet defiantly un-self-pitying thoughts, that I completely lost track of where the hell I was and missed my stop. I've never missed my stop, zoning out like that. Not in the eight years I've worked for Pearson & Co.

'Oh no,' I grumble, looking down at my watch.

I'm meant to be at work in five minutes and now I have to backtrack two stops. I walk as fast as I can through the crowd of commuters, trying to get to the opposite side of the platform.

'I was reading that,' a man in his sixties or seventies tuts as I plough past him so forcefully that I accidentally cause him to drop his copy of The Guardian onto the ground.

'Sorry,' I throw over my shoulder as I dash further along the platform.

The man shakes his head at me, before gingerly bending down to pick up his paper. I feel like a total pariah - the worst woman in London. Not only does my boyfriend, or ex-boyfriend as I should probably start referring to him, want to get away from me so badly that he's pawned his mother's engagement ring in order to jet halfway across the world, but I've just knocked a newspaper out of an old man's hands. I'm about to turn around and go back to help him, and properly apologize, but it's too late. The man is stooping down to grasp his paper from the ground, but just as he's about to reach for it, a train pulls into the platform and half a dozen commuters burst off, treading all over the pages.

I gasp, feeling terrible. The man shakes his head disappointedly and hobbles onto the train, abandoning his trampled paper. I try to push the shameful episode out of my mind and dash across the station to the opposite platform, where I stand, staring at the arrivals display, which informs me that the next train will be arriving in ten minutes. Ten minutes! Honestly! I tap my stilettoed toe impatiently against the ground, as if doing so might somehow make the train arrive faster.

Finally, after what feels like an eternity, the train decides to make an appearance and I hurry into the carriage, even though I'm fully aware that no matter how quickly I get onto the train, I'm still going to be late for work. Deep down, I know it doesn't really matter. I'm a partner at my firm after all, and in all the years I've worked there, I've always been on time. It's just frustrating that on the one day that I want to cling to the illusion that I might have just an iota of control over my falling-apart life, I'm going to be late, feeling as scatty and disorganized on the outside as I do inside.

I grab the overhead rail and try to push the negativity out of my mind and resume my pathetically weak mantra of telling myself I'm fine over and over again as the train chugs along.

By the time it arrives at my stop, I'm already fifteen minutes late for work and when I eventually get to the office, pounding the busy street in my heels, I'm a whopping nineteen minutes late. Fantastic. Just fantastic.

I swipe my pass against the sensor by the door and walk through reception.

One of the temps working at the reception desk looks over from her monitor and smiles sweetly.

'Morning,' she says brightly.

'Morning,' I chirp back, feeling a tiny bit more human.

The airy, light-filled, marble-floored reception area at work is a soothing slice of tranquility in the center of the chaotic city, and the receptionist probably doesn't know how much her friendly smile means to me on a morning like this.

I'm just about to head through the door leading to the corridor where my office is tucked away, when the CEO of the company pulls it wide open, stopping me in my tracks.

Albert Pearson, the founder of Pearson & Co, is standing before me, taking me completely by surprise. There are twenty-five Pearson

& Co branches across the country and Mr Pearson is the head honcho. I had no idea he was coming into the office today. Occasionally, he visits but I'm always well aware of it. Everyone is. We get so tense in the days and weeks leading up to a visit from him. The office is always impeccably clean. Everyone is always keen to appear effortlessly on top of their workloads. We all wear our neatest, most expensive suits and do our best to look like model employees. Of course, we muddle along pretty well at the best of times, but it's important to everyone that we give the CEO the best possible impression. Mr Pearson is quite intimidating after all.

He's an absolute force to be reckoned with, having created a network of leading law firms from nothing. He's from a single parent family in east London and his mum worked at the local launderette, yet through hard work and determination, he managed to rise from his humble beginnings to become a multi-millionaire powerhouse. Yet he's stayed true to his roots and firmly believes in supporting junior staff in getting ahead and having a workforce that's diverse and inclusive. Our firm probably has the highest number of state school educated lawyers than any other in the capital. As much as Mr Pearson intimidates me, I also have a lot of respect for him. He has better values than my boss, Nigel, who's your stereotypical money-hungry city lawyer, but Mr Pearson still unnerves me a lot more.

'Mr Pearson! What a surprise. How are you?' I reach over to shake his hand.

'Very well thank you,' Mr Pearson says, pumping my hand, his grip tight.

I suppress the urge to wince. Mr Pearson has a strong handshake, and when I say strong, I mean vice-like. I force a smile while he crushes my hand, my mind racing. What's he doing here? Why's he making a surprise visit like this? Should I be worried? One of our competitors made a huge round of redundancies recently. Could we be in for a similar cull?

'How are you doing, Rachel?' Mr Pearson asks.

Nothing about his placid friendly expression screams, 'You're about to lose your job' but he could just have a poker face. Or else his Botox is hiding how he's really feeling. Mr Pearson must be in his late sixties, but he's done everything he can to hold back ageing. His forehead is unnaturally shiny and smooth. He corrected his once-receding hairline with hair plugs a few years ago that provide a wispy and slightly unnatural-looking coverage, but it's coverage nonetheless, and his teeth have been whitened so much that they practically glow.

'I'm great, thanks!' I reply keenly, plastering on an enthusiastic smile, which I hope hides how rubbish I feel inside, although Mr Pearson will probably see through it.

Not a lot gets past Mr Pearson. I learnt that a long time ago. He has an extraordinary ability to see right through people, cutting to the quick of things. His ability to combine an almost psychic level of intuition with razor-sharp business acumen is probably what makes him so powerful. He's able to effortlessly grasp a person's strengths and weaknesses, assembling teams like an army general, with a unique ability to envision how relationships will pan out and how one person's strengths will complement another's weaknesses. I've seen him assessing new recruits on interview panels and his insights into candidates' characters and predictions of their performance have always been eerily spot-on. I often feel somewhat unmasked around him since he probably understands my strengths and weaknesses even better than I do.

'Good…' he replies hesitantly, narrowing his eyes, clearly not quite buying how 'great' I am.

He asks about one of the cases I'm working on. I specialize in tax law and I've recently been overseeing a case against a drugs company that's allegedly been underpaying tax. It's been going well, and I start to feel more confident as I fill Mr Pearson in on my progress. The case has certainly been proving more of a success than my rocky personal life.

'It sounds like you're doing an excellent job. Keep it up, Rachel,' Mr Pearson says, pumping my hand once more.

'Thank you! Great to see you again,' I say, pumping his hand back.

He smiles, but his smile is a little tight, as though something's still bothering him.

He releases me from his grip and slips past me, heading into reception. I'm about to walk down the corridor to my office when his voice pulls me back again.

'Rachel, pardon me for saying this, but I thought I should let you know, your jacket's on inside out,' he says, gesturing towards his own neat perfect-looking blazer, while smiling apologetically.

I glance at my jacket. It's a gorgeous tailored number I picked up in the Jigsaw sale a month or so ago and it's rapidly become one of my favorite items of work clothing. I put it on today because it usually makes me feel smart and confident, but in my warped emotional state, I clearly wasn't paying enough attention. I glance at the shoulder and spot an exposed seam. Mr Pearson's right. I put my jacket on inside out. Who does that?

'Thanks for letting me know,' I croak, cringing.

Mr Pearson nods, throwing a wave at me and the receptionist, before crossing reception and slipping through the revolving doors leading out of the building.

I glance at the receptionist who's now smiling at me in an awkward, sympathetic way like she's sharing in my embarrassment. I give her a squirming smile before slipping through the doors and racing to the office toilets.

Once inside, I take in my reflection. I'm a mess. My jacket's on inside out, my hair looks flyaway and messy from having been blown around on my mad dash to work and I have dark shadows under my eyes that lashings of concealer have failed to mask. My eyelash extensions, which were meant to look good for my date last night, now just look out of place and a little trashy. I look like I've been out on the town and I've crawled into work with a hangover. I groan, shaking my head. On the one day I look like this, Mr Pearson has to see me. Typical! He's probably regretting his decision to make me partner last year. I look nothing like the partner of a law firm. I don't even look like an intern; even they make an effort to look less scruffy than this.

Sighing, I pull off my jacket and put it on the right way around. I take a comb from my bag and smooth my hair. Then I lean close to the mirror and press gently on my eyebags, as if I might be able to zap them away, while staring blankly into my sad-looking eyes.

The toilet door swings open and I straighten up, plastering a professional smile onto my face in anticipation of whoever's coming in. Fortunately, it's my colleague, Priya, who I don't have to be fake around. Priya and I started working at Pearson & Co on the same day eight years ago. We were in the same intake of the firm's graduate recruitment scheme and we've been through a lot together over the years, from our first day as nervous new recruits, to our early years as bumbling trainees, to climbing the ladder with both of us managing to reach partner level. We're pretty much best friends. In fact, Priya and a couple of the other solicitors at my firm, Sasha and Julia, formed a, sort of, group. There's four of us, and it's a bit like Sex and the City meets Legally Blonde. When we're not all totally overrun with work, we go for lunches together, chatting about everything and anything, from our cases to sex and relationships and everything in between.

'Christ, what's happened to you? Heavy night?' Priya asks, raising her eyebrows.

She's never been one to mince her words.

'Hardly,' I grumble.

Back in the day, I used to have a bit of a work hard, play hard attitude, but like Paul made clear last night, my days of being fun are behind me. These days, I'm all about DIY and home furnishings, apparently.

'What's happened then?' Priya frowns at me, lingering by the sinks and eyeing my reflection.

I hesitate, wondering whether to launch into it when she starts squirming.

'Damn, I really need a wee. One sec.' She heads into a cubicle.

'So what's up?' she asks over a tinkling sound.

'Oh, I don't know,' I reply, gazing blankly at my reflection. 'I missed my Tube stop this morning, knocked a newspaper out of an old man's hand, then I saw Mr Pearson, updated him on my case, feeling all professional, only for him to inform me that my jacket was on inside-out.'

Priya bursts out laughing, before her laughter is drowned out by the sound of the toilet flushing.

She emerges a moment later, tucking her shirt into her trousers, while clearly trying to look more serious, although the corners of her mouth are twitching.

'Sorry…' she comments, still smiling slightly, before she clocks my downbeat expression and realizes that now might not be the best time to laugh at me.

'Shit, are you okay?' she asks.

'No,' I sigh. 'That's just the tip of the iceberg. Paul broke up with me last night,' I admit, flinching at how it feels to say it out loud.

'What?!' Priya balks, all traces of amusement gone from her face. 'Paul broke up with you?'

'Yes,' I croak, my voice tremulous as I fight the urge to cry.

'Oh my God,' Priya utters, her eyes wide with concern. She moves in to give me a hug.

'Err, wash your hands!' I tut.

'Ha,' Priya laughs. 'Even in the depths of despair you're still worried about hygiene.'

'Of course,' I reply as Priya rolls her eyes, squirting soap from the dispenser onto her palm before wringing her hands together under the gushing tap.

'So, what happened?' she asks. 'I thought he was going to propose.'

'Apparently not,' I sigh.

Priya has been almost as excited about Paul's proposal as I've been. Straight after I saw him outside the jewelry shop, I came back from the office and told her. Since then, we've both been gearing up to the big moment of Paul popping the question. Priya quite literally bought a hat. During her lunch break last week, she found a beautiful half-price wide-brimmed ocean blue hat in a boutique down the road and bought it to wear to the wedding. We both agreed it was a good investment. I can only hope that she kept the receipt.

I tell her the whole sorry story of last night, from how the restaurant wasn't quite how it used to be to how it turned out that Paul didn't even remember that we'd had our first date there. I recount him informing me he'd quit his job and explain that he's now jetting off to India to find himself and hadn't been buying a ring in Hatton Garden's, but pawning one.

'He pawned his mother's ring?!' Priya balks.

I nod weakly.

'That's awful. For a stupid self-discovery mission to India?' Priya sneers.

'You're Indian!' I remind her.

Priya may have grown up in north London, but her family hail from Delhi.

'Yes,' Priya rolls her eyes, 'but that doesn't mean I support people dumping my friends to gallivant around over there.'

I laugh, although I still feel a sinking sensation. 'I don't even think he's even trying to be a horrible person though, that's the thing. The things he was saying made it sound like our life together has been getting him down for a while. He hates my obsession with the house, he says he feels bored and trapped.'

'Sorry, but I'm not having that,' Priya scoffs, chucking her paper towel into a nearby bin. 'You don't just quit your job and disappear to India when you have a problem in a relationship. That's not how adults behave.'

'Unless you're totally unbearably sick of your life,' I counter.

Priya rolls her eyes. 'No. He's being a child,' she insists and it's a comfort to hear the anger and sense of injustice in her voice.

It makes me feel better. It makes me feel less like the boring insufferable noose around Paul's neck that I've been feeling like ever since I left the restaurant.

'I don't exactly love what he's doing, but it is what it is,' I reason.

'Really?!' Priya frowns. 'No. You need to sort this out,' she insists.

'What do you mean? I can't. He's a grown man. If he wants to hop on a plane to India, I can't stop him.'

I eye my reflection despondently in the mirror.

'Has he actually left already?' Priya asks incredulously.

'I don't know. He didn't come home last night. Some of his clothes were missing. He could have gone straight from the restaurant to the airport for all I know.'

'He's just left?' Priya gawps.

'Yep!'

'You know I've always really liked Paul, but this is some next level bullshit.' Priya shakes her head.

'Yeah, it really is,' I admit, taking a wand of concealer from my bag to top up the lashings underneath my eyes.

'You shouldn't tolerate this,' Priya insists.

'What can I do?' I sigh, dabbing the wand onto my eyebags, while meeting her pointed gaze with less enthusiasm.

'He's really taken the wind out of your sails,' Priya observes.

'What do you mean?' I ask.

Priya gestures at my reflection. 'This is not the Rachel I know. The Rachel I know doesn't slump her shoulders like that. She doesn't look despondent and defeated. She has a smile on her face. She's confident. She's a go-getter and she doesn't take shit.'

I laugh weakly. 'That Rachel didn't just get dumped!' I point out. 'Like I said, I can't force Paul to be with me if that's not what he wants.'

Priya shakes her head. 'No. He's clearly having some kind of quarter-life crisis. This isn't Paul. You need save the relationship and save him. It sounds like he's having a breakdown,' Priya observes.

'How can I save him when he's jetting off to the other side of the world? He's out of my hands,' I remind her, turning to face her.

'Okay, look…' Priya leans back against the sink, a pensive expression on her face. 'The guy clearly needs a holiday, that's understandable. Work's obviously got too much for him. Happens to the best of us. But I really don't think you should let your relationship go without a fight. You guys have been together for ages, that means something. One stupid argument in a restaurant shouldn't spell the end of all that.'

'One stupid argument and a getaway mission to India!' I add fretfully.

'Okay.' Priya meets my anxious gaze. 'Let him have his break in India. Give him a few weeks to unwind, relax, get some headspace or whatever it is he needs to do and then go and make up with him, talk to him, and get your lives back on track. You're not the kind of person who lets life just wash over you, Rachel. You're not just a piece of flotsam that gets swept up in the stream and chucked about. You're the kind of person who has a Life List, for crying out loud,' Priya reminds me.

We had a drunken heart to heart in the pub one night back when we first started at the firm and I told Priya about my Life List. She wasn't particularly fazed. She's just as ambitious. She's a strong believer that you forge your own destiny. Like me, Priya comes from a modest background and worked hard to get to where she is. But unlike me, she's the kind of person who wakes up at the crack of dawn every day, blitzes a protein-filled smoothie and listens to motivational podcasts while pounding the treadmill at the gym. When she broke up with her cheating ex-boyfriend, instead of wallowing in self-pity, watching movies and scoffing ice-cream like the rest of us, Priya stayed in hermit-like all weekend and emerged with an action plan. It was a detailed military-style dating strategy with clearly outlined objectives (namely, find a guy worth marrying) and key performance indicators (number of high-quality matches, dates per month, etc.). Within six months of actioning her plan, Priya had a new boyfriend, and within a couple of years, they were married. His name's Rene and she's totally smitten. Priya's methods may be unusual, and they're certainly not the stuff of Shakespearean romances, but they've worked for her.

'You're the master of your destiny, the captain of your ship,' Priya tells me. 'Are you really going to let Paul chuck your relationship away because of some childish tantrum or are you going to take control of this situation?'

She regards me with a look of impassioned intensity. Priya is known for her rousing speeches. She delivers them in meetings sometimes and has been known to alter the mood of an entire conference room. She's a natural born leader and has an incredible ability to fire people up. She's right that I am a confident go-getter most of the time, but there have been a few occasions over the years when a speech from Priya is what gave me the strength to conquer a task or situation that felt overwhelming. She's a good friend. And now is no different. Her words are affecting me. The look in her eyes and the passion in her voice is making me question myself. She's right, I shouldn't let a relationship I've invested six years of my life into simply collapse because my boyfriend has decided to jet off to India. No. I should fight for this. I'm not a piece of flotsam being swept along in the currents of life. I am the captain of my own ship.

'I'm going to get him back!' I announce, thinking out loud.

Priya smiles widely. 'That's my girl.'

'I'm going to go to India and I'm going to win my boyfriend back,' I assert.

'Damn straight you are. You've got this,' Priya enthuses.

I pull her into a hug.

'Thank you!'

'Anytime!' Priya replies, hugging me tightly back.

I look over her shoulder at my reflection in the mirror. My hair may still be a bit crazy-looking and my eyes are still lined with shadows, but there's a trace of my usual sparkle back in them now. My jacket is on the right way around and I'm back in action.

4 CHAPTER FOUR

Staring into space, eyes full of tears, while despondently nibbling at a piece of toast, was definitely not on my Life List. And yet that's exactly what I'm doing.

It's odd being home alone. This little terraced house has always felt like a symbol of mine and Paul's relationship. It's just an average two-bedroom red brick house midway along a suburban street in a not-quite-gentrified part of south London, but it was our home. When we bought it and began renovating it and making it our own, it felt like we were truly putting down roots, preparing for our future. It felt good. When we bought the house, it was run-down, old and neglected, but thanks to our efforts, it's been given a new lease of life. We weeded the garden, scrubbed the bricks, gave the front door and windowsill a fresh lick of paint, and made it look almost as good as new. I've been so proud of our efforts. It's gorgeous and cozy now, as my 2,398 followers on my Instagram account @rachnpaulspad would no doubt agree. And yet, this gorgeous house could have cost me my relationship. I sigh, nibbling my toast.

The truth is, there are reasons I'm borderline obsessed with home furnishings. There are reasons I inadvertently went from a cool fun girlfriend to a home-furnishings obsessed #interiordecor bore. And there are reasons I never really wanted to talk to Paul about it.

I don't really like ruminating over the past. I mean, where does that get you? It certainly won't help me reach any of the goals on my Life List, and yet since Paul left, I've been doing some reflection. I've been wondering if have taken the whole home furnishings obsession a bit too far. I might have done. And if I dig deep, I can sort of see why. There was definitely a turning point in my childhood that led me to be this way. I'm not about to pen a misery memoir. My childhood was pretty good. My mum and dad loved me. As their only child, they doted on me and my early years couldn't have been happier. We lived in a quaint little house not too dissimilar to the one I have now, except we lived in the village of Oxshott in Surrey. My parents had good jobs. My dad was a construction manager and my mum worked in sales. We had a nice life. I wanted for nothing. I had lovely clothes, all the latest toys, and a beautiful girly princess-like bedroom that was the envy of all my friends. My parents were happy too. We were settled. We had all the things that are so easy to take for granted – stability, a nice car, a couple of holidays a year, a good home, but then when I was 12, everything changed.

My dad suddenly suffered two heart attacks a few months apart and ended up in a wheelchair. He was made redundant. He had heart surgery and my mum became his carer while he was recovering, taking a break from her sales job. Except then, the company she'd been working for went bust. Both my parents were unemployed, and our landlady put our lovely house up for sale. My parents ran out of money and we ended up moving in with my mum's sister, Jill. My mum called the council one afternoon to ask if there was any support they could offer us, and cried with shame over tea and biscuits in Aunt Jill's kitchen after the council informed her we'd have to register as homeless before we could get any support. She swallowed her pride and gave in. The council offered us accommodation in a dodgy shelter known for drug use or a room in a cheap hotel on the outskirts of town, which would have left us totally isolated since my parents sold the car months before.

In the end, we just stayed with Aunt Jill, spending a year living in her tiny two-bedroom flat. She converted the living room into a bedroom for me, but it was never really a proper room. I slept on a sofa bed, which would be switched back to a sofa during the day, so my dad could sit and watch TV while I was at school. Aunt Jill did her best to try to make me feel some sense of ownership of it though and I had a corner where I kept all my things and a few posters on the walls, but it wasn't the same as having my own bedroom. I missed my old room and our house so much, but I didn't want to complain. My dad was in constant pain and I didn't want to make him feel even worse by admitting how unhappy I felt. Instead, I'd just ask my mum every week if the council had found us a house yet. I must have been asking too much, because eventually, my mum snapped, shouting at me to stop nagging her. So I stopped asking and resigned myself to Jill's sofa, when finally, we got a break.

The council got in touch and offered us a house! It was on the edge of town, but my parents didn't mind. What mattered to them was that we'd have our own space, our own home, a foundation upon which to rebuild our lives. I'd have my own bedroom again. No more sleeping on the sofa! My parents were so relieved, and their enthusiasm was infectious. We moved a few weeks later. My room was nothing like my old one. It was small and cramped and the walls were woodchip magnolia, but I still had a few bits of furniture from our old house, including my chest of drawers and dressing table, so I tried to settle in. My parents still didn't have any money and couldn't afford to decorate like they'd decorated our old house. Our place was furnished with mismatched second-hand stuff we found at charity shops or were gifted by friends. It took a while, but eventually we managed to get things feeling fairly homely, and then, just before Christmas, when we'd been in the house for about six months, the council informed us that the land had been sold to a housing developer and we'd have to move again. My parents were distraught.

We were allocated another house. It was slightly bigger than the one we'd had and it was closer to Jill, but my parents were so on edge and demoralized that they couldn't bring themselves to unpack half our boxes. They were convinced something would go wrong and we'd have to move again. For years, there were piles of boxes in the corner of each room. We never made ourselves at home and the house always had a slightly bare feel to it. There was no clutter, no decorations, no pictures on the walls. It was like my parents wanted it to be minimalist, so we could pack up and leave quickly and easily if need be. It wasn't until I was sixteen or seventeen that my parents finally accepted that the house was pretty much theirs and they probably wouldn't have to move again any time soon. It was only really when I was getting ready to go to university that they finally unpacked the last of the boxes and my mum began to adorn the house with little homely touches like scatter cushions and throws and fairy lights. My parents are still in the same house now, and these days, they're perfectly settled and happy, but their struggle affected me. It was the reason I came up with my Life List. I guess you could say I wanted to be in control. I wanted to have a stable, comfortable life with a good job, a good home and a safety net. I didn't want to end up moving around again. I promised myself that when I was finally in a position to get my own place, I'd make it as cozy and homely as possible. I'd make up for all those years of feeling a little bit lost.

That's why I fell so in love with my and Paul's house. It dates back to the Victorian era and it may be a bit shabby around the edges, the walls having distorted over the years to become slightly lumpy, with the floors and ceilings a little tilted and askew in places, but I've always considered those things to be quirks rather than flaws. It's an old house full of historical details that I just love, like a walk-in larder in the kitchen where I've always imagined families from a hundred years ago storing jam and pickled foods, nuts and grains and oats for winter. Paul and I get weekly Tesco deliveries, we don't exactly stockpile, so we filled the larder with books. I love that. It's like our own tiny library. I ventured nervously into it a few days after

Paul left, curious to see if he'd packed any books for his trip, but they were all still there. I didn't know whether to take that as a good sign or not. Is he planning to come back at some point? Will he curl up on the sofa with a cup of the lemon and ginger tea he's always loved and read them? Has he simply abandoned them? Or maybe a removals man will come knocking to collect the things he's left behind?

I let out a gusty sigh and get up to pop another piece of bread in the toaster. Everything in this house, including the toaster, has been carefully chosen. The toaster isn't just any old toaster, it's a really cool retro 1970s one. It's a pastel blue shade, which matches perfectly with the bone china hand-painted crockery I found at a craft fair and the vintage cutlery I got from Etsy, even the coasters. As I wait for my toast, I take in my coordinated kitchenware, and realize that Paul's right. I may have my reasons for wanting to make my house homely, but I have probably taken things a bit too far. The toaster pings and I pluck the hot slice, placing it on my plate. I head back to the dining table, where I sit down on one of the antique mahogany dining table chairs Paul and I picked up for a bargain price at a secondhand furniture shop, and upcycled at home over the course of a couple of weekends. I feel a twinge of unease as I picture Paul sanding each chair down in the backyard. He probably wanted to be doing other things with his weekend, and yet he was stuck in a backyard surrounded by wood dust.

I nibble on my toast and try to push the sadness and regret out of my mind. What's the use in wallowing in self-pity over all the things I've done wrong? No. There's no point in that. I need to think positively and stay focused on what I can do to salvage the situation. Once I'm in India, I'll explain everything to Paul. I never wanted to burden him with my sob story before. Paul went through far worse than me as a kid. His dad, who he adored, died suddenly from a stroke when Paul was just seven years old. My story of not having had a nice house always felt like a fairly minor inconvenience in comparison. But I can see now that it might have helped if I'd opened up. Hopefully, Paul will understand, and we can move forward.

I called Paul's mum the other day, and she was as shocked by the whole thing as I am. She confirmed that Paul is indeed in India and told me that he's staying at an ashram. An ashram! I googled it and I can't get over how strange the place seems. I take a sip of my coffee and reach for my phone. I scroll through the ashram's website for what must be the dozenth time. I've been trying to be positive about this trip, but I can't pretend the ashram isn't a dauntingly weird-looking place. It's pretty, full of lush trees and winding terracotta paths, but it's also populated by long-haired hippies who all wear white robes and look spaced-out in every picture. The founder is some yoga master and philanthropist known as Guru Hridaya. I looked up the meaning of 'Hridaya' and apparently, it's Sanskrit for heart. Guru Hridaya is a portly, not particularly attractive, man in his fifties and when I showed his picture to Priya and the girls at work, they giggled, cracking mean jokes that Paul had 'left me for him'. They know the best way to help me cope is to laugh, but I have to admit, I am surprised by Paul's decision. Of all the places and all the people he wants to escape to, a random guru in a strange ashram? I still can't quite wrap my head around the fact that this is what my tough, northerner, Manchester United supporting boyfriend wants. But maybe I'll see the appeal in person.

I spoke to my boss, Nigel, and booked off some holiday. Nigel was pretty surprised that I want to jet off to India, but I insisted it was an emergency and he reluctantly agreed. After all, Paul's right, I haven't taken a holiday for years, so Nigel let the short notice slide. My tickets are booked and in just a few weeks, I'll be on a plane, jetting far away from England and home furnishings.

I may be leaving my comfort zone, but I'll do whatever it takes to win back my man.

5 CHAPTER FIVE

I've got this, I tell myself as Priya drives along the deserted motorway towards Heathrow. It's 4.15am and the roads are empty, shrouded in an early morning mist. I went to bed at 8pm last night, setting my alarm for the early hours, but I didn't manage to sleep at all. I tossed and turned, plagued with last minute worries about whether I'm doing the right thing or whether I've completely lost the plot. I've never travelled as far away as India before. One of my close friends from school and I embarked on an interrail trip around Europe during our gap year, but the furthest away from home we got was St Petersburg. And yet now here I am, about to hop on a plane to southern India, alone.

I know in theory it should be fine. People go to India every day. Intrepid solo travelers go there all the time, just like Paul, in the spirit of exploration and finding themselves, but while struggling to sleep at midnight, all I could think about was everything that could possibly go wrong. What if I'm on a rickety Indian train and it derails like you see in those horrific news stories from time to time? What if I get bitten by a rabid dog and die? Sure, I had my jabs last week, but they don't always work. What if a sleazy guy takes a shine to me and I get harassed? What if someone mugs me on a dark street somewhere and I end up alone, in the middle of a strange unfamiliar place, with no money and no phone and… *Oh God*. The thoughts make my palms sweat even now so I quickly push them out of my mind. No. I'll make it to the ashram safely. But what if I get there and I've still got my phone and my wallet and I haven't been bitten by a rabid dog, and then I find that Paul's had some kind of epiphany and fallen in love with Indian life? What if he's found a beautiful hippy girlfriend and they've been experiencing all the joys of tantra together? The possibilities for disaster are truly endless.

'Are you okay?' Priya asks, glancing from the road ahead over at me.

I suddenly realize I've been gazing ruminatively out into the fog and Priya and I haven't spoken for quite a while.

'Umm, yeah, I guess,' I sigh, although the words don't exactly ring true.

'Are you sure? You've been tapping your toe non-stop for the past ten minutes and your nails are bitten down,' Priya points out.

I hadn't even realized I'd been tapping my toe. I glance at my fingernails, the polish chipped. Priya's right, I have bitten them down. My nail care has gone out the window lately and there have been a few times when I've caught myself absently biting my nails while imagining this or that nightmarish scenario about my trip. In my last apocalyptic daydream, Paul had reinvented himself as a yoga master and was touring India, leading workshops surrounded by dozens of lithe sexy hippy girls, all of whom were contorting themselves into bendy positions I'm not even remotely capable of.

'I suppose I am a bit stressed,' I admit. 'I am going quite a long way away.'

I decide not to tell Priya about my fears of Paul becoming a lothario yoga master.

'You are, but India's cool. It's different, but I think you'll be okay,' Priya assures me, nodding to herself, before glancing at a road sign towards Heathrow.

'You *think*?' I echo. 'You were the one who encouraged me to do this!'

Priya laughs. 'Yeah, I did, didn't I?' She pulls a face while I glare at her.

'Yes, you did!' I tut.

Priya laughs, sounding ever-so-slightly nervous.

'You're going to be fine!' she states, and I get the feeling she's trying to convince herself as much as me.

I stare at her, unimpressed. Is she having doubts now too?

She glances over at me, a bright enthusiastic smile plastered on her face. I raise an eyebrow.

'Look, the thing about India is if you smile at India, India smiles back,' she tells me. 'It's not like the UK. Nothing runs on time. Buses are always late. People are late. Trains are late. It's disorganized and chaotic and crazy, but you just have to go with the flow. It's a weirdly spiritual place. Honestly, if you put out good energy, you'll get it back.'

'Put out good energy?!' I parrot back, narrowing my eyes at her. 'Since when do you talk about *energy*?'

'Trust me. Smile at India, and India will smile back,' Priya insists.

'If you say so!' I reply skeptically. 'But what if the last thing I feel like doing is smiling?'

Priya gives me a sympathetic look and reaches over to squeeze my knee, her other hand on the wheel.

'Oh...' she murmurs. 'Okay, scratch that. Screw the energy side of things. Let's make sure you're fully prepared instead. Have you packed your mosquito repellent?'

She focuses back on the road.

'Yes,' I reply affirmatively.

'Anti-histamines?' she adds.

'Yep.'

'Sunscreen?'

'Got it.'

'Diarrhea medication, because no matter how good your energy is, every Brit visiting India needs that,' Priya warns, glancing over.

'Yep, I've got that too,' I reply, hoping I won't have to use it. The last thing I need on top of being dumped is a case of Delhi Belly.

Priya covers a few more essentials, from how many rupees I've taken out, to whether I'm aware of Indian toilet etiquette. She insists that people in India use their left hand to wipe after going to the toilet, and that it's culturally unacceptable to eat with your left hand.

'People eat with their hands in India, but if you eat with your left hand, *everyone* will look at you. It's totally gross!' Priya tells me.

'Okay, I won't,' I reply, even though I'm only half-listening.

I find myself gazing out of the window, unable to stop fretting.

'Have you got your toothbrush?' Priya asks.

'Yeah, I've got that,' I reply.

So far, I've packed all the things Priya insists I'll need, which makes me feel a little better. My vibes and energy and smile may be a bit lacking for this trip, but at least I seem to have packed the essentials.

'Flip flops?' Priya asks.

'Well, I've got my Prada wedges,' I tell her, knowing she'll be familiar with the ones I mean since I bought them during a shopping expedition we took a few months ago to a designer outlet centre just outside London.

The Prada wedges I found are utterly gorgeous and they were a total bargain. There's no way she'll have forgotten.

'You mean those pink suede ones? Don't those have a massive heel?' Priya asks.

'Kind of… I mean, it's only two or three inches,' I assure her.

'Only two or three inches?' Priya protests. 'You're going to an ashram, Rachel, not to the races. You can't stomp around in India in Prada wedges. The terrain can be really rough over there and even when you're in the ashram, people aren't going to want to listen to you clomping about. They going to be trying to meditate!'

I don't reply. I'm too busy picturing people sitting meditating. People don't really do that all day, do they? And anyway, I find it hard to believe that I'm going to be the only person wearing heels. Lots of people like wearing heels, regardless of whether they're in an ashram or not.

'You do realize that ashrams are about stripping back to basics, right?' Priya asks, and I can feel her giving me a stern look. 'No one's going to be dressing up. No one's going to be wearing heels, and certainly not designer ones! People probably won't even be wearing make-up.'

'No make-up?' I echo.

'Yes. It's an ashram! It's not the office or a City bar. You're meant to shun things like make-up,' Priya comments as she veers around a roundabout.

'But I look like a sick Victorian child without make-up,' I remind her.

Even Priya has been known to ask, on the very rare occasions when I've come into work without my usual lashings of foundation, blusher and bronzer, if I'm feeling okay.

'And anyway, how am I meant to win my boyfriend back without make-up on?' I scoff.

'Oh, come on! Paul isn't going to be swayed by a bit of eyeliner,' Priya laughs.

'Hmph,' I grumble. 'And anyway, thanks for denying that I look like a sick Victorian child without makeup!' I tease.

Priya snorts. 'Well, you could possibly do with a bit of sun!'

'Great,' I grumble. 'Guess I shouldn't have packed my fake tan either, then?'

'You didn't?' Priya spits.

'Of course not!' I insist, even though there might just be two bottles of the stuff in my suitcase.

I'm guessing people don't bronze up in ashrams either. But for all I know, it might be raining over there, and it's better to be safe than sorry. I'm definitely not going to tell Priya about the false lashes in my washbag though. My eyelash extensions fell off with all the crying, but Priya will no doubt find the idea of me wearing false lashes in India ridiculous, even though I imagined donning them for a romantic candlelit make-up date with Paul.

'You and Paul need to work on your connection,' Priya says, cupping her heart. 'Figure out where things went wrong, find your way back to each other. A little bit of blusher is not going to make him reassess whatever crisis he's in.'

'Maybe not, but it can't hurt,' I retort.

'Honestly,' Priya tuts. 'I think you'll have a different view once you get there. India's hot. Even if you do want to wear make-up, it's only going to melt off your face within seconds!'

'Hmmm…' I mumble, wondering whether false eyelashes can melt off your face too. That's something to Google while I'm waiting for my flight. The last thing I need is spidery lashes crawling down my cheeks while I'm trying to get my boyfriend to fall for me again.

'Have you got sunglasses?' Priya interrupts my thoughts. 'Because you'll definitely need them.'

'Yep, I even packed them in my hand luggage so I can put them on the moment I get off the plane,' I tell her, feeling a little smug.

I pull out my oversized Burberry sunnies. They're my favorite pair, featuring the brand's quintessential Nova check print. I love donning them in pub gardens for after work drinks, adding a cool edge to my work outfits.

'What the hell?' Priya says, taking in my sunglasses. 'You brought Burberry sunglasses?'

'Err… yeah?'

'Oh my God,' Priya half-laughs, half-sighs, shaking her head.

'What?!'

'You're going to an ashram with two hundred pound sunglasses! These places are meant to be about shunning materialism and you want to rep Burberry while you're out there!'

'But these are my *only* sunglasses,' I point out. 'Wouldn't it be more materialistic and consumerist if I'd gone to Primark and spent a tenner on a pair of cheap sunglasses for the sole purpose of my trip when I already have a pair?'

Priya lets out a long sigh. 'Well, technically, yes, but I mean, really? Are you just going to strut around the ashram in Prada heels, a face full of make-up and Burberry sunnies?'

I laugh awkwardly, hiding the fact that that's precisely what I'd intended to do. We pass another sign along the motorway for Heathrow, now only ten miles away.

'I guess I won't be needing hair straighteners either, right?' I venture.

Priya lets out a peal of laughter. 'Oh my God, you're not going to Marbella, you're going to In-di-a,' she says, enunciating each syllable.

'Doesn't mean I don't want good hair.'

'Oh man,' Priya groans, gazing incredulously at the road ahead. 'You are in for a shock.'

We lapse into silence for a few moments, both of us lost in thought as we pelt down the empty motorway.

'I know it sounds weird, but no one's going to care about how you look in India. It really is all about energy,' Priya comments.

'Maybe,' I reply, feeling unconvinced. 'It's just energy and vibes and gurus and ashrams and stuff. It's all a bit freaky.'

Priya laughs. 'Yeah, it seems freaky when you're driving along the M25 in the fog, but it will make sense once you get there.'

'Okay.' I shrug, although I'm not so convinced.

I decide not to tell her about the super fancy black lace La Perla underwear set and stockings I've packed for potential make-up sex, the business empowerment books I've got in my hand luggage and the iPad I loaded up with the latest episodes of Made in Chelsea. I doubt Priya would find them particularly in-fitting with my Indian quest either.

'I wish I could pack you too,' I tell her, my voice cracking, ever-so-slightly. 'I'm going to miss you.'

I look over at Priya, feeling emotional.

She gives me a sweet, encouraging smile as another sign announces that the airport is just a few miles away.

'You're going to be fine. And anyway, I'll be with you in spirit,' Priya insists.

I laugh, giving her a playful shove. 'Oh, shut up with your spirit crap, guru!'

Priya giggles and takes the next turn towards Heathrow.

6 CHAPTER SIX

'Coffee, tea, chai?' a woman's voice is saying. 'Good morning. Coffee, tea, chai?'

I blink a few times, waking up, baffled for a moment by my surroundings, until reality dawns on me. No, I'm not at home in my nice cozy bed, I'm on a flight to India. *India.* That's what I'm doing.

I look up at the woman, an incredibly pretty air hostess with smooth brown skin, sparkling eyes and a wide, pearly smile. She's holding a silver jug.

'Good morning,' she says chirpily.

'Morning,' I reply groggily, trying to muster some enthusiasm.

I glance out of the window, but all I can see is clouds. The last thing I remember was trying to read my book during take-off but finding I couldn't concentrate and deciding to watch a film from the in-flight selection instead. I opted for an action movie that was all the rage a few years ago, shunning the romantic comedies since I was pretty sure their brand of happily ever after would only get me down given my predicament. I watched a couple of action films in the end, but I must have fallen asleep during the second one as I hardly remember any of it.

'Where are we?' I ask the air hostess.

'We're flying over the Arabian sea,' she informs me. 'We'll be touching down on Indian soil in just under an hour.'

I realize I've slept for most of the flight, the exhaustion of a sleepless night hitting me.

'Great!' I reply, feeling a bit perkier.

The air hostess smiles warmly. 'So, would you like tea, coffee, chai?' she asks again.

'I'll have chai please,' I tell her, figuring that I may as well get into the spirit of Indian life.

'Of course.' She smiles, swapping the jug she's holding for another and pouring me a small cup of steaming milky liquid.

She hands it to me before moving on to the next row of passengers.

I hold the hot chai up to my nose and breath in its scent. It feels too hot to drink but it smells spicy and delicious, of sugar and cinnamon and tea leaves. It smells far more fragrant than the cups of chai I pick up every now and then from Costa.

As I hold the warm cup up to my face, breathing in its delectable smell, I peer past the man sitting next to me in the window seat and gaze out at a blanket of pillowy clouds, imagining the ocean beneath. Maybe it's the feeling of holding a nice warm drink or being surrounded by clouds, but my nerves about the trip momentarily dissipate and I feel positive – not quite excited but content.

'Business trip?' My fellow passenger – an Indian man who looks mid-forties – asks, taking me by surprise.

I hadn't had him down as the chatty type. He donned an eye

mask before the flight even took off and I got the feeling he wanted to keep himself to himself, which suited me fine, but now, holding a cup of what looks like coffee, he seems to have perked up.

'No, leisure,' I tell him, taking in the slightly crumpled white shirt he's wearing and the tie that he's loosened around his neck. He looks like he could be on a business trip.

His eyes wander towards my book, still abandoned on my lap: *Heels of Steel: How to Thrive as a Powerful Woman in the Corporate World.*

'Ah, right,' he says, frowning as though in confusion.

I'm aware my choice of reading material might not be standard for this kind of holiday, but why not use my time in India as an opportunity for self-improvement? I enjoy personal development, and if this trip goes according to plan, I'll come back to London with my relationship back on track and I'll be even more of a corporate bad ass, too.

'Oh, I'm just reading this for fun!' I tell him.

'I see!' The man replies.

'I'm on my way to see my boyfriend,' I elaborate, even though that's not quite technically true.

I should probably stop referring to Paul as my boyfriend, but it sounds weird to say I'm flying across the world to see my ex and it's not like I want to explain the whole sorry story to a total stranger.

'Where are you going?' The man asks, taking a sip of his coffee.

I tell him the name of the ashram.

'You are going to the Hridaya Ashram?' he says, looking me up and down, his face twisting into a puzzled expression.

'Yes!' I reply affirmatively. 'Why? Is that a surprise?'

'A little.' He smiles as though amused. 'I saw your book and I assumed you were coming to India for business.'

I laugh. 'Well, the ashram was my boyfriend's idea,' I tell the man. 'I'm going there to see him.'

He nods, seeming a little more satisfied with this answer. 'Very nice. Is your boyfriend a devotee of Guru Hridaya?'

'A devotee?' I echo, finding the word a little odd.

'Yes. Is he a follower? A renunciate?'

'A what?' I question.

The man eyes me strangely, as though baffled by my ignorance.

'A renunciate. Many of the people who visit the ashram give up their Western way of life. They abandon their material ways, let go of their ego and become divine followers of their guru,' he tells me, with a sincerity and reverence that surprises me given his formal attire.

'Oh, well my boyfriend isn't a renunciate. He's just…' I pause, looking for the right phrase. Having a crisis? Lost his way? Freaking out and embarking on a totally weird holiday? 'Travelling,' I opt for.

The man nods, taking another sip of his drink.

'Very nice. You will have a good time there,' he says slowly with a ponderous expression on his face, as though choosing his words carefully.

I get the feeling he's still slightly baffled by my travel destination.

We chat a bit more, making small talk as the plane soars above the clouds, but then another air hostess comes along, handing out newspapers and the man turns his attention to The Times of India.

I gaze out of the window as the plane pierces through the blanket of cloud and begins its passage across southern India. The sky is clear, and I take in the landscape below, amazed at how vast and rugged it is. There are huge swathes of rough mountainous land, blankets of palm trees and giant shimmering lakes, as well as sprawling cities, shanty towns and villages, loosely connected by a vast network of roads. The landscape is a far cry from the neat motorways and tightly packed suburban towns and cities I've left behind. It's incredibly vast and expansive, almost dauntingly so, and yet it's also kind of magical.

The plane begins nearing the airport and I get an even closer look at the city. It's built-up, urban and sprawling, a mix of skyscrapers, tower blocks, roads, railways and temples.

The plane begins to swoop down towards the airport. As it descends, slicing through the air, its engine whirring at full blast, my stomach starts to twist. I'm not sure if it's from the altitude or nerves. I open my book and attempt to read in an effort to calm my nerves.

A woman who knows who she is, what she believes in, and what she wants to achieve, is a woman who means business. She is a force to be reckoned with.

I start to feel a bit better. Who says enlightenment can't come in corporate packages?!

Eventually, the plane's wheels judder against the runway and after zooming along, the plane begins to slow down, drawing to an eventual halt. The pilot announces that we've arrived safely, and we're told we can remove our seatbelts. All the passengers begin rising from their seats and we collect our bags from the overhead compartments.

'Have a good trip,' the businessman says to me as he pulls down a briefcase and matching hold all. 'I hope you and your boyfriend have a wonderful time.'

He smiles kindly, turning to leave.

'Thank you,' I reply, as I stow my book in my bag. 'Nice to meet you,' I add.

I feel guilty for lying as the man walks away. If only I was just going on a trip to see my boyfriend. If only I was the kind of girlfriend who'd fly halfway across the world to spend time with her partner. I feel not only guilty that I lied but also that I'm not that kind of person. Maybe mine and Paul's relationship would be in a better place right now if I were, but instead of travelling, I've spent the past few years working and obsessing over interior décor.

I head off the plane, climbing down the metal staircase onto the runway. It must be around 7 or 8am over here, but it's already hot outside, the air dry and warm. I cross the asphalt towards the airport, glancing at my fellow passengers as we filter in. There are quite a few Indian people, some are in Western clothes but others, particularly the women, are wearing bright beautiful saris. There are a few Western travelers, who, like me, are dressed a little too thermally for the weather and wear slightly unnerved expressions on their faces. There are a couple of young travelers who have a hippyish look, sporting dreadlocks, backpacks and tans, as if heading off for the next leg of a gap year. One girl even has a yin yang tattoo on her tanned upper arm. They look more like the type of people who'd go to an ashram. I can see why the guy sitting next to me earlier might have thought I seem a slightly unusual candidate in comparison.

Inside, we wait for what feels like ages at the customs and immigration desk. I read my book, making my way through chapters on maximizing returns in negotiations and achieving strong but charismatic leadership by the time I'm finally, officially, allowed into the country. I wander towards luggage collection and eye the conveyor belt like a hawk until I spot my baby pink diamond faceted Ted Baker suitcase. It stands out by a mile compared to all the boring suitcases and dreary backpacks. I feel a twinge of pride as I pull my case off the conveyor belt. I got it on one of my shopping trips with Priya. Half-price, it was an absolute bargain, yet because I haven't been on holiday for so long, I've never had a chance to use it. It's so shiny and pretty.

I heave it off the conveyor belt and pull it through the airport, following the signs towards the exit, feeling an uneasy twinge in my stomach as I drift away from my fellow passengers. I may only have spoken to one of them, but there was almost a certain sense of camaraderie among us. Now, as I leave the airport, I feel weirdly alone.

I walk through the arrivals gate and try to feel strong and independent as I pass families waiting by the barrier for their loved ones. I don't even have a travel guide waiting for me like the guides holding up massive signs emblazoned with their guests' names. But it's fine. I don't need anyone. I'm only a few hours away from Paul now. It's all good.

Finally, I reach the end of the barrier and walk towards the exit. A couple of taxi drivers accost me, but I brush them off, not wanting to jump at the first offer I get. Hopefully I'll get a better price for my trip to the ashram if I pick one of the less pushy drivers waiting outside.

I emerge from the airport and wander towards a taxi rank, pulling my suitcase after me. The taxis are yellow, like New York cabs. I head towards them and once more, I'm struck by how hot the air is. Closer to people and the city, the air smells different. It smells of exhaust fumes from cars mixed with the scent of mint and cardamom. The air literally smells minty and fragrant. I breathe in deeply, smiling to myself, unable to believe that I can truly detect herbal aromas on the air itself. There's something charming about it, magical even. India's already presenting itself as a place both old and new, earthy yet modern, enchanting.

The dazzling morning light strains my eyes and I retrieve my sunglasses from my bag. As I approach the taxi rank, I find myself wondering whether Paul noticed the fragrant air when he arrived here too. I wonder whether the same taxi driver ran up to him as the one running towards me now, smiling goofily and beckoning me towards his cab. I let him take my bags and he grins, doing the Indian head wobble that I read about online but assumed was just an urban myth. It's a cross between a nod and a shake of the head, a funny and cute gesture that sort of gives the impression of 'yes' and 'no' and 'no worries' all at the same time. I hop into the back of the cab and yet again, it hits me how different India is. Cabbies in England tend to have little more than an air freshener or a pack of gum on their dashboards, but the front of this taxi driver's car is like a holy shrine in a Hindu temple. His dashboard is adorned with ornaments of Shiva and Ganesh, gaudy postcards of Hindu gods are tacked around the windscreen and there are even a couple of golden Hindu Gods dangling on chains and ribbons from the rear-view mirror.

Slamming the boot shut, my driver gets in the car. He asks where I'm staying and I give him the address of the ashram.

He seems surprised, just like the man on the plan.

'You're going to the Hridaya Ashram?' he reiterates, raising an eyebrow at me through the rear-view mirror.

'Yes!' I reply, feeling a little exasperated.

Why does everyone seem to find it completely baffling that I'd be going to the Hridaya Ashram? Just because I read corporate books and don't have a yin yang tattoo, it doesn't mean I can't dabble in a spot of spirituality.

'Okay!' My driver does another head wobble, before turning his attention to his dashboard.

He mumbles some words of prayer at one of his Hindu God ornaments, before twisting his key in the ignition and pulling away from the kerb. We drive out of the airport and start pelting down a main road. The road is lined with billboards for everything from toothpaste to Bollywood films. The style of advertising feels retro, lacking the irony and self-consciousness of London ads.

'Are you a follower of Guru Hridaya?' My driver asks, eyeing me through the rear-view mirror.

He keeps his eyes fixed on me, while speeding down the motorway at what must be at least seventy miles an hour. It's more than a little unnerving.

'Err, no, not really,' I mutter, staring at the road before us, as though, if I'm paying attention, that will somehow keep us safe.

As my driver focuses on me, he meanders out of his lane so that he's straddling two lanes, one of which is for cars heading in the opposite direction. It's empty for a moment, but a van appears in the distance and starts coming towards us at high speed, head on.

'Oh my God! That van!' I shriek, pointing at the oncoming vehicle.

My driver flicks his attention back to the road and swerves out of the van's path in the nick of time.

'So you don't like Guru Hridaya?' he asks, casually, looking back up at me, as though nothing's happened.

He's completely unfazed by our near-death experience.

'I don't know… Umm… Can you… look at the road, please?' I implore him, twisting my neck to watch the van speeding off into the distance.

I turn back to my driver who fortunately is now looking at the road. I glance at the Shiva ornament on his dashboard with pleading eyes as my heart pounds. Did the driver's prayer spare us a collision? I find myself torn between imploring Shiva to keep us safe and wanting to get the driver to stop and let me out of the cab so that I can hopefully get a lift with someone who actually pays attention to the road. Spirituality is all well and good, but a prayer's not going to prevent your car from crumpling in a head-on crash.

Adrenalin is still surging through my veins. My palms are sweating as I stare at the road, willing my driver to stay in his lane from now on.

'Hridaya Ashram is a good place. Very spiritual, very good for body and soul,' my driver tells me, gazing back up at me.

'Uh huh. Yep, yoga… Great,' I reply, staring at the road ahead and hoping he'll do the same.

The car begins to wobble once more, and I realize he's still looking at me.

'Please can you focus on the road. Please,' I beg.

'Okay!' he laughs, doing the head wobble as he looks back towards the road.

My heart slams in my chest. So much for India being a mystical otherworldly place, the home of meditation and yoga and enlightenment. I feel more stressed now then I've felt for months in London. In fact, I can barely remember ever feeling so stressed.

'Lots of great classes at Hridaya. Yoga, Tai Chi, art,' he says. 'And other things,' he adds pointedly, his eyes twinkling, almost mischievously.

'Yes, lots of great classes,' I reply. 'Please, please, look at the road,' I add desperately, my interest in preserving my life outweighing my desire to engage in conversation.

My driver seems to finally grasp how stressed I am and stops talking, turning his attention to the road instead. We lapse into silence and even though I'm keeping my eyes peeled on the motorway, I begin to relax a little. I think about the mischievous look in the driver's eyes when he said the ashram does classes in 'other things'. What did he mean by that? I went on the ashram's website a few days ago and checked out the activities on offer. There was the standard list of yoga, meditation and massage. But there were also quite a few weird offerings like tribal dance workshops, past life regression, and gong sound baths. I guess that's what he was referring to, and yet, the way he said it sounded almost naughty.

'So, you like yoga?' My driver asks as he pulls off the motorway.

He's clearly got bored of silence. I glance at a sign that indicates we're approaching a city, which we have to pass by on our journey down south towards the ashram.

'Err, it's alright, I reply, hoping he accepts my answer and we revert back into silence.

We start passing through narrower urban streets, which are far more chaotic than the motorway, full of zig-zagging rickshaws, motorbikes, cars, buses and vans, all weaving past one another. I can't make out lines in the road or any semblance of order. My driver speeds through the traffic, nipping at sharp angles between other motorists with reckless abandon. He's driving crazily but I don't know what to say. He's not talking anymore so it's not like I can tell him to keep quiet and focus on the road. He is focusing on the road, but he's still driving maniacally. The weird thing is, he's not the only one. A guy on a motorbike speeds along nearby, while his girlfriend sits on the back, her arms slung lazily around his waist. He turns his head to kiss her, while speeding forwards and neither of them seem at all tense. A man in another nearby car honks his horn incessantly while cutting up every single person on the road.

Go with the flow, I tell myself, trying to breathe evenly. *If you smile at India, India smiles back.* I remind myself of Priya's words as my driver continues to cut through the traffic like a five-year-old playing Grand Theft Auto after too many sweets. I plaster a smile onto my face, hoping India appreciates it. *Please India, smile at me*, I silently urge the country, my fear clearly making me deranged. Maybe I should say a prayer to Shiva? But what do Hindu prayers sound like? How do they start? Hi Shiva? Dear Shiva? What's up Shiva?

I close my eyes and begin to mentally draft a prayer.

Hi Shiva. Hope all's well...

A thud interrupts my thoughts. We've crashed. We've actually crashed. I'm not in pain. My heart's still beating. I look around to see that our car has gone right into a metal railing at the side of the road. The railing has bent badly out of shape. I stare, in disbelief, taking it all in. Cars honk irritably at us for obstructing the road. I can't believe it. We actually crashed! So much for smiling at India and praying to Shiva!

My driver gets out of the car to assess the damage. I edge towards the window and peer out. A large dent has now appeared in the bonnet, the metal scratched and warped.

'Oh no!' I gasp.

My driver kneels down and inspects his tire, pressing it with his thumbs. He nods to himself and stands up. He brushes some dust off his dented bonnet and does a head wobble.

'All is well!' he announces, as he gets back into the car and twists his key in the ignition.

I nod weakly as he swerves back into the road.

FLYING SOLO

7 CHAPTER SEVEN

'And this is your room!' The host of my ashram guesthouse says with aplomb, gesturing towards a ladder leading up to a treehouse. A literal treehouse. A small house, in a tree.

'What?' I utter, laughing uneasily.

She smiles back at me brightly, her gaze unflinching. She introduced herself as Meera when we met, telling me she's local and has lived in the ashram since she was a teenager. She seems friendly and she looks stunning in a dark red sequined sari with her jet-back shiny hair trailing in a long plait over her shoulder. Her hair reminds me of Priya's on the rare occasions when Priya doesn't wear hers pinned back for work. It's also long, jet black and enviably thick.

'But, it's…' I look up.

The ladder looks flimsy. The treehouse itself is constructed from what appears to be tightly bound bamboo stalks. It looks perilous, balanced among branches. I'm torn between appearing culturally insensitive and wanting a bed, on solid earth.

'I, err…' I mutter, wondering how the treehouse could possibly support my weight, let alone my suitcase too.

'I...'

'Is there a problem?' Meera asks, a little impatiently.

I'm pretty sure she already thinks I'm a bit strange since my first question upon checking in was whether there was a man called Paul staying at her guesthouse. She insisted she couldn't divulge guests' details but after I begged her to confirm either way, she eventually admitted that no, there's no one called Paul staying at the guesthouse at the moment. I knew the chances were slim, after all, there are several dozen guesthouses in the ashram, but it was worth checking just in case. I read online that most of the ashram guests congregate in the ashram's main hall for dinner, so I'll just go there later in the hope that I run into him.

'No, I just thought I'd have a room in a house… you know, with walls and stuff,' I venture, glancing away from the tree towards the main guesthouse, which is comprised of dwellings made of bricks and mortar.

Meera shrugs. 'You booked late, this is all we have left. The guesthouse is busy at this time of year,' she explains.

'But… I have a big suitcase. The treehouse doesn't look that strong,' I point out, unable to believe that I'm being presented with a treehouse to stay in.

After having travelled across the world, I'm now having to rest my weary bones in a treehouse. It feels like a cruel joke.

'It is very safe, I can assure you,' Meera insists, with a jaunty head wobble.

'But… But… What if it rains?' I ask weakly.

Meera laughs. 'The treehouse is perfectly comfortable!' she says. 'It is sheltered with palm leaves.'

Leaves?! I gawp.

'It won't rain anyway. We're out of monsoon season,' Meera assures me, but I can't quite bring myself to believe her and have faith that I'm not going to get soaked.

After all, I didn't think my boyfriend would leave me, did I? And yet, he did. I didn't think I'd be involved in a car crash straight after arriving in India, and I was. If I expect it not to rain, it probably will.

'So, make yourself at home!' Meera comments, plastering an overenthusiastic smile onto her face.

She turns and hurries away before I have a chance to raise any more objections.

Make myself at home? I look around me. I'm in the middle of the guesthouse garden. In the distance is a copse of palm trees with hammocks slung between them. And to the side of the garden is a row of outdoor toilets. Meera showed them to me after checking me in. Maybe she thought the awful outdoor loos would make the treehouse feel more palatable in comparison. If so, the tactic didn't quite work. I can't believe I've travelled all this way to perch up in a tree like a sparrow. Meera's clearly not going to offer me a better place to stay. I believe her when she says she doesn't have any other rooms, I did only book a few days ago, but I didn't realize that when I booked a 'private suite' that said suite would in fact be up a tree.

I sigh dramatically. I really need to whinge about this to someone. I'm dying to message Priya but of course, my phone doesn't work over here.

'Wait!' I call after Meera.

She turns, her smile still slightly fixed. 'Yes?'

'Erm…' I glance at the ground. 'Do you, umm… What's the WiFi password?' I ask.

'WiFi?!' Meera laughs. 'You're in an ashram!'

I stare at her blankly.

'WiFi!' she tuts, smiling to herself, before turning and heading back to the guesthouse.

No WiFi?! I mean, seriously? And what does she mean about being in an ashram, what if I wanted to look up meditation chants or yoga positions or something? I could easily have been planning to use WiFi for spiritual stuff.

I sigh, turning back to my treehouse. I look between my suitcase and the bamboo structure above me, wondering how the hell I'm going to get my stuff up there. I can't exactly lug my suitcase up the flimsy ladder. I guess this place is aimed at backpackers and not suitcasers like myself. So much for proudly parading my new Ted Baker luggage.

I pull my suitcase towards the ladder and tentatively step onto the first rung. The ladder is made of bamboo stalks too, bound together with reeds. I try to pull my suitcase up after me as I climb up onto the next rung, but it's too awkward. The ladder looks like it's straining and I don't trust my own balance. I'm going to have to unpack my case and take my stuff up bit by bit.

Sighing, I step back onto the ground and unzip my suitcase. Fortunately, I'm as anal about packing as I am about home furnishings, and I've compartmentalized different sections of my wardrobe into separate bags. I reach for the bag at the top, containing nightwear and another, containing dresses. I clamp the bags under my arms and begin ascending the precarious-looking ladder once more.

I take each rung steadily, worrying that the bamboo might snap, although it does seem surprisingly strong. The higher up I get, the more confident I begin to feel about the ladder's sturdiness. I can't help thinking about my staircase back home though, lined with a fluffy hand-tufted ivory carpet. Did Paul harbor secret longings for a bamboo ladder all along? Was our carpet too comfortable, too traditional, too boring? Did he crave something wilder? I ponder such questions as I reach the entrance of my treehouse. It doesn't even have a door, just a curtain made from tarpaulin.

I pull the curtain back, tentatively, almost hopefully. I don't know what I'm expecting to find behind it. My treehouse is hardly going to contain a plush suite with a king-sized bed, mini bar and jacuzzi, but even so, the sight of nothing but a mosquito net dangling from the centre of the roof over a thin mattress on the floor, still comes as a shock.

I look around, searching the rest of the tree house, but it really does contain nothing other than a mosquito net and a mattress with a blanket and pillow on top. My heart sinks. I dump my bags onto the floor and crawl nervously inside, expecting the floor to collapse under my weight. The last thing I need today is to fall through a treehouse. Although, like the ladder, the floor feels surprisingly firm. I consider standing up, but the treehouse is so small that I wouldn't be able to. I slide my bags along the floor towards one of the walls. I'd imagined unpacking once I got to India, putting my stuff in drawers, maybe even a wardrobe, leaving my book on a bedside table, but those things feel like luxuries right now. I take a closer look at my bed and pull the mosquito net back. The mattress is incredibly flimsy. It's one inch thick, if that. I give it a poke. It's rubbery, like a yoga mat. I reach for the folded blanket and roll its material between my fingers. It's thin and flimsy too. I feel like crying. The reality of my situation hits home. I'm sitting in a treehouse far away from home, I don't have a proper room, I don't have a proper bed, and I don't have a boyfriend, let alone an engagement. This treehouse, this crazy expedition, this whole situation, my whole flipping life, feels like a complete joke. What am I doing here? And what is so bad about me that my boyfriend would trade in our nice comfortable life for something so completely and utterly different?

Tears leak from my eyes. Hot, hurt, angry tears. They crawl down my cheeks and I let them, giving in, lowering my head. I've been so focused on my mission of coming to India and winning Paul back that the pain of the break-up hasn't really hit me, but it's hitting me now. I feel distraught, let down, confused and alone. I flick my tears away, but they're rapidly replaced. They crawl down my cheeks in torrents. I let out a pathetic sniffle, when suddenly I feel a stinging sensation on my arm. I glance down to see a mosquito sucking my blood, its transparent body growing red as its greedy insides fill up.

'Ahh!' I let out a shrill scream, flicking it off. 'You bastard. You absolute prick! Go away!' I shriek.

I sob again, as my arm stings, beading with blood.

'Everything okay up there?' A man's voice inquires.

Oh, great. It's probably another person who works at the guesthouse or a grumpy guest who wants me to keep the noise down. Screaming at insects is probably not considered very enlightened. Sniffling, I wipe the tears from my face and crawl back across my treehouse. I pull the curtain back and look down to see a guy who must be around my age peering up at me. He shields his eyes with his hand as he squints up, a friendly smile on his face.

'Are you okay? I thought I heard a scream,' he says.

He has an unusual accent, a mixture of European and American, that I can't quite place. He's incredibly tanned. It's hard not to notice the deep golden shade of his skin, given the loose tank top he's wearing, with shorts and flip flops. His body's lean and toned and the muscles in his arm bunch up as he continues to shield his striking blue eyes. His hair's shaven, but it's a golden blond shade.

'Oh… A mosquito was just sucking my blood,' I explain,

laughing, even though I still feel miserable, not to mention worried that the mosquito is still in my treehouse ready to strike again.

'Have you got any repellent?' The stranger asks.

'I think so… Somewhere in my bag.' I glance down at my suitcase.

He follows my gaze and raises an eyebrow as he takes in my massive, pink, overflowing case.

'I'm guessing you're not planning on keeping this down here?' he comments.

'No! It's just a bit hard lugging a suitcase up here, that's all,' I remark.

'Hmm… yes.' He nods, frowning at my suitcase, clearly appreciating my predicament.

I'm about to turn around and climb back down the ladder to get a few more of my things when he looks back up at me, with those startling blue eyes.

'I can help,' he suggests. 'I'll bring up some of your stuff.'

'Oh, okay…' I reply, although he's barely waited for my response and is already turning to my suitcase.

'Thanks,' I say, feeling grateful for the help.

'No worries!' he insists, flashing me a gorgeous smile.

His smile is dazzling and white, but he has the tiniest gap between his two front teeth that makes him look cute and endearing. I smile back, feeling a little shy. He's so handsome and I must look like such a state in comparison, having just been blubbing away in my treehouse, not to mention having spent the whole night on a plane.

As he reaches down for a bag from my suitcase, I find myself checking him out again, taking in his strong back, rippled with muscles. What am I doing? I'm in India to win back my boyfriend! The last thing I should be doing is checking out a guy from my guesthouse.

He takes a few of my bags – my washbag and another bag dedicated to skirts and trousers and comes back over to the ladder. He starts climbing up.

'So did you just arrive from England?' he asks, clearly realizing I'm not a seasoned backpacker on a round-the-world expedition.

'Yep! Straight from London,' I tell him.

He climbs higher.

'Bit of a culture shock, huh?'

I laugh. 'Yeah, a bit.'

He hands me the bags and I place them inside my treehouse.

He starts heading back down.

'Shall I come down and help?' I suggest.

'Don't worry about it.' He shrugs, with an easy smile as he heads to my suitcase to grab another bag.

'How long have you been staying here?' I ask.

'A couple of months,' he tells me.

He climbs up the ladder with another couple of bags, one containing a selection of tops and another full of towels and pajamas.

'I'm staying over there,' he says, pointing towards another treehouse in an adjacent tree.

It's practically identical to mine, except his treehouse is even smaller and even higher up.

'Right… Have you been staying there the whole time?' I ask, feeling baffled.

Surely, he hasn't stayed in a treehouse for two whole months?!

'Yeah, I love it!' He beams as he reaches the top of my ladder and hands me my bags.

I notice, as I take the bags, that he has a tattoo on his wrist. It looks like something in Hindi. I'm curious as to what it says, but it feels too personal to ask right now.

I want to ask him why he loves it here. The sun's shining, we're surrounded by tree and flowers and the beach isn't far away, but how can you love living in a treehouse? How could anyone love sleeping on a horrible thin mattress for months? What is it about hot guys – this one and Paul – abandoning real life in exchange for weird alternative lifestyles on the opposite side of the world? Am I missing something?

'So, err, what do you do here?' I ask, trying to sound tactful and no doubt failing.

He smiles placidly.

'I meditate. I read,' he tells me, as he retreats down the ladder.

Meditation is hardly my jam, but he reads. That's kind of interesting.

'What do you read? Novels?' I ask.

'No. Mostly spiritual texts,' he replies, hopping off the ladder and returning his attention to my suitcase.

'So what brings you here?' he counters, squatting down to

contemplate the bags remaining in my case.

Suddenly, a pang of terror hits me. A wave of panic floods through me – cold and icy. I remember something I stashed away at the bottom of the suitcase, right underneath the bag he's just about to lift up. My vibrator. A Rampant Rabbit Priya bought for me as a tongue-in-cheek birthday present back before I met Paul. I was single and I'd been going through a bit of a dry spell. I'd been complaining about my lack of action and Priya, being the practical problem-solver that she is, thought a vibrator would be the perfect birthday present. But then I ran into Paul on the Tube platform not long after my birthday and, as it happened, I didn't end up needing her gift. I stuffed it in the back of one of my drawers and forget all about it, but as I was packing for this trip, I stumbled upon it again. There it was, tucked away, neon pink and strange-looking, and yet also kind of intriguing. I figured I may as well pop it in my suitcase just in case I got a bit twitchy during my trip. And now, a random, and let's face it, rather attractive man, who is apparently my new next-door neighbor, is leaning over my suitcase, about to come face to face with my sex toy.

'One second!' I shriek, my voice piercingly shrill, as I spin around and scarper down the ladder.

I look over my shoulder, hoping hot guy (whose name I still don't know) doesn't delve into my case.

'What is it?' he asks, although he doesn't seem to fully grasp my panic and reaches for a bag – the bag I placed on top of the vibrator.

Any second now, he's going to expose a big fat plastic penis. With bunny ears.

'STOP!' I shriek, racing down the ladder.

'What?' he looks over, startled.

'Stop! Please!' I beg, as I jump off the ladder and rush over to the suitcase. 'I have some…ummm…'

He eyes me quizzically.

'I have some personal stuff in there. A, erm, chakra aligner,' I blurt out.

'A chakra aligner?' he echoes, still squatting worryingly close to my suitcase.

'Yep, that's right!' I comment as casually as I can, pulling the case towards me.

My heart is pounding. 'A chakra aligner. They're great!'

'Oh wow! A chakra aligner!' he enthuses, eagerly eyeing my case.

Damn it. I forgot these hippy types love stuff like chakra aligners, if that's even a thing. Dream catchers, crystal balls, meditation beads, tarot cards, or hemp bum bags. They're all over that crap. It's like candy to a baby, crack to a junkie. I may as well have said I have the secret to enlightenment stashed between my mosquito repellent and my socks.

'It's, erm, a personal chakra aligner. VERY PERSONAL,' I insist, pushing my suitcase further along the paving stones, out of his reach.

I slap the lid down and turn back around, meeting his gaze. He looks shocked and slightly bemused.

'Sorry, it's just… It's a very personal item. It's for, erm, connecting with my spiritual self. You know, it's kind of sacred,' I babble. 'It's just one of those things.'

'Of course,' he comments, smiling politely, with only a tiny hint of awkwardness.

He rises from his squatting position and stretches, while I remain hunched on the ground, shielding my suitcase. I look up at him as he flexes and I have to admit, he's hot. *Really* hot. Like chakra-aligningly hot. His body is perfect. He's muscular but not too muscular. He's toned and tall and his skin looks so silky and smooth, his arms and legs adorned with fine golden hairs. His physique is so good that he could model, but his face is gorgeous too. He has a few slightly questionable tattoos – the scrawling Hindi across his wrist and a couple of others too: I spot a peace sign on his ankle and a tattoo of a sun with swirling rays peeking out from under his top, but his tattoos don't detract from his sex appeal. In fact, they almost add to it. They add a slight quirkiness as without them, he might be too attractive, stereotypically so. I imagined the hippies at the ashram to be weird-looking, dressed in Jesus sandals and tie-dye clothing, with smelly dreadlocks, but this guy is nothing like that. He looks cool.

'Well, thanks so much for your help!' I say, still reeling from my near-miss with total humiliation.

'No worries,' he replies.

'I can take the rest of my stuff up.' I tell him. 'I'd better be settling into my room,' I add.

He raises an eyebrow. 'Room?' he echoes.

'Well, you know, treehouse,' I clarify.

He laughs, a wry twinkle in his eyes. I've always assumed that people who like meditation and spiritual texts and chakra stuff are weird and humorless, but I pick up on a teasing side to this guy, a sardonic edge.

'Okay… Maybe catch you later then?' he suggests.

'Sure!' I reply, smiling brightly.

'I'm Seb, by the way,' he tells me.

'I'm Rachel!' I reply, rising to my feet and without thinking, I reach out to shake his hand.

He raises an eyebrow, glancing at my outstretched hand. I look at it, extended between us, and cringe, realizing how formal shaking hands appears. Who shakes hands in an ashram? I'm not in the corporate world right now. I'm not at a networking event or meeting a new client. I'm in an ashram in India, for goodness sake!

But nevertheless, Seb reaches over and shakes my hand.

'Nice to meet you, Rachel,' he says, pumping my hand as a smile twitches at the corners of his lips.

'Nice to meet you too!' I reply, feeling his warm palm against mine.

His hand is so much darker than mine, which is pasty from hours spent indoors tapping away at a keyboard. His tan isn't the kind of light caramel hue you can pick up from five minutes in a booth at the Tanning Shop on Borough High Street, it's a proper deep brown glow gained from hours spent basking in the Indian sun.

'Maybe catch up later?' Seb suggests, with a friendly smile. 'We all tend to hang out and have dinner together.'

Having let go of my hand, he gestures towards an outdoor seating area by the guesthouse.

'All?' I echo.

'Everyone from the guesthouse,' Seb says.

'Cool! Sounds good,' I reply, wondering who else is staying here.

Could I have miraculously found myself in a remote corner of the world where I'm surrounded by hot hippies like Seb or is he a one-off? Could the secret appeal of the ashram be that this is where sexy travelers hang out? Did I miss some kind of memo informing me that this is where the free-spirited cool people congregate?

'Great, see you later then.' Seb smiles and turns to head back to his treehouse.

'Cool! See you later!' I reply.

I turn back to my suitcase. I reach for the handle and yank it up, forgetting, in my jet-lagged, disorientated state that I forgot to zip the lid closed after slapping it shut. The lid flies open and the contents of my case start spilling over the ground. My eye-popping pink Rampant Rabbit tumbles across the paving stones, bouncing a little in Seb's direction.

My heart flips. I jump forward, diving after it, but it keeps bouncing, ricocheting off the stone slabs like a bouncy ball.

Sensing commotion behind him, Seb turns as I leap onto the ground, plunging on top of the dildo.

'Are you okay?' he asks, looking alarmed as he takes in the sight of me lying on the ground in an awkward spread-eagled position.

'I'm fine!' I insist, the vibrator pressed between my stomach and the paving stones, just about concealed from sight.

'Did you trip?' Seb asks, holding his hand out for me, to help me up.

'Oh, it's alright!' I bat his hand away. 'I'm good,' I tell him, while remaining plastered to the ground.

'You're good?' He frowns incomprehensibly, clearly wondering why I'd want to lie belly-down on the ground next to my half-unpacked suitcase. 'You don't want to get up?'

'No, no, I'm fine,' I insist, smiling enthusiastically as though lying on the ground is the best thing ever.

I find myself extending my arm and prop my head on my hand in an effort to look casual.

'Thought I'd just chill for a minute.' I affect a yawn. 'Jet lag.'

Seb gives me an odd look, as though not quite convinced.

I'm worried he's going to try to help me off the ground again, and nervously, I reach for a nearby plant and start stroking one of its leaves.

'Just connecting with Mother Nature,' I hear myself saying, dreamily.

Surely if I appeal to Seb's hippy side, what I'm doing might somehow make sense to him, right?

'Okay!' he laughs.

I feel a strange rumbling against my stomach. Twisting to reach for the plant must have set the vibrator off and I realize it's buzzing under my belly. It makes a low rumbling noise and I cough loudly in an effort to cover up the sound.

'See you later then!' I say, my voice high-pitched and strangulated.

'Erm, see you!' Seb replies, eyeing me strangely as he edges away towards his treehouse.

I hum a weird tune to cover the sound of buzzing and continue stroking the plant, until Seb has climbed up the ladder and slipped into his treehouse. Once I'm confident that he's inside and not about to reappear, I peel myself off the ground and furtively scoop the vibrator up. I twist if off and stash it in one of the bags in my suitcase, cursing under my breath.

I carry the rest of my stuff up to my treehouse and finally take up the empty husk of my case. Then I lie down on my flimsy bed and silently die of shame.

8 CHAPTER EIGHT

I wake up, blinking at the mosquito net above.

Confusion floods through me. Where am I? I wonder, feeling completely discombobulated, and then it hits me – oh, yeah, I'm in India. I'm in a treehouse. I'm miles away from everything.

Great. Brilliant. I roll over, pulling the mosquito net aside. I look around for my phone. The light in my treehouse is soft, neither day or night, and I have no idea what time it is. I grab my phone and peer at the screen: It's 8pm. I've slept the whole day. So much for adjusting to the local time zone.

I want to check my notifications, read my messages, scan my emails, and scroll through Twitter, like I usually do when I wake up, but of course, there's no WiFi and I have no data over here, so I can't. I haven't gone so long without internet for ages. Probably for years. World War Three could have broken out since I left England and I'd be none the wiser.

Sighing, I place my phone down and realize I need the loo. I contemplate the outdoor toilets Meera showed me earlier, my heart sinking. I really don't feel like having to squat over a hole in the ground.

Voices from outside distract me. I think about Seb. Is that him? I creep over to the doorway of my treehouse and furtively pull back the curtain to take a sneaky look. I spot a few other guests, sitting around one of the tables by the guesthouse, but I can't see Seb.

I must have conked out the moment I lay down earlier. I'm still wearing my jeans and t-shirt and so fortunately, I'm dressed appropriately for venturing out to the loo.

I climb out and descend the ladder. I glance across towards Seb's treehouse, but there are no signs of life. I look beyond, at the tips of the palm trees, the gardens, and the rooftops of other guesthouses in the distance. The sky has a gentle orange, reddish tinge. Dusky. I realize I've stopped climbing down the rungs of my ladder. I'm just perching on it, gazing. But the fullness of my bladder snaps me out of my reverie, and I scurry down.

A few of the other guests look curiously in my direction as I head to the loos. I smile and wave. They wave back, looking like a friendly enough bunch. As it turns out, the ashram isn't an enclave of hot men like Seb and the other guests appear to be your standard bunch of travelers – people of all ages, races, heights and shapes.

I pick my way across the garden towards the toilets. Or should I call them latrines? They're outdoors. They don't have roofs. They don't even have cisterns. They're just holes in the ground, next to rusty old taps, with a bucket. Meera explained earlier that you 'flush' the toilet by filling the bucket with water from the tap and chucking it down the hole. Feeling a sense of dread, I step into one of the toilets and appraise the hole in the ground, scattered with leaves. A lizard darts across the ground, making me jump. I check out the next toilet along instead, but it's just the same, minus the lizard. I don't know what exactly I'm expecting to find. A dazzling toilet with a bidet? Luxury padded toilet roll?! A hidden jacuzzi? As if. I'm going to have to just bite the bullet and squat over the ground.

I close the cubicle door behind me. I feel weirdly shy about pulling down my jeans and look up at the dusky sky. The color's rapidly changing, the edges of the sky blurring, taking on a gentle blueish hue. A blackbird flaps its wings and perches on the wall of my cubicle. I hesitate before pulling my trousers down, feeling awkward, even though it's not like the blackbird is going to be checking out my butt.

Shrugging off my discomfort, I pull my jeans down and squat over the ground. I can't go at first. It feels too weird and my body tenses up. I miss my lovely cozy bathroom back home, but I take a deep breath and concentrate. The pee starts trickling out of me, making a high-pitched tinkling sound against the ceramic hole. I think of the other guests outside and hope they can't hear. This is why toilets have roofs.

Once I'm finished, I look around for some toilet roll, but I can't see any. There's none. Damn. I shake a little and stand up, pulling up my jeans so I'm just about decent. I open the toilet door and check the coast is clear, before waddling to the next loo along, but there's no toilet paper in there either, or the next. There's simply no toilet paper. At all.

Suddenly, I remember what Priya said about how in India, people wipe with their left hand and eat with their right. I thought she'd been winding me up, but could she have been telling the truth? Is that really a thing?

Groaning, I squat back over the hole and shake a bit more, but I can't bring myself to wipe with my hand, not as my stomach is now rumbling too and I'm going to have to get some food soon. I don't care if I wipe with the left hand and eat with the right, it's still not happening.

I give up. There's a jug and a rusty old tap by the loo. I fill the jug with water and pour it down the hole. Then I stand up, buttoning my jeans, and head out of the toilet. At the end of the row of cubicles are two sinks with a mottled mirror hanging above them. I check out my reflection.

My hair is mussed up and askew and the pillow I slept on has left an imprint on my face, probably thanks to the thin mattress and the lumpy treehouse floor. I don't look my best and even though I'm hungry, I could do with sprucing myself up a bit, especially as there's a chance I might run into Paul this evening. The way I'm looking doesn't exactly scream, 'Take me back'.

I wash my hands and head back up to my treehouse. The other guests are wrapped in conversation and barely notice me. There's still no sign of Seb. I sit on the bamboo floor of my treehouse, still unable to quite believe I'm here. I crawl over to my suitcase and sift through the bags by the wall, cringing at the memory of stroking an aloe vera plant while lying on the ground, humming to myself like a crazy lady in front of Seb. I'm torn between wanting to see him again and being utterly mortified at the thought. I root through a few of the bags until I find one containing gifts the girls gave me for the trip. They felt I needed hippy stuff so bought a collection of tie-dye hareem trousers and wacky tie-dye vests. I find a matching azure tie-dye vest and trousers. I'd never normally wear anything like this and take them in, feeling a little unsure. But I'm in India now, aren't I? And this is the kind of thing you wear when travelling. I want to jazz them up a bit though, so root through my suitcase until I find a pouch I filled with jewelry. I pull out some gold hoop earrings and a gold choker-style necklace. They'll give my hippy outfit a glamorous feel.

I get changed into my new outfit and put the jewelry on, before slipping on my Prada wedges. I grab my washbag, towel and make-up bag and head back to the toilets. There are still a few guests hanging around by the kitchen area, but I can't stop and chat. I need to get ready quickly before the sun sets and ashram life shuts down for the evening.

I hurry to the toilets and wash my face, dabbing it dry with my towel. Having a proper shower would be preferable, but I don't have time. I need to go and find Paul. I'm pretty confident he's going to be glad to see me. It's been a few weeks now. Surely, he's calmed down? He'll have had some time to think and gain perspective. Hopefully, he'll have realized that life with me wasn't really so bad.

Hopefully. I just need to make myself look pretty. I have a fairly standard make-up routine that I usually use for workdays – foundation, powder, blusher, a dusting of eyeshadow, eyeliner flicks and a bit of mascara. I usually add a touch of tinted lip balm after I've chugged a few mugs of coffee, but something about being dressed completely differently to how I'd ever dress in London makes me feel like experimenting with my make-up too.

I decide to go a bit wild with my eyeshadow, opting for an electric blue shade from my eyeshadow palette that I've never worn before. I dab it onto my eyelids, before blinking, inspecting my reflection in the mirror. My eyeshadow's pretty bright, but the look is lacking something. I add a dusting of a gold glitter that I've used only once or twice before on nights out. I check out my reflection. With my blue clothes and blue eyeshadow, I feel quite coordinated. I root around in my make-up bag and find a lipstick lurking at the bottom that I've hardly ever worn. It's a glowing pink shade, almost highlighter pink. I think it was a Christmas present from my mum several years ago and I've never got around to wearing it. But why not now? It's vivid enough to match my eyeshadow and will go well with my unusual new clothes. Now is the perfect opportunity.

I apply a slick of it to my lips and pout in the mirror. I don't look too bad! I run a hairbrush through my hair and then wind my locks up into a bun on the top of my head, binding it in place with a few clips. I pluck out a few loose tendrils.

I step back from the mirror and check out the final result. I look pretty nice, for someone who's not washed in quite a long time and spent the whole day sleeping in a treehouse. I gather my things, pausing to spritz my neck with perfume and then I head back to my treehouse. I leave my washbag inside and grab my wallet containing rupees. I place it in a little woven boho bag I bought online and sling it over my shoulder, feeling a tremor of butterflies as I crawl back out of my treehouse. This is it. The moment of reckoning. I'm going to be reunited with Paul.

As I climb down from my treehouse, I catch the sound of a Seb's voice – that hard-to-place European and American accent. I look over towards the guests. There he is. Sitting, having dinner with some of the others, leading the conversation. I can't help noticing how a few of the other female guests are hanging off his every word, looking enamored with him. I try to catch what he's saying, but he's too far away. He must sense me looking as he glances over and waves, his face lighting up.

I wave back, mirroring his enthusiastic expression. It's easy to see why people are drawn to him. He comes across as so genuinely friendly, as well as being seriously gorgeous.

I jump off the ladder and head over to the group. Seb breaks off his conversation and comes over to me as I approach.

'You're looking nice,' he comments.

'Thanks!' I reply, smiling gratefully, while noticing, over his shoulder, that the other women from the guesthouse are eyeing me with a strained, conflicted mixture of politeness, wariness and disappointment.

They're both quite a lot older than me and Seb, but I get the feeling they quite liked having him to themselves. Somehow, I don't sense that I'm a particularly welcome addition.

'I love your outfit!' Seb comments, taking in my attire.

I feel a sense of relief. I'm not exactly used to wearing hippy stuff so it's nice to be complimented.

'Really?' I ask. 'This stuff isn't my usual vibe.'

Seb nods. 'Yeah, you look good. It suits you.'

'Oh, thank you!' I reply, blushing.

I'm blushing. I'm actually blushing. I can feel the warmth rising to my cheeks. Damn. I look down to my feet. This is so embarrassing. It's the Indian weather. It's the heat. It must be. I try to pretend it isn't happening. The more I think about the fact that I'm blushing, the more I'm going to blush. Just think about something else. Brazen it out. Except, when I glance up from the ground, the first thing my eyes land upon is Seb's eyes, his wide smile, the dimples in his cheeks. Dimples. I hadn't noticed he had dimples before. And up close, now that I'm not talking to him from up in a treehouse or panicking as a dildo rumbles under my stomach, I can't help noticing that his eyes are really blue. Staggeringly blue. His irises are a cool pale hue with a darker border. They're stunning. They look almost Photoshopped. I don't think I've ever seen eyes as striking in real life.

'Are you settling in okay, then?' Seb asks.

'Pretty well, although I've slept all day,' I admit, a little sheepishly. 'I'm probably going to be up all night now,' I add.

Seb laughs. 'Well, there's not much night life here, I'm afraid. We tend to go to sleep not long after the sun's gone down.'

'Oh…' I look towards the setting sun, the darkening skyline. 'Not long then?'

Seb follows my gaze towards the red-tinged horizon.

'No, not long now,' he concurs.

He looks back to me 'So, shall I introduce you to everyone?' he asks, glancing towards the group.

'Sure, but I'm in a bit of a hurry. I wanted to meet someone in the main hall before it closes,' I tell him.

'Oh, you know someone here?' Seb replies, seeming taken aback.

'Erm…yeah,' I reply, wondering how much to tell him about Paul.

Do I admit that my ex-boyfriend is here? Do I admit that I followed him halfway across the world and that he has no idea? No. I might save that for later.

'Cool!' Seb enthuses. 'Where are they staying?'

'Umm, I'm not sure,' I reply, shrugging, affecting a casual air.

Seb frowns. 'Have you called them?' he asks.

'Uhhh… No, I thought I'd just, erm, surprise them!' I insist.

'Wow, okay!' Seb replies, still looking a bit bemused.

I look towards the path leading out of the guesthouse.

'I should probably head over there. I need to make sure I don't miss him. Is it that way to the main hall?' I ask, pointing in the direction of what I think is the center of the ashram.

'Yes, it's that way. I'll walk you there if you like?' Seb suggests helpfully.

The ashram seems quite sprawling and I am in a hurry, up against the setting sun and the entire place shutting down for the night.

'Sure, thanks!' I reply gratefully.

I glance towards the other guests, a few of whom are tucking into a big dinner.

'Are you sure you're done with dinner though?' I ask.

'It's fine. I've eaten. Let's go.' Seb smiles, beckoning me to walk with him.

'Okay, great,' I reply, noticing the women Seb was talking to before shooting slightly disapproving looks our way, clearly not overly pleased about me stealing Seb away from them.

I smile awkwardly at them, before turning to walk with Seb. We amble along a bit, heading out of the guesthouse. Part of me is a bundle of nerves over potentially seeing Paul, but even though I'm hurt over everything, I'm looking forward to seeing him. I've missed him. Desperately. I can't wait to be reunited and talk things through, properly for once. Not just in the form of a strained argument in a restaurant. And yet in spite of my eagerness to see him, I'm also a bit excited at the prospect of walking with Seb to the main hall and finding out more about him and what led him to end up in this strange place.

'So, your friend has no idea you're here?' Seb asks, as we head out of the guesthouse and begin walking along the dusty path.

'No, he doesn't,' I admit, a little sheepishly.

A warm breeze brushes past us, rustling the tendrils of hair around my face. It's so pleasant. The evening is ambient and balmy. There are no sounds of traffic, no sirens, no screeching foxes like there are at night-time in London. The ashram is calm and peaceful and yet inside, I'm on edge. Now that we're outside the guesthouse, I could run into Paul at any moment. He could walk past us right now.

'So you just flew from London to surprise this guy?' Seb asks, looking curiously towards me as a man and a woman appear in the distance.

The man is about Paul's height with similar dark hair. My stomach twists with nerves, but then he gets a few paces closer and I realize it's not Paul, it's a stranger.

'Yep, I guess I did!' I admit, feeling a little ridiculous.

My plan made sense back home. Priya helped convince me that it was a good idea, a sensible move, a way of fighting for my relationship and my future, but now, walking alongside an easy-going person like Seb, I feel a bit crazy and out-there. Am I a bunny boiler? Is jetting on a plane and following your technically-ex boyfriend halfway across the world actually a bit weird?

'He must be really special to you,' Seb observes, a tender expression in his eyes.

'Yeah,' I reply. 'He is.'

I feel a pang of emotion and look down at the path.

A moment of silence passes between us as we pace ahead. I'm thinking about Paul, that night in La Dolce Vita and how wrong I got everything. But I force those sad thoughts out of my mind. I'm here now. I'm trying my best to salvage what Paul and I had. I'm giving it my all. There's nothing more I can do. There's no point wallowing.

'So...' I look over to Seb. 'Where are you from? What brought you here?' I ask.

'I'm from Quebec,' he tells me, which explains his accent since Quebec is a French-speaking part of Canada. 'And as to why I'm here. Well, that's a long story,' Seb laughs, rolling his eyes.

'Okay,' I laugh, feeling unsure whether to press him.

Perhaps his reason for being here is really personal. Maybe

someone died or he had a breakdown. Maybe you shouldn't ask people staying in ashrams what brought them there? It's not like going to stay at an ashram is like booking a couple of weeks in Ibiza. You don't go to an ashram to party and catch a bit of sun, you go to reflect and unwind. Perhaps asking someone at an ashram what brought them there is like asking someone at a rehab center what led them to end up in rehab – it's probably unlikely to be a particularly happy story. I need to get a better handle on ashram etiquette.

'It's okay, you don't have to answer!' I add, with an awkward laugh. 'Sorry to pry.'

'Don't worry about it.' Seb smiles, looking pensive as we walk along. 'I guess it was a bit of a mad time though. Things got a bit crazy back home. I was working at a ski resort and it was pretty full-on. Lots of partying, hanging out with tourists, lots of girls, drinking, drugs.'

I look over at him, shocked. *Drugs?*

'When you're working in a place like that, life's just one big party. I got sucked into it. All I was doing was partying,' Seb admits.

He glances over at me, a rueful look in his eyes.

'Sounds fun!' I comment.

'It was fun. Too much fun!' Seb jokes.

Another silence passes between us. I'm curious to know more, but I also don't want to pry. I glance towards Seb. He looks reflective and I wonder whether he'll elaborate. In the darkening sky, his face looks different. The shadows make his face appear more angular, emphasizing his chiseled features, his perfect bone structure. He's seriously handsome and I can imagine I'm not the only person to fall for his looks. I've known him less than a day and I've already been drooling over his eyes, his dimples, his muscles, even the golden hairs on his arms and legs. And I'm meant to be here to win back my boyfriend! I can easily imagine how Seb would have been on the receiving end of a lot of attention from tourists, free and single and ready to have a good time. But most guys would love that attention. Most guys would love their lives being one non-stop holiday, with partying and women and endless fun.

'It must feel different being here after all of that?' I venture.

Seb shrugs. 'It is, but I love it.' He glances over at me, smiling softly. 'Life's completely different here. I gave up all my vices. Sex, drink, drugs. I decided I'd have a year off. A year of complete abstinence. It's been hard at times, but I feel like it's helping me clear my head,' Seb tells me, with complete sincerity, seemingly unaware of how strange such a pledge sounds.

'You've given up sex for a year?' I balk.

'Yeah!' Seb laughs, his eyes flickering with amusement at my reaction.

Maybe I shouldn't be shocked. Perhaps everyone in the ashram has taken some kind of abstinence vow. That sort of stuff could be the done thing around here.

'Wow, okay...' I murmur.

I spot a large building in the distance which I'm pretty sure is the main hall. I vaguely recognize it from the pictures I browsed of this place online, and even though I feel a twinge of nervousness, I'm still distracted by Seb's confession. He's given up sex for a year! The idea that anyone would do that voluntarily is bizarre to me. Was he a sex addict? A total player? Is this some kind of self-imposed punishment for a life of depravity? I'd never voluntarily go without sex for that long. The thought is horrible. I haven't had sex since Paul and I broke up, which has been a month now and I'm already beginning to feel frustrated. We had sex just a few days before he dumped me. In fact, our healthy sex life was one of the reasons I didn't realize that there was anything wrong with our relationship. Sex with Paul was always good, really good. We've had chemistry ever since we first clapped eyes on each other and it's stayed strong throughout our relationship, even during the past few years when our life apparently became insufferably dull, according to Paul. He's always been a passionate lover, sparks have always flown between us. Maybe our healthy sex life is one of the reasons I've been so reluctant to let him go. I haven't wanted to give up on those sparks and that intimacy.

'So, how's the celibacy going then?' I ask, bemused.

'It's okay. I went to Thailand for my birthday though a few months ago and messed up, but otherwise it's been fine,' he tells me.

It's none of my business, of course, but I can't help feeling an almost sordid sense of intrigue. I want to know more. What happened in Thailand? I try to think of a way of subtly getting Seb to elaborate, but I can't think of a way to phrase the question that isn't just downright nosy.

We arrive outside the main hall and I realize the moment's passed. If there ever was an appropriate moment to pry into someone else's sex life.

'So, this is it!' Seb declares, gesturing towards the hall.

It's a striking building, with pillars and a towering roof like a temple, yet it's been painted in eye-poppingly bright shades: neon yellow, glowing orange and fuchsia pink. It's so cheerful and rainbow-like that I feel like laughing. It looks like something from a children's storybook. It couldn't be more different from the slick colorless office blocks I walk past every day on the way to and from work

'Wow!' I gawp, awed by the sight of the place.

'It's quite something, isn't it?' Seb comments, skipping up the steps towards the entrance.

I peer through the open door. I can see people milling about inside: a few people carrying plates of food, others waiting to be served at a canteen, diners sitting around tables. Paul could be one of those people. He could be among that hubbub. My nerves intensify, my stomach squirming at the thought.

'Are you coming?' Seb asks, turning around at the entrance, eyeing me expectantly.

'Uh, yes, definitely!'

'Well, come on then!' Seb beckons me towards the hall.

I laugh awkwardly and head up the steps towards him.

'Do you want to come in?' I ask as Seb lingers by the entrance.

'Well, I don't want to ruin your reunion,' Seb replies, backing away slightly.

I realize I really don't want him to go. He's so laid-back that he's a comforting presence. Even though I haven't known him for long, I feel relaxed around him. It was a bit surprising how he just opened up about his sex life or lack thereof, but it was also kind of cool. He's an open person. He doesn't seem fake or cold or wily, like people in London can sometimes seem. He comes across as genuine and flawed, humble and sweet. His easy demeanor is soothing. It's the perfect antidote to how wound-up and stressed I feel right now.

'Come! It'll be fine,' I insist.

'Really?' Seb replies, sounding unconvinced, but he narrows his eyes and seems to register something on my face. An expression of unease no doubt.

'Okay, if you want me to,' he relents with an encouraging smile.

'Thanks,' I reply, feeling genuinely grateful.

We walk into the hall. It's huge. There must be a couple of hundred people inside. The canteen is bustling. People are sitting at tables, eating their dinner from silver trays, chatting convivially. There's a stage area at the back and quite a few people are sitting on it, just hanging out. A lot of the people in the hall are wearing ashram robes – loose white linen tops and trousers. I read about the robes online. They're meant to encourage the individual to relinquish their ego and the trappings of Western life. I can sort of see the logic, but there's something a bit creepy about them to me. After all, where else does everyone wear uniform robes like that, but in mental hospitals and prisons.

I look around, scanning the hall for Paul, but I can't spot him. He might not even be here anyway. After all, the ashram is huge.

'Where's your friend?' Seb asks.

'I'm not sure…' I reply, looking along each row of tables, trying to spot Paul's familiar face, but to no avail.

'Shall we eat?' Seb suggests, checking out the canteen's enticing array of fresh salads and curries and naans.

It does look incredible.

'Yes, let's,' I reply.

We wander over to the canteen.

'Haven't you already eaten though?' I ask Seb, recalling the dinner he was having back at the guesthouse.

'I'll eat again!' Seb laughs.

We walk up to the canteen. The food looks so delicious and my stomach instantly starts rumbling. I realize I haven't eaten since I was on the plane – hours ago. I've barely even registered my own hunger as I've been too focused on reuniting with Paul.

Seb and I take plates and trays from a stack and begin working our way along the canteen. The food looks so mouth-watering that I nearly stop thinking about Paul. Nearly. I still find myself looking over my shoulder every now and then, half expecting him to be behind me, registering my presence in disbelief, but he's not there. I get the feeling he's not in the hall at all. He's probably having dinner at his guesthouse or one of the other eateries in the ashram.

I load my plate with food, unable to resist the delicious dishes. Seb practices a little more restraint, opting for just a couple of spoonfuls of the tastiest-looking curries and salads, rather than turning his plate into the towering mound of food that mine is.

We pay and then look around for somewhere to sit. The hall is pretty packed, but Seb spots a few free seats at the end of one of the tables. I do another scan for Paul as we sit down, but he's nowhere to be seen.

I feel myself relax a bit. Even though I'm disappointed, I have a plate of tasty food and, although I probably shouldn't think it, a rather tasty companion, too. Life could be a lot worse.

'This looks so good!' I gush as I tuck into my heaped plate.

'Yeah, the food here is amazing. I put on weight at first. That's why I try and eat at the guesthouse more now,' Seb explains.

I eye his bicep, flexing as he raises his fork to his mouth and I'm tempted to say something about what great shape he's in, but I resist. He might think I'm coming onto him and given that he's avoiding sexual contact right now, it probably wouldn't be appreciated.

'Is there a gym here?' I ask, before taking a bite of a garlic naan.

'Yeah, there's an outdoor gym,' Seb says. 'The equipment's pretty basic, but it's nice being able to work out in the sunshine.'

He tucks into his salad.

'Sounds cool,' I comment, although it didn't occur to me for a second to bring gym clothes on this trip.

I try not to think about Seb working out in the sunshine, although images pass unwittingly through my mind. I picture him flexing in the sun as I chew my naan. What am I thinking? So he's a hot guy and I haven't had sex for a few weeks, but that's no reason to be such a pervert! Could it be that ever since he's mentioned that he's taken a vow of abstinence, he's suddenly become even more appealing? Like forbidden fruit in the sense that now I know I can't have him, I want him even more.

'So, tell me about this friend you're surprising? What's the deal with that?' Seb asks.

'Oh, yeah…' I reply, having momentarily forgotten about Paul in favor of thoughts of Seb's muscles.

'He's, uh…' I hesitate, not knowing quite where to begin.

Should I tell Seb the truth or will he think I'm weird? I could just brush him off and be vague about it, say something about surprising an old friend, except Seb seems like such an honest person that it might feel uncomfortable to be so vague with him. I take a sip of water as I consider how to answer, when I feel a tap on my shoulder.

'Rachel?' A familiar voice says.

My heart skips a beat. It's Paul. I turn to see him standing behind me, his face practically white from shock.

He looks completely different. He's wearing the white ashram robes, he's grown a beard and his hair has been wound into shaggy dreadlocks. No wonder I didn't spot him. And yet, despite how different he looks, I feel a surge of affection for him. Finally, I'm here with him. Finally, we can talk things through.

'Paul!'

His eyes are wide.

'What are you doing here?' he croaks.

'I, erm…' I try to think how to answer, but I'm aware of being watched.

A girl's standing behind him. She's also wearing the ashram robes. She looks mid-twenties and quite severe. She has no make-up on and her brown hair is scraped back into a tight ponytail. She eyes me coldly.

I glance back from her to Paul, trying to focus on him instead.

'I'm here to see you. Why else would I be here?' I say.

I look imploringly into his eyes, trying to transmit just how much I've missed him over the past few weeks and how determined I am to save our relationship, but my expression, which is meant to be tender and meaningful appears to be having no effect. The look reflected back at me is one of anger and frustration. Paul's eyes are blazing.

'I can't believe this!' he hisses. 'I came here because I needed to get away from my life back home. I needed space and you've chased me!'

'I haven't chased you!' I object.

After all, he's been here for several weeks without me. He's had loads of time to himself. It's not like I just hopped on the first plane.

'I wanted SPACE!' Paul states, raising his voice.

A few more people look around and I feel my cheeks begin to burn up. I can't even bring myself to look at Seb, who is no doubt watching this horror show in complete shock. He'd naturally have thought that whoever I was here to surprise would be happy to see me, and instead they're shouting at me, wishing I'd never shown up.

I lean a little closer to Paul.

'I just wanted to show you how much I cared. I want to save our relationship,' I tell him, trying to keep my voice low.

Paul sighs exasperatedly. 'Rachel, if you cared, you'd have respected my right to move on with my life. You wouldn't have stalked me halfway across the world!'

I shrink away from him. I've hardly ever seen Paul look so angry. I feel a rush of shame. Have I got this all wrong? Perhaps for once, I should have ignored Priya's advice. After all, it's not like she has a track record of taking the most traditional approach when it comes to matters of the heart.

'I'm sorry. I was hardly stalking you though,' I comment feebly.

Paul laughs sarcastically, shaking his head in disbelief.

'I can't believe this,' he scoffs. 'We break up, then you show up here, all the way from London, dressed like Princess Jasmine from Aladdin and you expect me to greet you with open arms.'

He gestures up and down at my outfit. The pale girl behind him snorts with laughter, before cupping her hand over her mouth.

Princess Jasmine? I hadn't thought of her while I was getting ready this evening, but Paul's right. I do resemble her. I have the same blue outfit, exaggerated make-up, even similar jewelry. I thought Paul would appreciate my efforts to dress differently and acclimatize to my new surroundings. I thought he'd realize I can be adventurous. I figured it would show him that I can be more than just the furniture-obsessed lawyer bore I've become in recent months. But no. I just look like a joke to him – a Disney character. My cheeks blaze with embarrassment. I feel two inches tall.

'Can we talk about this privately, Paul?' I suggest, eyeing him fretfully, before glancing at his bitchy sidekick, who is still sniggering.

Who is she, anyway? Surely, he's not dating her?

'No!' Paul scoffs. 'No, we can't talk privately You just don't get it, do you? I WANT TO MOVE ON!' he stipulates, loudly and clearly, like he's talking to an idiot.

He turns to the girl behind him, who's now smirking at me.

'Come on, let's go,' he says.

He turns on his heel and marches away, towards the exit. The girl throws a mean, pitying look my way before following him out.

I watch them despondently as they leave. Then I realize there's a hush in the hall, protracted seconds of silence rolling by. I look around. Mine and Paul's argument has somehow silenced the entire place. I suppose the ashram isn't used to drama. People here are probably too busy meditating to have domestics. I look sheepishly down at my lap, hoping people will turn their attention back to their meals.

Eventually, I glance shyly up at Seb, aware that my cheeks are burning.

He looks at me sympathetically. I can't think of a single thing to say and silence passes between us.

I reach for my naan and take a bite.

'How's your naan?' Seb asks, smiling sweetly in spite of everything.

I swallow.

'It's great,' I reply awkwardly, trying not to cry.

9 CHAPTER NINE

'Damn!' I grumble, pushing Seb's laptop across the picnic table.

I give up trying to talk to the chat operator of my airline, who keeps parroting the terms and conditions of my flight at me.

I'd booked what I thought was a fancy flight insurance package that included the option of changing the return date of your journey home, but what I didn't realize was that I could only change the date if I had 'extenuating circumstances' like bereavement or illness. Apparently, being ruthlessly rejected by your boyfriend in the middle of an ashram dining hall and being ridiculed for resembling a Disney character doesn't count.

'No luck?' Seb pulls a face.

'Nope,' I sigh.

'So you're stuck here for two full weeks then,' Seb remarks, fully aware of my predicament.

I told him everything last night once I got over the initial shock. Unlike Priya, Seb wasn't particularly on board with my plan to win Paul back and seemed to be of the opinion that if he wanted to come to India to 'find himself' then that's what I should have let him do.

He made me sound like some sort of self-discovery saboteur, which was a little awkward, but of course, if anyone's going to be able to relate to Paul's quest for enlightenment then it'll be Seb. Even though Seb didn't exactly agree with my endeavor to win Paul back, it was good to talk things through with him. He was so sensitive and understanding, and even though I still feel a bit bruised, it was good to have someone supporting me. One thing Seb and I definitely were in agreement on is that Paul was a complete dick last night. We both firmly agreed on that.

'Yep, I'm stuck here for two weeks,' I reply.

Two whole weeks. God. I honestly don't know how I'm going to cope. Thanks to my jet lag (and general stress), I was up most of last night tossing and turning. But it turns out that no matter whether you lie on your left side or your right side or your back, trying to sleep on bamboo stalks is simply not comfortable. It must have been 4am by the time I finally passed out, and then I was up a few hours later at dawn when it turns out that the ashram becomes an aviary. I've never heard so much birdsong in my life: hooting and chirping and singing. It was impossible to sleep over the cacophony, and just when I thought it couldn't get any noisier, there was human singing and chanting too. I mentioned it to Seb earlier and he said it was Meera. Apparently, she does it every morning, performing a 'vocal sun salutation'.

'It could be worse,' Seb reasons, gazing over the garden of the guesthouse, which I have to admit, is rather pretty.

'I suppose,' I admit.

The area where we're sitting has been decorated in paving stones carved into the shape of leaves, which fan out across a grassy expanse, dotted with flowerbeds bursting with exotic lilies, sunflowers, marigolds, lotuses and small buds with petals like stars. In the distance are the palm trees and hammocks. I might curl up in one later and see if I can get some shut eye, although if I'm stuck here for two weeks then I really should stop sleeping during the day.

I drum my fingernails against the picnic table, eyeing Seb's laptop again, even though I've just pushed it aside.

'Do you mind if I...' I reach for it.

One thing I've learnt about Seb is that while he may have given up sex, drink and drugs for an entire year, fortunately, he hasn't given up the internet. Working in the travel industry has clearly made him a savvy traveler, because he managed to pick up an internet dongle at Mumbai airport, loaded up with a ton of data, enabling him to get online despite our guesthouse's no WiFi policy. Although he insists he hardly goes online at all, only logging on once every few weeks to send emails to family.

'What do you need to do?' Seb asks, eyeing me warily.

The truth is, I want to check my work emails. I've already checked my personal account and let my family and friends know I got here safely, but I want to know what's happening in the office. It's 9am on Monday morning. Well, here it is. Technically, back home, it's three or four in the morning. But it still feels really weird to not be working. I've set up my 'out of office' reply, but nevertheless, I'm curious to find out if there are any updates from the office, especially given Mr Pearson's surprise visit, which still bothers me slightly since I have no idea what it was about.

'I just... I, err...' I stammer.

'You want to go on Twitter?' Seb raises an eyebrow accusingly.

He's been keeping a pretty close eye on me ever since I got online, watching a display in the left-hand corner of the screen to see how much data I was using. I suppose when, like him, you're here indefinitely, you want to make your data last. Apparently, there are a few computers in the main hall, but you have to book a slot to use them. This place is barbaric.

'I... just...'

'If it's online shopping, they don't deliver here,' Seb jokes, smiling cheekily.

'It's not online shopping!' I tut. 'But it's nice to know that in your eyes I'm a vapid consumer!'

Seb laughs. 'Okay, fine. My bad. Work then?'

I smile guiltily. 'Rumbled.'

Seb shakes his head in mock disappointment and reaches for the laptop. For a moment, I think he's going to push it back across the picnic table towards me and allow me to indulge myself, but instead he just presses a few keys and ejects the dongle.

'I'm doing you a favor,' he insists, regarding me over the top of the screen, before snapping the laptop closed.

'How?' I balk.

'You're here in India and you want to check your office emails. I mean, come on!' He rolls his eyes indulgently.

I feel like explaining to him that something's going on with my company's CEO and that it could potentially mean something significant, in terms of redundancies or restructuring, and yet, I still get the feeling that office politics, no matter how drastic, will be of no consequence to Seb. That kind of talk is kryptonite to ashram-dwellers like him.

'Alright, fine,' I relent. 'No office emails for me.'

Seb smiles.

A peacock struts into the guesthouse garden, its beautiful feathers vibrant and pearlescent, shimmering in the sun.

'Wow!' I utter as it approaches our table, looking regal and proud.

Seb and I both admire it as it parades ostentatiously around the garden before strutting back out onto the path and disappearing from sight. As it retreats from view, I realize Seb's right. I am in India and office politics is irrelevant right now. If I'd been staring at his computer screen, clicking through my inbox, I might have missed the sight of that beautiful peacock. What else might I miss if I keep obsessing about life back home? I don't exactly expect I'm going to fall for ashram life, but I may as well at least try to appreciate it.

'So what do you do here then?' I ask, fixing Seb with a curious look.

'There's plenty to do,' Seb insists, smiling.

His smile really is ridiculously cute. The narrow gap between his front teeth gives him such an adorable look. Combined with his hippy tattoos and his shaved head and his slightly quirky character, his handsomeness has an intriguing and uniquely captivating quality.

'Like what?' I ask.

'Well, there's yoga, meditation, Tai Chi, massage, art classes, swimming, gardening, whatever you want!' Seb insists, gesturing expansively.

I smile weakly. Yoga? Yoga is the one craze I've never even remotely got on board with. Show me a yoga studio and I'll show you a wanker magnet. I've tried it, once or twice, but it's just boring. And I've never experienced any kind of physical benefit. People talk about yoga bodies but I think it's a con. I mean, have you ever seen someone overweight walk into a yoga studio and leave slim? Hardly. The type of people who go to yoga classes always seem to be in good shape in the first place. I reckon yoga is just an excuse to wear nice Lycra and have tasty smoothies afterwards and catch up with yoga pals. And gardening? Do I look like an OAP?

'Cool,' I reply weakly. 'So, erm, which of those activities are you doing today?' I ask, hoping that his itinerary might offer something slightly better in the way of entertainment.

Even checking out this outdoor gym he frequents would be a lot more interesting than getting green-fingered.

'I'm going to meditate for a few hours,' Seb tells me.

Meditate? For a few hours?

I must be gawping, because Seb starts to laugh.

'It's not that bad,' he claims.

'A few hours?' I echo.

'Buddha meditated for forty-nine days to achieve enlightenment,' Seb tells me.

'Oh, come on,' I scoff.

'He did!' Seb insists.

'What? So he didn't eat? He didn't go to the toilet?' I protest.

'No, he reached a higher plane,' Seb insists, although his eyes lack conviction. 'He rose above bodily functions.'

'Hmm...' I eye him cynically.

'That's what his followers believe.' Seb shrugs.

'Well, obviously that's rubbish! Even if he was grabbing the odd bug here and there off the ground to sustain himself and drinking rain, he would have needed to go to the toilet,' I point out.

Seb snorts with laughter. He looks down at the picnic table and shakes his head, his lips tight, as though he's biting his tongue from saying something.

'What?' I ask.

He looks up. 'It's just you. I haven't met anyone like you in this place. Two minutes into contemplating meditation and we're discussing Buddha's bowel movements.'

I smirk. 'I just think you need to consider the practicalities,' I comment, when an idea hits me. 'Maybe Buddha was wearing a nappy of some description. Did they have nappies back then?'

'Seriously?' Seb tuts, standing up. 'You need some spirituality in your life.'

He gestures for me to get up.

'Come on. Let's meditate,' he insists.

10 CHAPTER TEN

'Where are we going?' I ask as we leave the guesthouse, the morning sunlight illuminating the same path we walked along last night, revealing pretty flowers and shrubbery that I hadn't noticed before.

'To the meditation studio,' Seb explains, marching along.

'The meditation studio?' I echo. 'What the hell is that? Buddha didn't have a "meditation studio", he just had a tree. Isn't going to a meditation studio defeating the point?'

'What point?' Seb asks, eyeing me with amusement.

'Well you're meant to use meditation to transcend your surroundings, right? Reach a higher plane and all that, but if you're already in a boujee meditation studio then aren't you kind of cheating? Or is this, like, meditation for beginners?' I ask.

Seb laughs. 'It's not "meditation for beginners"!' he insists, doing air quotes.

Suddenly, he stops, drawing to a halt, as though a thought has occurred to him.

'Hey, maybe you're right, actually,' he says. 'Maybe we should meditate under a tree.'

He peers along the path, squinting into the distance at a copse of trees.

'Err…' I utter.

A mangey-looking stray dog wanders along the path. Seb is too focused on peering into the distance at the trees to notice, but I back away, eyeing the dog warily. It sniffs at the ground and doesn't look remotely interested in me or Seb, but the last thing I need is to get bitten by a possibly rabid dog. Animals of the dog's ilk would almost certainly bother us if we decided to meditate under a tree for hours, and then there's the mosquitos to worry about. And the blistering sun, which will be beating down by mid-day and…actually…

'Well, I have only just arrived from London, and I suppose I am kind of a beginner,' I reason. 'I think maybe the meditation studio will do for now.'

I start pacing along the path, trying to ignore Seb smirking out of the corner of my eye, having totally called my bluff.

The walk to the studio isn't quite what I imagined. I thought the ashram was all exotic gardens and temples and pretty guesthouses, I didn't realize parts of it are built-up. Well, when I say build-up, what I mean is that the ashram has an ashram version of a shopping center. Winding off the path is a development that looks quite modern and plush, containing a gift shop, a supermarket, even a clothes store. I hesitate as we pass it, in shock.

'Can we…?' I edge a little closer, squinting towards the windows of the gift shop. 'Can we just take a little look?' I suggest.

'Buddha didn't shop before meditating,' Seb points out, irritatingly.

I ignore him and wander a little closer, catching sight of the display within the gift shop. There are so many cute things: candles, crystals, dream catchers, bath products, and *cushions*. The most gorgeous cushions! I edge closer. They look handmade, each one emblazoned with the most beautiful embroidered designs featuring emblems quintessential to India – elephants, lotuses, tigers shells, peacocks and more. They're *so* gorgeous. IKEA doesn't have anything like them. Not even remotely like them. Or Dunelm. Or even Habitat. They'd look so perfect in my living room. It's been in need of a pop of color and these cushions are just the ticket.

'Rachel? Rachel?!' I hear Seb saying, his voice weirdly distant.

The cushions had me under a spell. I tear my attention away, and turn back to him, blinking.

'Yep?'

'Aren't we meant to be meditating?!' he reminds me.

'Yes, but…' I steal another glance at the cushions. 'I think I should get a cushion, you know, to sit on…'

I edge towards the shop.

'They have cushions in the studio. They have mats too,' Seb informs me.

Of course, they do.

'Well, I might just buy a few anyway. They look amazing!' I enthuse.

Meditation can wait. It's not every day that you find cushions this gorgeous.

'Alright,' Seb sighs, looking a little despondent. 'I mean, the shop's still going to be here on the way back though. It would probably be easier to get the things you want on your way home, rather than lug stuff all the way to the studio and then back, but it's up to you.'

He perches on a nearby wall.

He has a point. It's not like, if I'm totally honest with myself, I intend to buy just one cushion. I definitely want two or three. Okay, more like four, or five, or half a dozen since I may as well round it up. I picture my living room. Six of those cushions would look amazing. And maybe I could grab a few candles, put them on the coffee table. I could get a dreamcatcher too as a souvenir or a present for Priya. That is a fairly sizeable haul and it would be a bit of a drag to lug it all the way to the meditation studio and back.

'I just hope the cushions won't have gone by the time we're done meditating,' I comment, thinking out loud.

'They'll be there,' Seb insists. 'I've been walking past that shop every day for weeks and those cushions have been there the whole time.'

I hesitate, not sure whether to leave it. Seb may well be right and the cushions may still be in the shop by the time we're done meditating, but it's still a game of chance. After all, you never know when a savvy shopper is going to swoop in and grab the thing you've had your eye on for weeks. I've been burned that way before and I don't want to be burned again, and yet, I feel kind of bad on Seb, sitting boredly on the wall. He's clearly keen to crack on with some hardcore meditation, and he has taken me under his wing since I got here, helping with my suitcase, accompanying me to the main hall last night, and letting me use his computer and his dongle. It is probably a bit unreasonable of me to leave him sitting out here while I splurge in the gift shop. Also, if I know he's out here waiting, it's not like I'll be able to give the task my full attention. I need to have a clear head. If I'm feeling pressured, I might make the wrong decisions, like the time I panic-bought a truly awful space age lava lamp in IKEA because Paul was hassling me to wrap things up since a footy game due to start.

'Okay, I'll leave it. Let's go meditate,' I relent.

Seb glances up from watching a bright red caterpillar make its way across the paving stones at his feet. 'Are you sure?'

'Yeah, I'll get them on the way back. You're right, that's a better idea,' I say.

Seb smiles. 'Okay, cool.'

We walk along the path and I know I should probably be thinking about deeper stuff, spiritual stuff or whatever, but I'm still thinking about those cushions. They really are going to look great in my living room. I can't wait to get them. At least some good will have come from my trip to India. Paul may not want to be with me, but the plus side to that is that I no longer need to pretend that I don't love home furnishings. I can splash out on cushions to my heart's content. I can make my living room look as cute and cozy as I like, and I don't have to feel remotely bad about it.

I glance over at Seb. While I've been daydreaming about my living room, he seems to have been lost in thought about something too. He's frowning slightly to himself, his expression faraway. I wonder whether he's thinking back to his time in the ski resort, to his wild days. I'm still curious about what he got up to back then. Was it really so bad that he had to become celibate? I still want to pry, but I don't feel it's my place. I have only known the guy for just over a day.

We carry on walking, lost in our own private worlds of thought. Ordinarily, I'd probably find walking in silence with someone I hardly know to be quite uncomfortable, but I don't feel like that around Seb. Instead, I feel relaxed. Maybe it's the effect of being on holiday, or the radiant glow of the sun, or the gorgeous soaring palm trees dotted along the path, but I feel quite peaceful. The humiliation of my encounter with Paul last night has faded surprisingly rapidly. I still have some work to do to get my head around the fact that he doesn't want to be with me. It still feels raw and my trip to India has certainly not gone to plan but maybe being here will be a good thing. As long as I stay out of his way, having a bit of sunshine and some free time to think and come to terms with the end of my relationship is probably exactly what I need. I packed a few notebooks too. Maybe I can try journaling. Or at least jotting down some thoughts on how I'm going to overcome the latest stumbling block in my Life List.

'Here it is!' Seb says, stopping at the end of a winding path leading to a small building with plate glass walls, which is presumably the studio.

'Looks nice,' I note as we wander down the path.

Whoever looks after the gardens at the studio clearly has a love of horticulture as they're beautiful, blooming with the most colorful array of flowers. Although the studio has glass walls, it's shaded by palm trees at the back. In front is a tiered, stone fountain. A stream of water trickles out of it, making a gushing, relaxing sound. The fact that I can hear the fountain so clearly reminds me once again just how peaceful the ashram is. All of the sounds I'm used to aren't apparent here. There are no London buses chugging along, no honking cars. There are no harassed-looking office workers, pounding the pavement, barking into their phones. There are no train announcements or planes swooping overhead. There's no ding on my phone because someone's liked a post on Facebook or shared a cat video on WhatsApp. There's certainly no sound of a ringtone because Paul is calling. It's just *quiet*. Perfectly quiet. Weirdly and entrancingly quiet. I smile to myself.

'You're really taken with that fountain, aren't you?' Seb comments, piercing my thoughts.

I look over at him.

'Oh, yeah, I guess. It's pretty' I reply, taken aback.

'Maybe they do fountains in the gift shop. Do you have a garden back home?' he asks.

I feel my eyes widen as the thought sinks in. I've never even thought about water features.

'Yes, we do have a garden actually,' I muse.

'We?' Seb echoes.

'Me and…' I hesitate. 'Paul. We were living together, but I guess we're not anymore.' I smile awkwardly.

'Oh, I'm sorry,' Seb replies, grimacing. 'I didn't mean to remind you.'

'It's fine! I need to get used to it.' I shrug, although I don't feel quite as carefree inside as I'm making out.

'I didn't realize you two were living together,' Seb comments.

It occurs to me that I didn't mention that part when I explained about our break-up last night.

'Yeah, it was pretty serious,' I laugh, my voice chipper but unconvincing.

'I see,' Seb replies, smiling sympathetically.

His smile is so sweet and inflected with concern that I feel something lurch inside. A feeling of self-pity and deep disappointment that I've been trying to keep at bay through making jokes about Buddha's bowel movements and fantasizing about cushions threatens to raise its ugly head. The trickling of the fountain could soon mirror the flow of my tears if I'm not careful.

'So, let's meditate!' I suggest brightly.

'Okay, let's do it!' Seb concurs, with equally strained enthusiasm.

I can tell he's a bit worried about me, but what can I do? I can't let it out, unleashing a torrent of suppressed tears. Seb has witnessed quite a lot of drama in just 24 hours of knowing me, the last thing I need to do is start blubbing away on his shoulder.

He approaches the meditation studio and pulls one of the sliding doors aside.

'Do they just leave things unlocked here?' I comment. 'Don't you need to ask anyone to use this place?'

'No.' Seb gestures for me to step inside. 'They just leave it open so anyone can come and meditate whenever they feel like it.'

'That's very trusting,' I reply, not really sure who 'they' are, but I'm guessing it's whoever owns the studio, be that the guru or someone else.

I follow Seb inside. I can see immediately why he'd rather meditate here than under a tree. The studio is so lovely. Dreamcatchers dangle from the ceiling and the floor is covered in overlapping rugs, all mismatched and threadbare and spread out at odd angles, but the affect is charming and homely. Alongside one of the walls are some rolled up yoga matts, cushions, even blankets.

'This is so cute! I love it,' I gush.

'It's nice, isn't it?' Seb comments, as he wanders over to a cabinet in the corner of the studio.

He pulls open a drawer and retrieves a long thin stick from a narrow packet. It takes me a moment to realize it's incense.

'Sage and bergamot okay with you?' Seb asks, looking up from the packet.

'Yep, fab! Love a bit of sage,' I insist, even though I barely know what sage smells like.

Seb smiles as he takes a box of matches from the drawer. He lights the incense stick and then places it in a holder on top of the cabinet. It begins gently burning down, emitting spirals of fragrant smoke. I pluck a cushion from the selection alongside the wall. The cushion I choose is made from cheap purple satin and it's nowhere near as pretty or unique as the ones in the gift shop, but it's large and soft and should be good for meditating.

'So, where shall we sit?' I ask, appraising the floor of the studio, and wondering if there's a special meditation spot.

'Wherever you like,' Seb replies, grabbing a cushion for himself.

'Okay.'

I plonk my cushion down in the middle of the room and sit down cross-legged on it, feeling pretty happy with my choice of spot. I have a good view through the floor-to-ceiling windows of the fountain and the garden outside. With its glass walls, the studio's a bit like being in a pod within a botanical garden. It's really quite lovely.

Seb places his cushion next to mine and sits down, effortlessly adopting the lotus position.

'Wow, you can do that!' I remark, surprised.

'It took me a while, but I got there in the end,' Seb tells me, as he lowers his hands to his knees and places them palm upwards, drawing his forefinger and thumb together to form a circle. He closes his eyes.

'Are you… starting?' I ask.

'Yes,' Seb says, keeping his eyes shut.

'Okay, well I suppose I'll start too,' I state, placing my hands palm upwards on my knees and mirroring the thumb forefinger thing.

I close my eyes. A few moments pass. I try to get into the zone, but I feel ridiculous and the silence in the room is deafening. Something about us both sitting here like yogis, not talking, amuses me. It's too much for my British uptightness and I can't help laughing. A giggle escapes my lips. I attempt to conceal it with a cough.

'Sorry,' I mutter, opening my eyes to peek at Seb.

He opens his eyes a crack and gives me a side-long look, the corners of his lips curling into a reluctant smile. Relieved that he's smiling, I allow myself to laugh more freely.

'Oh god! I'm sorry! It's just this, and us, and the way we're sitting and… Oh my God!' I laugh, dabbing my eyes.

Seb laughs too, but it's more a polite laugh than the hysterics that seem to be taking hold of me.

'You'll get used to it,' he insists, still maintaining his meditation pose perfectly. 'It'll feel less weird soon. You just have to give in to it.'

'Sorry Seb. I'm just not very spiritual. I'm sorry,' I say, as I desperately try to stop laughing.

I force myself to draw in a deep breath, but it's shaky and I'm still worried I'm going to crack up.

'You'll get there.' Seb frowns slightly. 'I think.'

I draw in a deep breath, trying to calm myself down. This place is crazy. One minute a fountain is practically bringing me to the brink of tears and now sitting cross-legged pretending to be a yogi is making me hysterical. I need to pull myself together. I take another, longer, raggedy breath.

'Right, I can do this,' I assert, attempting to regain my composure.

I sit, back straight, legs crossed, palms up, and close my eyes again.

'I've got this,' I tell myself, aloud.

'Yes. You do have to be silent though,' Seb remarks.

'Okay, will do. Do you have any tips? Like, what am I meant to do? Just keep quiet and try to clear my mind?' I ask, getting my question out there before Seb gets too into the zone and is no longer accessible to the outside world.

'You're right. I should have given you some tips,' Seb says. 'Sorry.'

I open my eyes to find him turning to me.

'So, what you do is close your eyes and concentrate on your breathing. In, out. Long, deep breaths. Focus on your breath. The goal is to clear your mind and rise above all those thoughts that are always clamoring for attention in our minds, but it's not easy,' Seb says. 'You'll have loads of thoughts coming in, but you have to just try not to get too caught up in them. It takes practice.'

'Okay…' I utter, feeling a bit boggled. 'So I just need to not think?'

Seb smiles encouragingly. 'The best way to do it is to think of your thoughts like passing cars or buses. One comes along and you go, "Oh, a red bus", and another comes along and you go, "Ah, a grey car" and you just observe the thoughts but you don't get carried away with them. You just let them pass you by. You don't hop on board, if that makes sense?'

I nod. 'Yes, it does actually,' I concur, warming to the concept.

'Good,' Seb replies, looking pleased.

'So, what's the end goal?' I ask, clearing my throat and sitting up a little straighter.

Seb laughs. 'The end goal?' He raises an eyebrow.

'Yeah.' I shrug. 'Like, the objective?'

Seb smirks. 'I can tell you work in an office. Next, you'll be asking if there are meditation KPIs,' he teases.

I give him a gentle shove. 'Shut up!'

'Objective!' Seb scoffs, pushing me back.

'Okay, okay, I may come from corporate London and all that, but surely there's some sort of end goal?' I huff.

'The end goal is just to still your mind and feel peaceful. Seriously, when you can tune out all your thoughts simply by closing your eyes and focusing on your breathing, it's liberating. Meditation is like a home for me now. I know I have this peaceful place to go, no matter where I am,' Seb tells me, his eyes sparkling.

I can feel how much meditation means to him and his enthusiasm is infectious. Even though I still don't really know what his life back home entailed and what mistakes led him to come to the ashram, it's clear that he's finding happiness and contentment here.

'Okay, that sounds like a pretty good end goal, actually,' I admit.

'Cool. Now let's action that objective!' Seb grins.

He starts closing his eyes when I poke him in the side, making him laugh.

We stop laughing and settle down, closing our eyes. The way Seb described meditation, of having a peaceful place to go wherever you are – a home – did make it sound appealing. I close my eyes and try, sincerely this time, to meditate.

I inhale deeply and exhale. My mind is blank. Weirdly blank. White and clear. I picture tumbleweed rolling across it. I breathe in again and out. My mind's empty. Almost too empty. Am I a natural at this? I wonder. Or am I just vacant? What if I'm just so vapid that meditation is easy for me because I don't have any significant thoughts? I picture myself, becoming a spiritual guru, like Buddha, being lauded internationally for my remarkable meditation abilities. Maybe I'll become a guru. I wonder whether I'd feel like a fraud, knowing that I didn't have to sit under a tree for forty-nine days to achieve this state, but that it just came to me. Would that make me a fraud or a natural?

Suddenly, I realize I'm thinking. I'm actually thinking quite a lot. Damn. What kind of a moving vehicle would that thought be? A bus, I reckon.

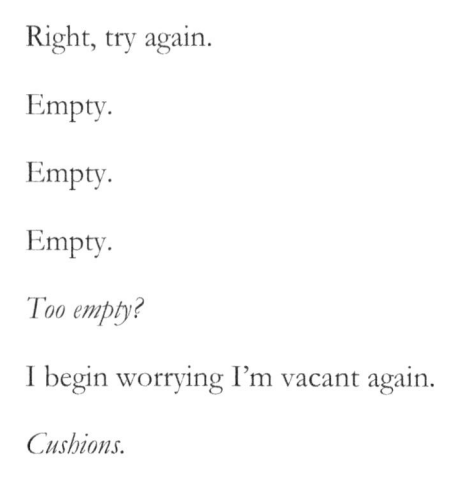

Right, try again.

Empty.

Empty.

Empty.

Too empty?

I begin worrying I'm vacant again.

Cushions.

They were so pretty. Must get some later. Definitely. They really would look so great in the living room.

Damn, another thought.

As far as thoughts go, it was just a car though. A little Nissan. No big deal. I barely hopped on board. I picture the thought retreating into the distance, disappearing down the road.

Gone.

Right, clear my mind.

Empty.

Empty.

Empty.

Seb.

Sex with Seb.

Wait? What?

Where did that come from?!

Talk about a DOUBLE DECKER.

And yet, I can't quite seem to hop off board. I don't even want to. I picture Seb's tanned brown skin, the light blond hairs on his arms, the dimples in his cheeks when he smiles. I think of his arms, his build, his gorgeous muscles.

I imagine turning and moving towards him, kissing him. The thought is insanely hot. Maybe it's the fact that we're in this nice private studio and we're meant to be meditating. Or perhaps it's the forbidden fruit aspect of Seb having taken a celibacy pledge. The idea of naughtily breaking his vow and making this meditation session a whole lot more fun is far too appealing.

Could he be having similar thoughts?

I open my eye a crack and take a look at him, but he looks perfectly serene, eyes closed, back straight, hands still palm up on his knees. He doesn't look like he's having erotic fantasies at all, but surely the thought must have crossed his mind at some point? We're both around the same age, both here, both alone. I'm not hideous looking, he must have at least considered it.

I close my eyes again. Perhaps he truly is committed to his pledge. Or perhaps he just thinks I'm a no-go zone because of Paul. He probably respects my broken heart. Maybe I should too, except don't they say the best way to get over someone is to get under someone else? I might be in rebound mode, but the idea of a fling with Seb is *very* appealing.

I open my eyes once more and subtly peer at him. Could I make a move? What would I do? It works in my head but reaching out and touching his tanned brown leg might be really sleazy in real life. Is it really uncool to disrespect someone's celibacy pledge like that? Probably.

Seb must feel me looking as he opens his eyes a crack.

'What?!' he asks.

'Oh, sorry, err, nothing. Just got distracted,' I reply.

Seb raises an eyebrow.

I got distracted by you, Seb. By you, I think, hoping he somehow picks up on my thoughts.

'Remember, thoughts are like cars, just watch them come and go, try not to get on board,' Seb reminds me.

'Yep. Got it, thanks,' I reply, feeling irked.

Bloody cars. If Seb was a car, he'd be a Rolls Royce and I'd definitely hop on board.

Seb closes his eyes, returning to his meditative state.

His face is completely serene. He looks truly peaceful. He doesn't look even remotely horny. I should just leave him be, respect his pledge.

Suppressing a sigh, I close my eyes again and try to meditate.

At first my mind is like a suburban street with cars coming and going, a few pull me along and a few just drift past. Then I get bored and my mind becomes a motorway in which I'm hopping from car to car, and then it calms down and I'm back to the suburban street. I don't know how much time has passed. It feels like forever, but it may only have been twenty minutes. I get that for Seb, meditation is his happy place, but I just feel crushingly bored. Life feels too short to meditate. There are books I could be reading right now. I could be exploring the ashram. I could be eating. I could be shopping. I could be trying to have fun. And instead I'm simply thinking about not thinking. Why on earth did Buddha do this for forty-nine days?

I sneak another look at Seb. His eyes are still closed and he still looks perfectly serene. Urgh. I could get up and go but surely he's going to get bored fairly soon? I close my eyes again, reasoning that I'll wait it out.

I'm back on the suburban street, cars coming and going, the odd bus, the odd cyclist. Then the cars get hazy, the buses morph into cyclists, then back to cars, then dissipate to nothing. I realize I'm falling asleep, the tiredness suddenly hitting me.

I lie down and place my head on the cushion. Just for a moment. Just until I'm ready to get back into proper meditation.

'Rachel? Rachel?' Someone says.

I open my eyes to see Seb looking down at me, gently nudging my arm. The studio is dark. I glance out of the window. The sun has set. What the hell? How long have I been sleeping?! How long was he meditating?

I realize I've left a puddle of drool on the satin cushion. Damn it. So much for enticing Seb to break his abstinence vow!

'Hey,' I grumble.

I sit up, rubbing the sleep out of my eyes.

'You were meditating for ages,' I comment, my voice raspy.

'Yeah. I got really into it. Hours flew by,' Seb says dreamily. 'When did you go to sleep?'

'Oh, I'm not sure. I meditated for a while too,' I tell him, while trying to subtly wipe the drool from the side of my cheek with the back of my hand.

I flip over the cushion.

'That's good,' Seb says.

His stomach rumbles loudly, making both of us laugh.

'Hungry by any chance?!' I ask.

'Yeah,' Seb laughs. 'Shall we go back to the guesthouse? We could make something?' he suggests.

I'm still pretty bleary and out of it, but I nod.

'Sounds good,' I reply.

We get up, picking up our cushions and placing them back by the wall. I feel a little guilty that mine is damp with drool, but never mind. We leave the studio as we found it and head back to the guesthouse. The cool air wakes me up as we walk.

'So, how did you find meditating?' Seb asks, looking over at me as we walk along the path, the sun setting in the distance. 'Before you fell asleep, of course!'

I laugh. How did I find it? Boring, if I'm totally honest, but Seb looks so hopeful that I can't possibly say that.

'It was…' I search for the right word. Something that isn't an outright lie. 'Relaxing,' I tell him.

'Relaxing? That's good,' Seb replies, a little weakly.

I can tell he'd been hoping for something a bit more enthusiastic.

'I'm sure I'll get more into it,' I add. 'Enlightenment takes time after all!'

'Ha! That's true,' Seb concurs.

We walk in silence for a few moments. No longer racking my brains for pseudo-spiritual things to say, I take in my surroundings. The dusty path we're walking along is lined on one side by cute little houses, set back from the path with hedges and gardens, and on the other side, are verdant fields, the grass long and overgrown like reeds. A buffalo grazes in the distance. The gentle fading glow of the sun shimmers off its fur making it look copper-colored, almost reflective. I'm about to comment on how beautiful the buffalo looks to Seb, when he turns to me.

'What is it about Paul?' he asks, taking me completely by surprise.

I raise an eyebrow. 'What? What do you mean?'

Seb shrugs. 'I was just thinking about you two last night. Maybe it's not my place to say anything…' he trails off. 'Actually, ignore me. It's not my place.'

He looks ahead, concentrating on the path stretching into the distance.

I laugh. 'Oh, come on. As if I can just ignore you! I need to know now. What is it? I won't be offended.'

Seb eyes me wryly. 'You won't be offended? How do you know?'

'I'm thick-skinned! I can take it,' I insist.

'You might be offended. No one ever knows if they're going to be offended. You can't predict that,' Seb points out.

'Okay. Well if I'm offended, I won't hold it against you. Hit me.' I smile encouragingly at him.

Seb laughs. 'Okay, if you insist. I guess I'm just a bit surprised that you came all this way to win Paul back. You two seem kind of…' he pauses, searching for the right word, 'different.'

'Different?' I frown, pacing along as I take in his observation. 'I guess we are different, but aren't all couples a bit different? It's not like I'd want to date my clone,' I point out, although I can't help thinking how few arguments my clone and I would have about going to IKEA at the weekends and how perfectly our home décor visions would align.

'Yeah, different. Paul seems kind of uptight, I guess. A bit… bland,' Seb notes, with a sneer to his voice.

It's clear he's not the biggest fan of Paul. A butterfly flaps across the path before us. It's larger than the butterflies back home. Much larger. Almost three times the size and I take it in, full of wonder, as it flaps its colorful wings, disappearing into the distance. It's so pretty. Everything in India feels heightened. The grass is longer, the buildings are more vivid, the food is tastier, even the butterflies are bigger.

'Well, I suppose he isn't exactly *edgy*,' I reason, 'but what did you expect? Paul's just a normal guy.'

I find myself feeling oddly defensive of him. I think of his habits: how he'd always have a sketch pad on the coffee table in our living room and would idly doodle characters from TV shows in the evenings. I think about how he had a thing for baking bread when he was stressed out or had something on his mind. He'd knead dough in the kitchen, his brow knotted with thought, and he'd always seem happier once the bread was baked, as though he'd worked his way through his problem. I think of how he used to buy expensive rose scented Neal's Yard bubble bath. The first time he bought it, after we'd moved in together, I assumed it was a present for me, and then there was a slightly awkward moment when he admitted that no, in fact, he'd bought it for himself. He liked to take long luxurious rose-scented baths on Sunday nights. He'd even light candles. It was adorable. Paul definitely wasn't an edgy guy. In fact, he was about as edgy as a satsuma, but I was fine with that. I liked him just the way he was.

I snap out of my thoughts and realize Seb is looking at me in a strangely penetrating way.

'Yeah, he's cool. Ignore me. I don't really know him,' he says. 'I told you I shouldn't have said anything!'

'No, it's fine. What did you mean though?' I ask, my voice lower than before, more serious.

'It's just *you*. You're funny and sparky and full of life. I thought Paul was going to be more like you, that's all,' Seb comments, smiling wistfully.

Funny? Sparky? Full of life? How is any of that offensive? I feel my heart swell. I feel genuinely touched. What a lovely way to describe me! And I can tell from Seb's sincere expression that he means it too.

'And there was me thinking I was just a boring, interior design obsessed, career-focused corporate bore,' I laugh, still feeling bamboozled by his compliment.

'There's so much more to you than that!' Seb scoffs, as though the idea that law and cushions and furnishings are all I'm about is insane.

I smile at him, feeling a weird combination of touched, relieved and genuinely grateful. The way Paul's treated me recently has really got under my skin, more than I think I even realized, and it feels nice to be complimented and appreciated.

'Thank you,' I say.

Seb smiles back at me, as another butterfly, even larger than before, flaps between us.

11 CHAPTER ELEVEN

Maybe it's because I spent most of the day sleeping, or perhaps it's because I went to bed early, at around 10pm after having dinner with a few of the other guests, but I wake up bright and early with the birds and this time, they don't annoy me.

I lie in my treehouse, blinking at the mosquito net above me. I listen to the chorus of owls, blackbirds and sparrows. The sound of chirping is joyful and I smile to myself, enjoying the sound of nature beckoning in a new day. I think about my getting up routine back home and the awful nagging alarm on my phone that I keep meaning to change, which goes off every morning at 7am. I usually hit snooze a few times, before eventually dragging myself out of bed. I tend to be tired and not particularly well rested. I work long hours and don't usually get home until gone 8pm, sometimes around 9pm, and I'm not normally able to fall asleep until I've spent some time winding down. Usually I eat in front of the TV, chat with Paul for a bit, and just watch whatever's on until my brain has relaxed and I'm ready for bed. It takes a while though and it's often not until around 1am that I crash. Thinking about it, I've probably got more sleep in the past few days, albeit at weird times, than I've had for months in London. I've simply been getting by during the week, high on ambition and hunger and then by the time the weekend comes, all I've wanted to do is catch up on rest. I haven't been up for much apart from trips to IKEA; I've simply been too tired.

Yet when Paul and I first got together, we did all sorts. We'd go on the Time Out website and find random events taking place, from silent discos and pop-up theatre shows to gin-tasting workshops and cheese festivals. We'd go along, just out of curiosity, for the ride. I remember one time we went to a traditional Scottish cèilidh dance in a village hall and it turned out to be one of the best nights ever. We were explorers back then, living our lives to the full, striving to experience our city in as many unique and interesting ways as possible. I was a junior paralegal and Paul was still doing waiter work while freelancing in graphic design. Our jobs didn't stress us out. I clocked off every day at 5pm and the moment I left the office, work couldn't be further from my mind. But then, as the years went on, we started doing those fun adventurous things less and less. I moved up in my job, from paralegal to solicitor, and Paul quit his waiter job and got an in-house graphic design role. I was working longer hours and so was he. We were both tired more often, and instead of having adventures every weekend, we'd manage one or two a month. And then eventually I got promoted to Partner and Paul became more senior too and somehow, we forgot all about Time Out and its catalogue of quirky, random events. I can't even remember the last time Paul and I did something like that. I cast my mind back, gazing at the net above me. I think it was a vegan supper club night three years ago, that we left early because we were both so exhausted.

I sigh, feeling deflated. Guilty almost. I know I've been working too hard recently. When I was first made Partner, I thought the long hours would be a teething period in which I was adjusting to my new role. I kept thinking life would go back to a slightly less intense state, but then every time I thought I was about to get some reprieve, a new case would come along, or someone would leave the company and there'd be more work to pick up. After a while, I stopped fighting the intensity and the long hours and just, sort of, adjusted. I forgot what life was like before. Working all the time became my new normal. I'd never have taken this holiday and slowed down if I hadn't considered coming here to be an emergency. I didn't think I needed a break, I thought I was fine, but it's taken being pulled out of my office, and having flown thousands of miles for me to realize that maybe I have been working too hard and perhaps I did lose a sense of myself along the way. Maybe there are reasons why Paul might have wanted out of our relationship. We haven't been how we used to be for a long time. I haven't been how I used to be.

A tear crawls down the side of my face, dampening my pillow. I sit up and flick it away. But another tear falls. I flick that one away too, when another falls. And another. I don't want to give in to the tears. What use is crying? But they won't stop. So, I just let them fall. I feel sad, but it's not a tormented feeling. My tears aren't angry tears or hurt tears or frustrated tears. I'm not upset that Paul's left me, it's not about that. I'm crying tears for myself. Tears that almost feel like grief for the person I used to be. Where did the person I used to be go? How did I get so carried away with work? How did I forget about having fun? And about being me?

The tears eventually dry up, the raw sadness passing. I dab my face dry and crawl out from under my mosquito net. I peer out of my treehouse and look towards the guesthouse. No one's up and about yet. No one's having their breakfast or enjoying their coffee in the sun. I look out over the treetops, taking in the lush blanket of palm trees, mango trees, willows and ferns. The sun's rising, tinging the edges of a soft blue early morning sky. I spot a few chirping birds sitting on tree branches. I sit for a minute, just taking the view in. It's funny to think that only a few days ago, I felt having to stay in a treehouse was a living hell, and now I feel quite grateful to be here. Blessed even. I can see now why Seb's stuck around.

I grab some napkins I nicked from the main hall a few nights ago that I've been using as toilet paper and climb down my ladder. I walk through the gardens towards the toilets. Even the prospect of using the toilets isn't as horrifying as it has been, although it's still not exactly great. I don't care how much this place grows on me, I'd still rather have a nice modern bathroom than a roofless hole in the ground. I use the loo as quickly as possible, trying not to dwell on the experience, and then check out my reflection in the mirror by the sinks. I look good. Well-rested, relaxed. My skin has a natural glow about it that I haven't been able to achieve in recent months in London no matter how many high-end products I've been applying.

I splash a bit of cold water onto my face and head to the guesthouse kitchen to make a coffee. The birds are still chirping their early morning chorus but no one else has risen. The kitchen in the guesthouse isn't much – just an old oven with a gas hob, a fridge and a couple of rickety shelves where everyone keeps their supplies. I still haven't gotten around to finding the supermarket or buying anything, but I know which shelf is Seb's and I figure he won't mind too much if I help myself to some of his instant coffee.

I look around for a kettle, but there isn't one, so I pour some water from a huge communal water dispenser into a saucepan. I light the hob and stand in front of it, waiting for the water to boil. I'd sort of hoped that Seb and I might have the kitchen to ourselves last night, when we got back from meditating. I'd hoped we could get to know each other better while we cooked, but there were a few other guests milling around – a 50-something American woman called Saskia who clearly has a soft spot for Seb since she kept touching his arm and calling him 'sweetie', and an extremely chatty Indian guy called Sayed. Sayed was lovely but he seemed to have no idea when to stop talking and spoke for about 45 minutes straight on the history of India's railway system. Meera was also there, and now that she's no longer laughing at me for wanting a WiFi password in an ashram, she's really warm and sweet.

Meera and the others hung out with us while Seb made everyone a curry and we all sat outside together, eating and chatting. I'd sort of wanted to continue the conversation Seb and I had been having on the way back from the yoga studio, when he commented that I was 'funny and sparky and full of life'. I wanted to find out more about his past – the experiences back home in Canada that led him to come here. He told me a few things about his background. He mentioned that he'd studied International Relations at The Sorbonne in Paris and used to want to be a government diplomat like his dad, but lost interest, getting swept up in the romanticism of Paris instead: drinking, dancing and chasing girls. He said he lost interest in working in politics but hasn't quite found another career path that feels right for him, which is why he ended up in the travel industry. I wanted to dig deeper and find out more, but it was difficult, with Sayed going on and on about India's rail network.

My water starts boiling and I remove the pan from the hob, turning the heat off. I grab a mug from the drying rack and spoon in some coffee, pouring in the steaming water. Instant coffee is a far cry from the Costa flat whites I pick up every morning back home on the way to the office, but it's fine. Like my treehouse, I'm getting used to the quirky ways of life here.

I take my steaming mug outside and sit down at one of the picnic tables on the patio, the same one we had dinner at last night. A few items from our evening remain: a couple of burnt down candles, a pack of cards we never got around to playing, and a few leaflets Saskia left behind about life in the ashram. I pick one of them up. It lists workshops and events. Smirking slightly, I flick through it and check out today's listings.

Tuesday March 17th

Nirvana Yoga Dance

Brazilian Dance Fighting

Hatha Yoga

Spiritual Ascension Snakes and Ladders

I snort as I read the last one. Spiritual Ascension Snakes and Ladders?! They have to be joking, right? Someone has to be having a laugh.

'Morning!'

I look up to see Seb coming towards me, wearing just a small pair of shorts.

'Oh, hey,' I reply.

His hair is mussed up from sleep and he's rubbing his eyes, looking like he literally just rolled out of bed. His small shorts don't leave a lot to the imagination. Is he trying to torture me? He looks incredible. He has a six pack. Not even a six pack – an eight pack – with all these other muscles that I didn't even know existed rippling across his sides. His pecs are perfectly defined. His skin is smooth and caramel brown and just…

'What were you laughing at?' Seb asks, glancing towards the leaflet in my hands, interrupting my ogling.

'Oh, just one of the events on today,' I comment, hoping he's still too sleepy to realize just how much I was perving on him.

'What event is that?' Seb asks, yawning, as he lingers by the table.

'Spiritual Ascension Snakes and Ladders!' I scoff.

'Oh, I've been to that. It's not so bad,' Seb tells me, sitting down opposite.

His bare knee brushes against mine. Painfully aware of the contact, I edge my knee away. I feel a little self-conscious. I'm still in my pajamas, my hair is a mess and I haven't even washed my face properly. I definitely do not look my best and I'd really rather Seb didn't see me like this. Unlike him, I require soap, a hairbrush and preferably a spot of make-up to look good. A grubby face, tangled locks, not to mention crumpled PJs, is definitely not the best look.

'I don't know… It sounds a bit ridiculous,' I remark.

Seb smiles lopsidedly, causing one of his dimples to appear adorably on his cheek.

'Well, it's a little quirky for sure, but it was interesting. Snakes and Ladders is an ancient Indian game. It was originally called Moksha Patam,' Seb explains. 'It's all about karma. The ladders are good karma and the snakes are associated with vices, like anger, theft, lust.'

I raise an eyebrow. 'Right, I had no idea it was so deep!'

'Yeah!' Seb shrugs. 'I feel I took something from it. Why don't you check it out?' he suggests.

'I don't know. It sounds a bit weird. I don't think so.'

'Oh, come on!' Seb says, giving me an indulgent weary look. 'You agreed that since you're stuck here for two weeks, you may as well make the most of ashram life?'

'But Spiritual Ascension Snakes and Ladders? That's just too much!' I protest.

'It's fun!' Seb insists.

'Hmm… I think hatha yoga sounds a bit more…' I search for the right word, 'sane.'

Seb laughs. 'Well I think you should throw yourself in at the deep end,' he remarks standing up, his knee brushing against mine once more.

'They have hatha yoga in London. I bet they don't have Spiritual Ascension Snakes and Ladders!' he comments, before padding off to the kitchen, probably in need of coffee.

'Yeah, for a good reason,' I mutter as he walks away.

I look back down at the leaflet. Spiritual Ascension Snakes and Ladders? I mean, how batshit can this place get? And yet Seb does have a point. I can do hatha yoga any day of the week in London, but will I ever get to play Spiritual Ascension Snakes and Ladders back home? Hardly. But despite that, I can't help rolling my eyes at the thought. Surely there are other ways to connect with the ashram than playing really loopy versions of board games? The players will no doubt be a load of weird hippies. Maybe Seb's right though. Maybe I should do unusual stuff while I'm here. When in an ashram in India and all that.

I flick through the leaflet, checking out what other weird stuff is on.

Past Life Regression Meditation

Ayurvedic Massage Training

Get in Touch with your Spirit Animal Workshop

I laugh out loud at the Spirit Animal Workshop. I read about that one online, but I barely believed it could actually be a thing.

'What's that?' Seb asks, leaning through the open window of the kitchen.

'There's a workshop on getting in touch with your spirit animal!' I tell him.

He sniggers, shaking his head. Even he can't stay straight-faced at that one.

'What do you think I am?' he asks, still leaning out of the window.

'What?' I reply, unsure what he means.

'What do you think my spirit animal would be?' he asks, smiling, eyeing me expectantly.

The first animal that pops into my mind is a lion: beautiful, striking and strong, but I feel too embarrassed to admit that to him. Lions are majestic. Lions are captivating. They're enchanting. Is it flirting if I tell him he reminds me of a lion? Surely if I admit that he'll know I'm attracted to him.

'Erm, I don't know, maybe a…' I pause, trying to think of an animal that isn't flirtatious. 'A badger?' I suggest.

Seb's face falls.

'A badger?' he echoes.

'Yeah, I don't know… A badger.' I shrug.

'Oh, right, okay…' Seb murmurs, looking crestfallen.

He smiles weakly and steps back into the shadows of the kitchen.

Oh no! He's clearly really upset. A badger was not the right choice. Couldn't I have said something cool like a wolf or a shark? Something masculine and powerful but not flirty? Why did I come out with a badger?! I feel like such a bitch. Especially after how sweet Seb's been to me, helping me get settled in the ashram, letting me use his computer, trying to teach me meditation, cooking for me. Not to mention his compliments last night. He tells me how funny and sparky and full of life I am, and I return the compliment by telling him he reminds me of a badger? What is wrong with me?!

I take a sip of my coffee, feeling terrible. I try to think about something else and let the awkwardness of what just happened go, but I can't. I'm acutely aware of Seb in the kitchen behind me, making his coffee or whatever else he's preparing, feeling like the human equivalent of a badger. I need to patch things up.

I take another sip and get up, venturing into the kitchen.

Seb smiles awkwardly as I wander in, but quickly looks back down at the egg he's scrambling.

'Erm, Seb?' I say.

'Yep?' he replies, although he keeps his eyes fixed on the pan.

'I, umm, I…' I stammer.

What am I meant to say? *I didn't mean to call you a badger.* How ridiculous does that sound?

'I… I wanted to say that really, I think your spirit animal is a lion, but I felt too embarrassed to admit that and then badger came out,' I tell him.

Seb turns to me, and looks at me, quite intently, as though checking how sincere I am. He must realize I'm telling the truth, because the tension dissipates from his eyes and his expression relaxes.

'Why would you be embarrassed to tell me you think I'm a lion?' he asks, as he takes his pan from the hob.

'Because lions are beautiful,' I comment, thinking of his eyes, his smile, his chest, his dimples, as he tips his egg onto his plate.

I gulp. I feel like I've just confessed my undying love for him. I feel like I've propositioned him. My comment hangs in the air between us.

Lions are beautiful.

You are beautiful.

Seb places his pan down and looks at me, his eyes wide, tender, piercing.

'Thank you,' he says. He smiles, holding my gaze.

Thank you. Is that it? I feel like I've just laid my heart bare. I've told him how I really feel and all he has to say is 'thank you'? God. Is this what a year of celibacy does to a man? If I were to do a striptease right here, right now, slathering my body in ayurvedic massage oil, would he just smile and say 'thank you'?

'No worries!' I reply.

Seb's toast pings out of the toaster.

'A lion's way better than a badger. No offence to badgers!' Seb comments, as he reaches for it.

'Totally!' I agree, still full of shame, bristling with rejection. 'Right, I'm going to go and get ready for the, err, Snakes and Ladders. See you later,' I babble as I edge towards the door.

'Do you want company? At Snakes and Ladders?' Seb asks, placing his toast on his plate.

'Nope. No, it's cool! I'm good. You, err… do your thing!' I smile way too artificially, but Seb doesn't seem to notice.

He's too distracted by trying to find a knife and fork in the cutlery drawer, which I discovered last night is a disordered mess of utensils.

'Okay, I was going to go to the gym anyway,' Seb comments, not looking up from the drawer.

'Sounds good, enjoy!' I urge him as he pulls out a fork.

'Bingo!' he says, grinning, completely oblivious to my embarrassment.

'Cool!' I laugh as I skulk off to my treehouse.

12 CHAPTER TWELVE

'Namaste,' a woman dressed in white ashram robes greets me, holding her hands together in prayer.

I smile and awkwardly mirror her gesture.

'Namaste,' I reply, without much conviction.

'I'm Amala. I'm waiting for the rest to arrive and then we'll start the game,' she tells me in a soft slow voice with traces of a German accent.

'Great! I'm Rachel,' I reply, almost reaching for a handshake before stopping myself.

I really need to stop trying to shake hands with people in the ashram.

'Welcome, Rachel,' Amala smiles beatifically. 'Please make yourself comfortable.'

She gestures for me to enter the hut behind her.

'Thank you,' I reply.

I wander into the hut. It's adorned with wall-hangings,

embellished with shards of mirror that dazzle with the reflection of dozens of tea lights, flickering around the room. The Snakes and Ladders board is laid out on the floor, with half a dozen cushions placed around it. A couple of players are already sitting cross-legged, waiting for the game to begin. One of them, a woman, who looks around my age, is sitting with her eyes closed, breathing deeply, as though in an intense meditation. A man with long scraggly dreadlocks sits next to her and gives me a friendly smile.

'Hello,' he whispers. 'Welcome.'

'Hi,' I whisper back, smiling as I sit down on the cushion next to him.

Hypnotic windchime music plays in the background.

I take a look at the Snakes and Ladders board. It's nothing like the ones I remember from my childhood, and is covered in illustrations of gods, angels and demons. Seb was right, the slides do represent vices, with each one adorned with symbols of doom — hellish flames, ghoulish demons, scary spiders, deathly skulls and ominous bats. The ladders, on the other hand, are decorated with butterflies, angels, flowers, sun beams and doves.

'Wow!' I remark, glancing at the dreadlock guy.

He smiles.

'It's a special game,' he says. 'First time?'

'Yes,' I reply.

'You'll enjoy it,' he promises.

'Hope so!' I say, although I'm still struggling to see what all the fuss is about.

It's just Snakes and Ladders after all. I only played it as a kid when I was bored and it was so-so then, how great can it be these days? Even if the board is quite pretty.

We sit in silence for a few minutes as the sound of the music washes over us, the candles twinkling. I have to admit, the atmosphere of the room is quite relaxing. An incense stick burns in the corner, emitting a fragrant lavender scent. I begin to feel quite relaxed, when none other than Paul walks into the hut.

Paul.

I gawp at him, eyes wide. He stops in his tracks, staring back at me.

The pale girl that accompanied him in the main hall the other night wanders in after him with Amala.

Amala looks between me and Paul.

'Is everything okay?' she asks.

I consider getting up and bolting, but I got here first. Surely, he should leave?

'It's fine,' Paul grumbles, shooting me a look before sitting down on the cushion furthest from me.

I glance towards the exit of the hut. Should I make a run for it? But as I'm considering escaping, Amala sits down next to me and smiles widely, gesturing expansively around the group.

'Thank you for coming to share in this wonderful experience,' she enthuses, her eyes sparkling. 'I am so grateful to have you all here.'

I smile weakly back, feeling resigned. I can't make a run for it now, that would just be rude.

The pale girl settles down next to Paul, adjusting a long cotton scarf that's got caught under her leg. She pulls it free and then places her hand proprietorially on Paul's leg. She shoots me a cold, smug, mean look, as though to say, 'He's mine now.'

I gawp back and look to Paul. He glances back at me with a guilty expression. The anger that was in his eyes the other day is replaced with a look that's even more cutting: guilt. He looks genuinely contrite and I realize with a pang that he's moved on. He's with this pale girl. He's moved on from me. Just a few weeks after dumping me, he's found someone else: a bitchy, hippy girl.

I can't believe it. We were together for six years. Six years! And he's just moved on, like our relationship meant nothing. We had a home together. A history. I thought he was going to propose to me, for goodness sake. So much for winning him back.

I experience an intense sinking feeling. I thought Paul just needed a change of scenery. A break. I thought he needed time to think. I thought he needed perspective but that he'd come back to me, realizing that what we had was important to him. I thought he'd see that our life together meant something to him. But now I understand that it really is over. He's moved on. He doesn't care.

Suddenly, I notice that Amala's talking, introducing herself and explaining her background. I've missed the first part, having been so distracted by Paul, but from what I gather, she gave up a corporate job back home in Germany and has reinvented herself under the guidance of Guru Hridaya, who she says re-named her Amala, meaning, 'The purest one'.

'My life is completely different now,' she says, smiling happily.

I glance at Paul, wondering if this is the life he wants to? Will he change his name? Reinvent himself? Will he be leading a spiritual board game session in a few years' time too? Meditation Monopoly? Or Believe-in-yourself Buckaroo!

'Let's introduce ourselves,' Amala suggests, turning to Paul's new squeeze.

'Hi everyone,' she says in an American accent. 'I'm Blossom.'

Blossom? I suppress the urge to roll my eyes. I shoot Paul a look, but he ignores it. I wonder if Guru Hridaya named her Blossom? Weed would have been a better choice.

'I've been living here for three years. I came from Wisconsin one summer to volunteer and when I got here, I realized I was home,' she says with a nauseatingly cheesy smile.

'That's wonderful,' Amala enthuses.

'I've settled here and I'm very happy. I'm a different person now, way more enlightened, and I'm so grateful for all the incredible people who are coming into my life, who I'm making wonderful, fulfilling connections with,' she says, squeezing Paul's thigh.

She shoots me a self-satisfied smile. I roll my eyes. For someone so enlightened, she's certainly petty. I get that she's with my boyfriend, or ex-boyfriend, but does she have to rub it in like this?

Now it's Paul's turn to introduce himself.

'Hi everyone,' he says, looking around the group, but avoiding eye contact with me.

'I'm Paul. I'm from London. I came here because I guess I needed a break from the rat race,' he explains.

I scoff. The rat race?! Is that how he saw his life? He lived in a cozy, terraced house and designed logos and brochures all day in an office with a bean bag break out area, it's not like he was The Wolf of Wall Street.

'Are you okay, Rachel?' Amala turns to me, looking concerned and a little confused.

'I'm fine!' I insist.

'Please continue, Paul,' Amala insists.

'Yes, so I was unhappy in London, so I came here to do some self-exploration,' Paul tells the group, while avoiding eye contact with me.

Self-exploration? I raise an eyebrow. It doesn't look like it. It looks more like he's been busy exploring the local totty.

The woman who had been meditating before introduces herself as Madeleine from France and the dreadlock guy tells us in a sleepy, stoned voice that he's called Silas and he's on holiday from Amsterdam.

I mumble something vague about being on holiday from London, and with everyone acquainted, Amala begins describing the rules of Spiritual Ascension Snakes and Ladders. I try to focus on what she's saying, even though I still feel completely rattled.

'The stairways represent spiritual ascension, growth, escape, dreams and hope. And the snakes are all the things in life that hold us back and prevent us from reaching the higher plane of our being,' Amala explains.

She picks up the die and rattles them in her hand.

'Before you throw the die, close your eyes and look inside your soul. Meditate on it. This game is about karma. Our souls will guide us and when you throw the die, your karma will manifest,' Amala says.

She hands around a dish containing counters

She turns to me. 'Would you like to start, Rachel?' she asks, offering me the die.

'Sure,' I reply, taking the dice.

'Close your eyes and look inside your heart,' Amala advises. 'Meditate on it before you throw the die.

I close my eyes. I'm still thinking about Paul and Blossom, but I push them out of my mind and try to look inside my heart, whatever that means. I focus, shaking the die in my hand, and breathing deeply. When it feels right, I throw the die.

The die land on a four and a six. I move my counter along the board and land on a ladder, a long ladder that stretches three or four rows up the board.

'Excellent!' Amala gushes, eyes wide. 'That's incredible karma, Rachel!'

She seems genuinely impressed.

'Thank you!' I reply, feeling pleased.

I shoot a look at Paul, who looks impassive. Blossom, on the other hand, pouts grumpily.

Silas takes his turn and like me, lands on a ladder. He makes it up the board, but I remain half a dozen spaces ahead.

Madeleine manages to inch along the board, but misses the ladders, and then it's Blossom's turn.

She clutches the die in her hand and holds them close to her heart. She frowns, clearly in deep concentration. Moments pass. The candles flicker. The music plays. She breathes in and out. I glance at Silas and he raises an eyebrow. Then finally, Blossom opens her eyes and throws the die.

She gets a one and a two, and moves her counter along the board, missing the ladders.

'Better luck next time,' I snipe.

She glares at me.

Paul closes his eyes as he shakes the die, but also fails to land on a ladder. Ha! Go me. I'm the most spiritually enlightened of the group. Amala throws the die too. She lands on a ladder, but even she fails to get as high up on the board as me.

We carry on playing and my luck is in. I keep landing on ladders and within half a dozen throws, I'm just two squares away from reaching the final square, labelled 'Nirvana'.

It's clear that I'm going to win. There are no snakes between me and the finishing point. I'm way ahead of everyone else, even Amala. The only person who's remotely close is Silas, eight squares behind me.

Blossom is sweating, huffing as she takes her turn. She's still at the bottom of the board, having continually landed on snakes. Paul is somewhere in the middle.

'Come on,' Blossom pleads, eyes closed as she shakes the die.

She throws, getting two threes. She moves her counter along the board, but lands on another snake, which drops her right back at the bottom. I can't help smirking.

'Don't be discouraged,' Amala says, as Blossom sulks.

'You just need to work on yourself and your personal growth. You'll get there eventually,' Amala assures her, but it's clearly not what Blossom wants to hear and she smiles tightly back at Amala, her eyes daggers.

Eventually, it's my turn again and I throw the die. I don't even have to concentrate, because it's clear I'm going to win. Die thrown, I move my counter to Nirvana. I've won!

'Congratulations, Rachel!' Amala gushes. 'Very impressive, especially for your first time. You must be really in tune with your spiritual self.'

'Thanks, I guess so!' I gush, feeling pleased with myself.

I may have had a bit of a rubbish few weeks, and Paul may have moved on from me quicker than you can say 'reincarnation' but, according to this game, I'm enlightened, and what's more important than that?

'Well done,' Silas remarks. 'Impressive.'

'Thank you!' I smile.

'Really good! Congratulations,' Madeleine adds.

I'm about to thank her, when Blossom butts in.

'I'm sorry, but there must be something wrong with the game,' she says. 'Rachel is not spiritual. She's not!'

Amala looks at her, completely shocked. 'Excuse me?'

'She's not enlightened. Paul told me all about her. She's a lawyer. All she cares about it furniture and wallpaper and stuff. She doesn't care about spirituality,' Blossom sneers.

I gawp at Paul. So, he's been bitching about me to his new girlfriend. Really?

Paul looks away.

'She's not spiritual. She's a corporate lawyer!' Blossom shrieks.

'This is a divine game,' Amala tells her, looking genuinely offended. 'It reflects what's in your heart. Rachel is clearly more enlightened than you give her credit for.'

I smile at Amala, feeling grateful.

'Thanks, Amala,' I say.

She smiles back at me, kindly.

'But I'm spiritual. I meditate every day! I live here! I do yoga! I'm vegan!' Blossom protests.

'I'm sorry, Blossom, but I think you still have some work to do on your spiritual path,' Amala tells her.

I smile smugly.

'Maybe she'll get there one day,' I comment, unable to help myself.

I get up, thanking Amala for the opportunity to play, but excuse myself, not wanting to be around Blossom and Paul any longer.

Amala thanks me for playing and compliments me once more on my enlightened state. I leave a donation of rupees in a dish by the door, say goodbye, and head back towards the guesthouse.

I may be enlightened, but I still feel like crying. My boyfriend of six years has dumped me and moved on to a stuck-up horrible wannabe hippy called Blossom. I mean, seriously? I wander down the dusty path, feeling rotten. There's only one thing for it: I'm heading to the gift shop. It's time to buy cushions.

13 CHAPTER THIRTEEN

'Wow, do you have enough cushions?!' Seb jokes, glancing up from his book, as I lug my haul into the guesthouse.

'Just about!' I reply, laughing weakly.

Seb's eyes linger on me. He frowns slightly. He seems to register my downbeat mood.

He springs up, leaving his book on the picnic table in front of him.

'Let me help,' he says, coming over.

He's no longer topless, having donned a t-shirt, a pair of cut-off jeans and a New York Yankees cap.

'Thanks.' I smile, handing him a bag of cushions.

We lug the cushions to my treehouse.

'What's up? Are you okay?' Seb asks.

I sigh. 'It's a long story.'

'Okay…' Seb murmurs as we approach my ladder.

I start climbing the ladder, carrying my bag of cushions up with me. Once I'm at the top, I shove the bag through the doorway of my treehouse, before climbing down and reaching for the bag Seb's holding. I take it back up to the treehouse and deposit it inside, before hesitating. Should I stay here and cocoon amid a pile of cushions or should I chat to Seb for a bit? I'm not feeling particularly sociable and I still feel quite embarrassed that I basically came onto him this morning through a spirit animal chat-up line and he didn't seem that bothered. I get that he's doing a year of celibacy, but he has been flirty. Not lots, but there's clearly something between us. I'm not delusional. It hasn't totally been in my imagination. He's been a bit flirtatious and he's been wanting to spend time with me. He must realize that it will have crossed my mind that the connection between us might be more than platonic? Just because he's taken a vow of celibacy, it doesn't mean the rest of the universe has.

'Do you want a cup of tea?' Seb suggests as I linger at the top of my ladder.

'How very English of you,' I tease, looking down at him.

'Well, actually I was thinking of making chai. But you look like you could do with a chai.' Seb smiles.

'I could,' I admit. 'Actually, I could do with a large glass of wine, but a chai will have to do.'

I start climbing down the ladder, feeling heavy-footed and weary. Seeing Paul has really taken it out of me.

'I can bring it up to you if you want?' Seb suggests, clearly noting my lethargy.

'Oh! Thanks,' I reply. 'Are you sure?'

'Of course. No worries,' Seb says, before heading off to the kitchen.

I watch him go for a moment. I wonder whether he's thought about what I said this morning. Isn't it obvious that I fancy him? Maybe we should have a conversation and get things out in the open, dispel the tension, so he can continue with his celibacy and I can focus on getting over Paul. I crawl into my treehouse.

It's become a total mess. Since there's no chest of drawers, wardrobe or storage of any kind, I've taken to living out of my open suitcase, chucking my laundry into a few carrier bags. But there are clothes all over the place, bottles of sun cream, mosquito repellent, face wipes, make-up, sunglasses, unread books and empty notebooks scattered about. I grab all the bits and pieces and shove them into my suitcase, making sure my Rampant Rabbit is safely stashed away. Then I empty my bags of cushions and arrange them in a corner of my treehouse. It's a far cry from the homely chic vibe I'm envisaging for my living room back home, but it looks kind of cozy.

Just as I'm rearranging a few of the cushions, I feel the weight of the treehouse shift a little and realize Seb's coming up. I sit down, making myself comfortable, as he crawls in carrying a steaming mug of chai. He hands it to me.

'Thanks,' I reply, smelling the chai, as he checks out my cushions.

'Very nice,' he comments.

I laugh. 'Thanks!'

'I'm just going to get the other mug,' Seb says, disappearing back down the ladder.

A few moments later, he comes back up, with another mug of chai. He settles into the cushions and takes a sip. Despite my low mood, I feel immediately better at having personalized my treehouse a bit, making it a little more homely. And having a cup of chai helps too.

'Do you ever miss your home comforts?' I ask Seb.

'A bit.' Seb shrugs. 'But you get used to it.'

He picks up a cushion emblazoned with an elephant.

'These are nice,' he says, admiring the stitching.

'Yeah, they're lovely,' I reply, somewhat sadly. 'Paul never really appreciated my love of home furnishings. It was one of the reasons he ended things.'

I take a sip of my chai.

'What? He ended your relationship because you like cushions?' Seb balks.

'Well, not just because I like cushions,' I explain. 'We used to be fun and adventurous and then we just started shopping at homeware stores every weekend and I'd spend my evenings scrolling through Instagram checking the #myhousebeautiful hashtag.'

Seb laughs. 'Really?' he asks, almost disbelieving.

'Yeah! I got really into it,' I admit, realizing that since I got to India, it's been the longest time in months that I haven't hit 'like' on an interior décor snap on the gram.

'So how come you guys stopped being so adventurous then?' Seb asks, taking a sip of his chai.

I smile to myself, realizing just how little Seb bothers with small talk. It just doesn't seem to be his style. He says exactly what he wants to say and somehow, over the past few days, I've opened up to him more than I'd ever open up to a stranger back home. People become so closed off in London, but with Seb it hasn't been like that; we've been open around each other since day one. Maybe it's because we're here, in this strange place, and normal rules don't really apply.

I consider Seb's question. Why did Paul and I stop being so adventurous? It's the question I've been unpicking ever since we broke up, and it's rooted not only in my busy work schedule, but in my genuine obsession with our house. I allowed that to overtake my old interests and my old self, and I had no idea how insufferable Paul found it.

'We bought a house together and I just really wanted to make it nice,' I tell Seb. 'I know that sounds really sad. I know there's more to life than cushions and wallpaper and nice furniture, but I somehow got really into it.'

'Hmm…' Seb frowns slightly, taking another sip of his chai, as though he's not quite satisfied with my response.

I feel like he expects more, and of course, there is more to it. There's my childhood and all the moving around and not having a stable home. It's pretty personal, but I find myself opening up and telling Seb all about it as we drink our chai. Our mugs are empty by the time I get to the end of the story. Seb's reclining in the cushions, sprawling out to make himself more comfortable and I've relaxed a bit too, lying back, as I cast my mind down memory lane.

'So, you were homeless as a teen,' Seb observes.

'Not homeless!' I bristle. 'I always had a roof over my head.'

'But you didn't have a stable home for quite a long time,' Seb says.

'No, we didn't,' I admit.

Seb's comment about being homeless jogs a memory of my mum crying on my Aunt Jill's shoulder in her kitchen. She'd been in the changing room at the swimming pool, and while getting changed in a cubicle, she'd overheard a couple of her swimming pals talking, and one of them, not realizing my mum was there, commented how she wasn't inviting 'that homeless couple' to her dinner party. My mum was devastated that her friend saw her and my dad that way. Even though we didn't have a permanent home, my mum couldn't accept that we were homeless, even though we were, technically, or the council would never have come to our rescue and found us a home.

I've never wanted to accept that we were homeless either. I've always carried some of my mum's shame. It's why I'm so obsessed with having a home these days.

'Does Paul know about all this?' Seb places his empty mug down.

I shake my head.

'Really?' Seb balks. 'But you were together for ages, weren't you?'

'Six years,' I confirm.

'And you never told him?' Seb asks incredulously.

'No. His dad died when he was a kid. I always just felt it wasn't important, you know? I felt like what I went through was nowhere near as bad, so I just didn't talk about it,' I tell him. 'Also, I didn't really know there was an issue until he broke up with me.'

Seb nods. 'Maybe you should talk to Paul,' he suggests.

I shake my head. 'He's already moved on.'

Seb shoots me a curious look and I explain about Paul's new girlfriend and how they were together at Spiritual Ascension Snakes and Ladders.

Seb grimaces. 'God, I'm sorry,' he says.

'It's okay. I think it finally dawned on me that we really are over. And not just because he says so. I think I'm getting over it now too,' I muse. 'Paul said he needed time to be on his own and think, but he's just latched onto someone new straight away. It's hurtful, but it's also just made me respect him less. It's like he can't stand on his own two feet for five minutes.'

'And how do you feel? Do you need time alone too?' Seb asks, looking into my eyes.

In spite of everything, I feel a frisson of electricity as I hold his gaze. I search his blue eyes, trying to figure out how he feels. He's meant to be celibate and yet, he's holding my gaze in that intense, penetrating way. Does he care about me needing time alone simply because he's concerned about my well-being or is he asking because he might be interested in me? It feels like the latter, but maybe I'm deluded.

'I… I…' I hesitate, trying to find the right response.

'Rachel!' A voice interrupts my thoughts. It sounds like Meera.

Grateful for the interruption, I place my empty mug down and crawl across my treehouse, pulling back the curtain. I peer out to see Meera standing below, gazing up.

'Hey! I was going to head out for some food soon. Thought I'd go to a restaurant. Do you want to come?' she asks.

'Oh, I'm with Seb,' I tell her.

Meera wiggles her eyebrows mischievously. 'Oh really?'

I smile but decide to ignore her implications.

'Come up,' I suggest, beckoning her to climb the ladder.

'Are you sure?' Meera wiggles her brows again.

'Yes, I'm sure!' I laugh, rolling my eyes.

'Okay!' Meera giggles, climbing up.

Seb sits up, making himself look a lot less leisurely and relaxed, as though he's also self-conscious about us appearing too intimate.

Meera pokes her head into the treehouse.

'You're both clothed! That's something,' she teases, climbing in.

'Of course, we're clothed!' I tut, laughing.

'Okay, okay!' Meera trills as she crawls across the treehouse, joining us on the cushions, eyeing them approvingly.

'I just thought you two might have finally got together, you know,' she says.

'Finally?' I balk, feeling my cheeks flush. 'Seb and I have only known each other a few days!'

Meera gives me and Seb a knowing look. Seb affects a casual expression, but his ever-so-slightly blushing cheeks give him away.

'Oh, come on! You guys clearly have a connection! Everyone's noticed,' Meera insists.

I laugh awkwardly. Everyone's noticed? By everyone, she can only really mean a handful of people at the guesthouse, but still! The thing is, though, Meera is probably just projecting. I ran into her husband in the kitchen the other day, an American guy called Fred who left his job as a trader in Seattle to relocate to the ashram ten years ago, where he met Meera. He's a shy, dreamy character and I got the impression he likes to keep himself to himself, but he said hello to me and explained how he came to the ashram, fell in love and never left. I think Meera expects everyone else's stories to be as romantic.

'We're just friends!' I tell her.

'And I've taken a vow of celibacy,' Seb adds.

My ears prick up. He didn't outright deny having a connection with me. Or even deny wanting to sleep with me. Is his vow the only thing stopping him?

'Oh yeah,' Meera grumbles. 'Your celibacy pledge.'

I smile at Meera, mentally giving her a high five. As much as I respect everyone's reasons for being at the ashram and engaging in self-discovery, Seb's pledge is kind of irritating. What's it even achieving? Surely sex can be about different things with different people? He may have engaged in some regrettable flings back when he was a ski instructor, but alcohol isn't even available here at the ashram and sex between us wouldn't be regrettable anyway, it would be great.

'I swore off sex for a year and I'm only five months in,' Seb reminds us.

Meera gives me a sympathetic smile.

'I just think if you connect with someone, it's a shame not to go for it. Life is for living!' she insists.

I laugh, loving how unfiltered Meera is. She's right though, life is for living! I look over at Seb, curious to see how he reacts. Is he going to deny our connection? Admit it? Give up his pledge? But he just smiles mysteriously.

'So, if you guys aren't busy, shall we go and get some food?' Meera suggests.

'Sure!' I reply.

Seb concurs and we climb out of the treehouse. We leave our empty chai cups in the kitchen and set off for the restaurant, chatting about our days as we walk. The sun is beginning to set, the sky taking on a tinged look. I realize sunset and sunrise are my favorite times of day here.

'So where is this place?' I ask, as we get further and further away from the guesthouse.

'It's my uncle's place. It's outside the ashram, but it's not far. It's worth the walk, trust me,' Meera insists, smiling encouragingly.

'It is worth it!' Seb concurs, having clearly already paid a visit. 'Their parathas are incredible.'

'Cool!' I reply, pretending I know what parathas are.

I think they're like chapatis, but I'm not entirely sure. Seb and Meera chat about the restaurant while I daydream, my mind wandering to Seb. I can't seem to help myself. I think about kissing him, connecting with him, touching him. I need to stop obsessing! Maybe he's got the right idea taking a vow of celibacy. Perhaps I should do the same, because I clearly have sex on the brain.

I contemplate this, feeling uneasy, when I spot Blossom, Paul's new squeeze, coming towards us, with a couple of others, all of them wearing the white ashram robes.

I quickly divert my gaze, but it's too late. Blossom has clocked me and turns to her friends. She whispers something and they all look towards me, smirking. So much for enlightened. I feel like I'm back at school dealing with mean girls.

I decide to take the high ground and carry on walking with my head held high, tuning them out.

I breathe a sigh of relief once they're safely behind us

'Who was that?' Meera asks in a hushed voice once they're out of earshot.

I explain how I met Blossom and how she tried to make out that I wasn't sufficiently enlightened to win Spiritual Ascension Snakes and Ladders.

'I mean, sorry, but what is so enlightened about wearing crappy white robes and having a dumb name like *Blossom*?! That doesn't make you spiritual!' I rant.

Meera nods. 'It's Guru Hridaya. He makes them think they have to wear those robes in order to reach a higher plane of consciousness. He claims it's all about relinquishing the ego, but really it's just about stripping people of their personalities,' Meera muses, looking oddly sad.

I haven't seen her appear anything other than cheerful and happy and cheeky ever since I arrived in the ashram. The sad, resigned look on her face comes as a surprise.

'What do you mean?' I press her.

'Guru Hridaya. He doesn't actually care about enlightenment or helping people achieve some sort of higher state. All he cares about is money. All these westerners come here, feeling lost. They're usually going through something, looking for answers. The guru offers them some guidance, support. He's like a father figure. He tells them what to do – wear these white robes, meditate, eat this food, do this kind of yoga, and they just do it, thinking they're becoming spiritual,' Meera explains.

I sigh, realizing how easily taken in people can be.

'Once you've been here a few weeks, Guru Hridaya's followers start asking you to do work to contribute to the ashram. They call it a form of meditation – "selfless sacrifice". The guests are already so brainwashed by that point that they do it. The don't realize it's just free labor. It's crazy,' Meera adds.

'What kind of work do they do?' I ask, feeling shocked.

'Everything! Cleaning, cooking, gardening. And then once they've been here a while, they're given a laptop and told to reach out to other Westerners online, convincing them to come over here,' Meera explains.

'Really?' I balk, thinking back to the ashram's website, which was packed full of useful information and even had a chat service.

Looking back, it was an oddly efficient site for an ashram. I didn't really think about it at the time. I'd assumed that whoever was running the site was paid, but it must just have been some gullible guest, being exploited.

'Ultimately Guru Hridaya just wants loads of lost Westerners to come here and work for him for free,' Meera says.

'But why?' I ask.

'It's about money. It's as simple as that. Once you've been here for a while, he pressures you to make a donation to the ashram. People are so brainwashed by that point that they donate thousands. Sometimes their entire life savings. They beg their families for money. He tells them the donations are essential to continue the spiritual work that the ashram's doing, but it's all bullshit,' Meera sneers.

'That's crazy,' I comment, in shock.

I may not have been on board with a lot of the goings-on at the ashram, but I didn't realize things were quite so sinister. Is this what's going to happen to Paul? Is he going to end up donating a ton of money to a corrupt guru and becoming an unpaid brainwashed slave? Should I warn him?

'It's a scam,' Meera sighs. 'He just keeps all the money.'

We walk a few paces, the sky darkening as I take what they're saying in.

'Why do you stay here then? If things are so messed up...' I ask.

Meera shrugs. 'I like it here. It's beautiful, right?' She looks at me for confirmation as we amble along the path.

I nod. This place is truly beautiful. I've never been as touched by the beauty of nature as I have been during the past few days since I got here.

'So, the fact that this place is a scam doesn't bother you?' I question.

Meera does a head wobble. 'A bit, but a lot of the Westerners are happy here, even though this place isn't as authentic or spiritual as they'd like to think. I just do my own thing. I mind my own business. I run my guesthouse my way. I stay out of Guru Hridaya's way and he stays out of mine. There are different rules for Indians. We don't get hassled. We lived on this land before the ashram came along,' Meera explains.

'Fair enough,' I reply, still feeling bamboozled by what she's said.

I look to Seb, who appears completely unphased, as though he's already fully aware of the situation.

'How do you feel about Guru Hridaya?' I ask, a little surprised at his seemingly cavalier demeanor.

The ashram may be beautiful, but Meera's take on it does put a negative slant on things. How can Seb be so focused on spiritual enlightenment in a place that's corrupt? According to Meera's description of the kind of Westerners the guru targets, Seb fits the bill perfectly. He's a little lost. He'd been struggling back home. He's looking for clarity, a new path, direction. And yet even though he's determined to find a sense of enlightenment, he doesn't seem to have been sucked in by Guru Hridaya at all.

'I'm interested in some of the things Guru Hridaya talks about, but I'm reading spiritual texts from lots of different thinkers –

Buddha, Rumi, the Dalai Lama, Deepak Chopra, Eckhart Tolle… I'm just enjoying being here. I'm reading, reflecting. I'm doing my own thing,' Seb insists.

I smile at him, feeling totally convinced. Seb is an independent spirit. I've been able to see that since we first met. He wears a New York Yankees cap in an ashram for goodness sake! He may be going through a slightly challenging period of his life, but he's not totally lost. He's still got his head screwed on and it's clear he's not going to become brainwashed or get exploited. Yet, although I feel reassured about Seb, I'm a little worried about Paul. Paul seems a bit more vulnerable. After all, he immediately found a new girlfriend. What if he finds solace in Guru Hridaya too?

We leave the ashram and walk along a main road, alongside the sea. The sky has darkened now, but it's still warm out. The road is pitted with potholes, which we weave around. Cars intermittently speed past us, and the sea stretches into the distance, waves crashing against the shore.

'There it is,' Meera says, pointing into the distance at a roadside joint, with an outdoor oven and half a dozen tables laid out under the sky. Most of them are occupied with a combination of locals and Westerners.

'The food is amazing,' Meera enthuses.

'It really is,' Seb insists.

As we approach, Meera's uncle, emerges from the kitchen and greets us, chatting to Meera in Hindi. She tells me and Seb to go and find a table as she catches up with him.

There's only one table free and Seb and I sit down opposite each other. The sun has fully set now, the sky thick with darkness. I look out into the distance, towards the ocean. It's so dark and the streetlights are so sparse that I can barely see anything, just a faint glimmer of the moon reflected on the water.

I look around at the other diners sitting at their tables. They seem relaxed, at ease, chatty. The atmosphere is more laid back than the ashram. No one is wearing the weird ashram robes. A few people are even swigging from bottles of beer.

'Hey guys!' Meera calls out over the hum of conversation.

We look her way.

'Do you want the vegetarian option or meat?' she asks.

I smile, amused by the simplicity of the menu.

Meera takes our requests and turns back to her uncle. She chats away, perching on a stool next to him as he chops vegetables. She doesn't seem to have much interest in coming over and joining me and Seb. I can't help wondering if she's done this on purpose, creating an almost date-like situation to bring us together.

'This place is cool,' I comment.

'Yeah, it's nice. It's good to get out of the ashram from time to time,' Seb muses.

The headlights of a passing car flash over his face, illuminating his striking eyes and chiseled features. He really is gorgeous, and I'm clearly not the only person who thinks so. A few other diners glance in our direction, with a couple of hippy girls checking Seb out.

'Definitely.' I smile, although I still feel a little troubled by what Meera said on the way here.

'Do you ever worry that the ashram might get under your skin?' I ask.

Seb smiles. 'No, I like being here, but I'm definitely not going to become some weird devotee,' he insists.

'That's good.' I smile, relieved, feeling grateful that of all the people I could have met in this ashram, I met Seb.

It's nice to be around someone with a healthy sense of skepticism, balanced perfectly with a spirit of adventure and open-mindedness.

'How long do you think you'll be here?' I ask.

'I'm not sure yet. Maybe when I've figured things out, I'll be ready to leave,' Seb replies.

'When the year of self-denial is up?' I ask.

Seb laughs. 'Probably before. I can deny myself in Quebec too. At least, I want to be confident I can,' he explains.

'What were things like back there?' I press him.

'Oh God,' Seb groans. 'I made a lot of bad decisions.'

'Like what?'

Meera comes over with our dishes, placing them down on the table, with some cutlery.

'Just catching up with my uncle, I'll be back in a bit,' she says, heading back to the kitchen.

Seb and I tuck in. The food is delicious, and I see exactly what he means about the parathas. It turns out they're wheat flatbreads and they really are exceptionally good, especially when served drenched in butter.

We gush about how good the food is, but Seb frowns, a distracted look on his face, and I can tell he's still thinking about life back home.

'I… I got someone pregnant,' he blurts out eventually.

'Oh, okay,' I reply, taken aback.

He meets my gaze, his eyes sad and ashamed.

'I hooked up with this girl, Vanessa. She was on a ski break with a few of her friends to celebrate finishing her first year of uni. We had fun together, but then she went home and I didn't think about it that much. I just moved on to the next thing,' Seb tells me, shaking his head.

'But she got in touch on Facebook a couple of months later to tell me she was pregnant. She said she was getting an abortion. I didn't know what to think. It really messed me up. I kept thinking about that unborn child we'd created. I kept worrying about her. We used a condom, but I guess it didn't work,' Seb recalls sadly.

'So, what happened?' I ask.

'She got an abortion. It really affected her. She got depressed, dropped out of uni. I felt terrible. I guess it hit me that my lifestyle had consequences. I was living for the moment with all the drugs and drink and sex, but it wasn't as simple as that. Other people were getting hurt,' Seb comments ruefully, his eyes full of sadness.

His pain and regret are palpable, and I want to say something to help.

'It could have happened to anyone,' I tell him. 'I don't think you should beat yourself up.'

Seb shakes his head, tearing his paratha.

'No. I realized my actions have consequences. Her whole life changed. I'd just been acting like I was the center of the universe and all that mattered was having a good time, but life isn't as simple as that,' Seb says, taking a bite of paratha.

'I suppose,' I reply, not knowing quite what to say to make him feel better.

I don't want to say anything trite or meaningless. A pregnancy and an abortion and a young woman dropping out of university are big things and I can see now why Seb has ended up here, desperate to change his life and gain perspective. He clearly needs to heal just as much as the mother of his unborn child.

'Do you speak to the girl much?' I ask.

'No,' Seb replies. 'We're friends online, but she's living with her family now, taking time out. I don't think she particularly wants to talk to me.'

I nod, not knowing what to say. The whole situation sounds intense and I can see that it's probably the sort of thing that time heals. I'm about to say something to that affect when Meera comes barreling over, carrying a few dishes.

'Brought you some more parathas!' she enthuses, placing a plate of steaming parathas on the table.

She sits down next to me and begins tucking into her food.

'Cool!' Seb replies, smiling brightly. 'Thanks.'

He reaches for a paratha and gives me a small, sad, private smile. I smile back, wishing there was something I could do to help.

14 CHAPTER FOURTEEN

Sun streams through the beams of my treehouse. I pull back my mosquito net and watch particles of dust swirling in the light, while listening to the sounds of the birds chirping. Eventually, I crawl out of bed and pull back my treehouse curtain. I gaze out over the treetops. The sun is rising and it's already a warm, ambient, gleaming day. Weirdly, as I take in my surroundings, I feel almost at home. It's been a while since I arrived now and funnily enough, despite how unplanned and unexpected this trip has been, I feel like I'm settling in. I've made memories since I've been here. I've had conversations with new friends – deeper conversations that I've had for ages with people back home in London. I suppose that's the kind of thing that makes a place a home – it's memories and connections, not necessarily cushions and soft furnishings.

Seb interrupts my thoughts, appearing from the kitchen with a bottle of water in one hand and a towel in the other. He's wearing a loose vest, gym shorts and running shoes.

He must sense my eyes on him because he suddenly looks my way. I feel happy noting the way his eyes light up when he catches sight of me.

'Hey,' he says, waving up at me.

'Morning,' I reply as I make my way down the ladder.

Seb approaches as I climb down. He looks incredibly gorgeous – all blue-eyed and tanned and healthy and handsome. I should really be getting used to his good looks by now, but I still feel girlish and almost giddy every time my eyes land upon him.

'Are you heading to the gym?' I ask, stepping off the ladder and glancing towards his bottle of water and running shoes.

'Yeah! I felt like I should burn off the parathas,' he laughs, rolling his eyes a little.

I wonder if either of us are going to mention the conversation we had last night. When Meera came along, we instantly switched to lighter topics. I can't help wondering how Seb's feeling now, and yet I don't want to bring it up and make him uncomfortable.

'Cool! I should probably do the same,' I comment, even though I have absolutely no intention of working out right now.

'Do you want to come?' Seb asks.

'No, I'm alright. Maybe tomorrow.' I shrug.

Seb nods. 'So what are you up to this morning?' he asks.

'I'm not sure yet. Coffee!' I laugh.

The truth is, I have no plans. My only real plan is to make coffee, sit down at the picnic table and hope the peacock reappears so that I can admire him, but I don't feel like telling this to Seb. Peacock-spotting doesn't seem anywhere near as valid as a gym session.

'I think I'll just relax, unwind, maybe check out the hammocks and do some reading,' I say, gazing over at the hammocks slung between the palm trees at the bottom of the garden.

'Sounds nice.' Seb smiles. 'Well, see you later then.'

'See you later!'

Seb breaks into a light jog and runs out of the guesthouse. He's clearly in the mood for exercise. The Swoosh on his Nike trainers becomes a blur as he jogs away. He must be one of the only people in the ashram who wears Nike running shoes. Other people here would probably deem such shoes to be emblematic of Western consumerism - the antithesis of enlightenment, but Seb just does his own thing. He doesn't feel the need to put on a performance of being 'spiritual'. He makes his own rules and I like that about him.

I head to the kitchen to make my coffee. I still haven't gotten round to buying my own kitchen supplies so pinch a bit of Seb's coffee again and boil up some water on the stove. As the water's boiling I think about Seb and the things we spoke about last night. I knew there would be a significant reason for him coming here. After all, you don't just up sticks and relocate to India over nothing, but I had no idea quite how serious the reason would be. I thought he was just a player who had drunk too much and taken too many drugs and was having a quarter-life crisis. I didn't realize how much more there was to the story. I'd never have imagined that there was a pregnant girl, an abortion, and that Seb would be feeling so much guilt and sadness over everything. It's like he's punishing himself in some way, denying himself the things he took pleasure in before this girl got pregnant, as some kind of penance. Poor guy. He may think he's made a mistake, but he's a good person, that's obvious. He wouldn't even be here beating himself up over everything if he wasn't. I hope if this trip teaches him anything it's that he has a good heart and he's not a bad person.

As much as his celibacy frustrated me before, I now respect it. He needs to do whatever it is he needs to do in order to process what's happened. Hopefully, he'll come out on the other side of all this feeling less guilty and no longer beating himself up. I might have found his celibacy vow annoying before, but I'm definitely going to stop lusting after him now. Or at least try. I'm certainly going to stop wishing he'd give up his vow for me. He needs this. He needs to do whatever it is he feels is right to move on. He needs to get over his past just as much as I need to get over Paul and move on from that stage of my life.

My water boils. I make my coffee and head outside.

I sit down at the picnic table and take a sip. Something catches my eye on the table, and I look down to see a snail, slowly streaking its way along the table leg. I feel a pang of sadness. Paul and I always had an in-joke about snails. He told me once that the first time he realized he was in love with me was when he watched me leave his flat for work one morning, back when we were first dating, and saw me stoop down and pick up a snail from the front drive, before carrying it over to the garden and placing it safely within the shrubbery, where it wouldn't get stamped on. Apparently that small caring gesture made Paul realize I was the woman for him. I thought it was hilarious when he told me and from then on, whenever we saw a snail, I'd joke that it was 'Cupid' – the snail that made him fall for me. We were once in the Royal Botanical Garden in Kew back in London when we stopped by a tank of snails and I shrieked excitedly, pointing at the glass.

'Look, it's Cupid!'

Paul rushed over and planted a massive kiss on my lips as a pair of elderly ladies eyed us strangely.

'Things haven't really worked out, Cupid,' I sigh, plucking the snail of the picnic table and placing it in a nearby bush.

I sit back down, wishing the peacock would make an appearance. But never mind. The leaflet about activities in the ashram is still on the table. I pick it up and flick through to see what's happening today.

I scan the listings. The 'Get in touch with your spirit animal' workshop is taking place.

A mischievous part of me feels like going. It sounds so bonkers and yet it would no doubt make for a hilarious story. Priya and everyone else at the office would laugh out loud if I told them I'd tried to channel my inner goat, or dog, or whatever animal I truly am.

I check out the time and place the workshop is being held, cross-checking the map at the back of the booklet to try to figure out how to get there.

As it turns out, the workshop is being held in a studio not far from the guesthouse and it's on in just a couple of hours. I figure I can have a shower, read my book or maybe attempt to write in my diary for a bit, lounge in the hammocks and then make my way there. I may as well. When in an ashram and all that…

Just as I'm having this thought, the peacock saunters into the guesthouse. There he is! He looks even more beautiful than I remember, his striking feathers shimmering in the bright morning sunlight. He approaches, looking regal and proud.

As he nears my table, I realize I have a massive goofy grin spread all over my face. It hits me that two weeks ago all I wanted was for Paul to propose. All I wanted was for him to put a ring on it. I was so desperate to tick the goal of getting engaged off my Life List and now here I am, sitting in an ashram, smiling at a peacock, feeling completely mesmerized and content. This moment was never on my Life List and yet I couldn't be more grateful for it. Maybe life is better when it's not planned.

'Morning,' Meera says, distracting me.

'Morning!' I reply, glancing her way.

She looks almost as colorful as the peacock, wearing a beautiful purple sari, her hair falling in shiny waves over her shoulders. She smiles and heads into the kitchen, emerging moments later with a steaming cup of chai. She sits down opposite me.

'So how was last night then, huh?' she asks, taking a sip of chai and giving me a cheeky look.

She clearly suspects something happened between me and Seb, or at least suspects something is going to happen.

'It was good!' I laugh, before sipping my coffee.

'And…?' Meera perseveres.

'Well, Seb's obviously gorgeous and I really like him but I don't want to stand in the way of his pledge,' I explain. 'He seems to be taking it really seriously.'

'Yeah,' Meera sighs. 'I understand. It's a shame though.'

'I know,' I admit. 'Under different circumstances maybe it would work out, but I suppose we both have stuff to deal with right now.'

Meera smiles, a little sadly. She clearly liked the idea of matchmaking.

'That makes sense,' she admits.

We chat about the restaurant last night, the amazing food and the peacock, who it turns out, is called Raja, meaning king, and is like a pet to Meera. I tell Meera that I'm thinking about going to the spirit animal workshop.

'Oh yeah, that's a good one!' Meera insists, her eyes flickering almost wickedly.

I'm about to ask her to elaborate when some new guests arrive, ready to check in.

I head back to the kitchen to wash up my mug and then go to get ready.

Having had a shower and got dressed, I take my book on female corporate empowerment and make myself comfortable in one of the hammocks. My book may not be the most spiritual choice of reading material in the world, and I can see now why the man on the plane seemed surprised that I was heading to this ashram with such a book. I'd feel embarrassed to read it in the mail hall or somewhere where other people could see. It's like caring about corporate success makes you a sell-out here. But I'm proud to be a lawyer. This ashram wouldn't even be possible were it not for laws protecting people from anarchy and crime.

That's the problem with the hippy narrative. It depends upon privilege. Fortunate Western hippies who happen to be able to take months out of their lives to do yoga and meditate in India, act like they're above the 'sell-outs' who facilitate their 'enlightenment' in the first place. While going on about the importance of doing yoga all day and meditating and leading alternative lifestyles, they forget about the pilots who flew the planes to get them here, the engineers who designed the roads, the tech geniuses who run the social networks that keep them in touch with their families back home, the banks that facilitate the funding of their trips, the medics that can provide care if something goes wrong, and all the workers who maintain the irrigation systems and waste disposal and food provisions that keep them healthy and well. Those people aren't spending their days meditating and yet their contribution to the community is invaluable.

I guess that's why I can't identify with hippies. I don't need to spend all day meditating to feel enlightened. In spite of how much I may have been over-working in London and losing touch with myself and my sense of happiness, I'm still proud to be a lawyer. Upholding the law is important and reading books that help me do that is fine, it's nothing to be ashamed of. I rock my hammock gently and gaze at my toes. Birds chirp above me as I open my book.

I get through a couple of chapters, broken up with a lot of daydreaming and then I realize it's time for the spirit animal workshop. I feel a twinge of unease. Am I really doing this? Part of me wants to simply carry on lying in the hammock, but I should do something unique while I'm here.

I leave my book in my treehouse and head over to the hall where the workshop is taking place. There are quite a few people hanging around outside, waiting for the workshop to start. There must be a couple of dozen people. Most look a little nervous, as though, like me, they can't quite believe they're doing this. Although there are a couple of die-hard hippies who look completely relaxed and confident as though they do this sort of thing all the time.

I linger at the edge of the group. I'm not really sure whether to speak to anybody. No one is really chatting. The atmosphere is quiet and anticipatory, almost tense.

I begin to feel awkward, when a man who must be in his early forties appears, striding confidently towards the front door of the hall. Everyone turns to him and I realize he must be the teacher. He's wearing baggy harem trousers and a slouchy grey t-shirt over a lean, yoga-toned body. He's bald but has a long wispy grey beard that he's gelled into a point.

He takes a key from the pocket of his trousers and unlocks the door, pulling it wide open.

'Welcome everybody. Namaste!' he says, gesturing for us all to head into the hall.

'Namaste,' a few people reply.

'Welcome. Hello. Good morning!' he says enthusiastically to each person as we file into the hall.

He has a thick American accent and I find myself wondering what led him to end up teaching spirit animal workshops in an ashram in India.

The hall is incredibly beautiful inside. It's circular with a domed glass ceiling, and it's flooded with light. In spite of the looming weirdness of the workshop, the atmosphere of the hall is still uplifting.

'Welcome to this workshop!' The instructor says, striding into the center of the hall once everyone has filtered in.

'Hello everybody and welcome,' he says, smiling beatifically.

'My name is Jasper and I will be your guide today, assisting you in getting in touch with your spirit animal,' he says.

I try not to smirk.

'Have you ever had a recurring dream about an animal? Have you ever been followed by an animal or connected with an animal in a way that feels unique or special? Have you ever crossed paths with an animal and helped that animal in some way? That animal might be your spirit animal.'

Jasper carries on talking about the unique connection between people and animals and how our spirit animals may represent a part of ourselves we have not yet 'manifested'. He claims that by engaging with our spirit animals, we can reach our true potential.

'Now let's start with some stretches,' he suggests, launching into a lunge.

Half the attendees start doing serious yoga moves. One girl even drops into the splits.

I opt for a lunge and a few arm stretches. While I'm lunging, feeling a strain in my left hamstring, I gaze across the room, experiencing the odd sensation of someone looking at me. I spot none other than Blossom. Urgh. She's lying on the ground, performing some kind of sun salutation, while giving me daggers.

I quickly look away, but I can't help rolling my eyes. What's her problem?! Has she not had her fill of getting at me? Why does she feel the need to glare at me today as well? It's not like I'm trying to compete with her for Paul, I'm not even bothered about that. She can run off into the sunset with him for all I care. All I'm interested in right now is doing my lunges and trying to get in touch with my spirit animal. Maybe I am more enlightened than her after all, because she could clearly do with taking a leaf out of my book and getting into this workshop instead of giving me evils.

I swap legs, stretching out my right hamstring and even though I know I shouldn't, I glance over at her again. She's still shooting me daggers!

I turn around, presenting my back to her and continue with my stretches.

'Okay now that we're all limbered up, let's get in touch with our spirit animals!' Jasper suggests.

I shoot him a look, trying to catch a trace of humor or wryness. Surely, he can't say something like that with a straight face? But apparently, he can. He looks completely sincere. In fact, he's folding his hands together in prayer and closing his eyes. What the hell?

'I call on the spirit of the eagle, the wisdom in the eyes of the owl, the fragile flutter of the butterfly's wings, the growl of the bear, and the grumble of the gorilla…'

I snigger and glance around the room, expecting others to be as amused as I am, but everyone else looks somber. Some people are even praying too, with their hands together and eyes closed. How do these people take everything so seriously? I feel so out of place. I'm beginning to wonder if I should have stayed in my hammock, reading, after all.

Finally, Jasper opens his eyes and looks around the room, taking us all in.

'I hope you'll all find this workshop a very enlightening experience,' he says.

I raise an eyebrow. I have my doubts.

'Now, it's time to channel your spirit animal. Close your eyes and be at one with your animal self,' Jasper insists.

I need to stop smirking and at least try to take this seriously. I chose to come to this workshop after all. I close my eyes.

Right. What animal am I?

Am I a bird? No. A bird doesn't feel quite right. If I was a bird, I'd be the one flying around, travelling the world. I wouldn't have simply followed Paul over here.

Am I a sheep then? A follower? No, not quite. If I was a sheep, I'd probably be wearing the white ashram robes by now and be a follower of the guru. I'm a bit more independent than a sheep.

Perhaps I'm a lion like Seb? No. I'm hardly a lion.

Could I be a peacock? No, that would just be arrogant.

A caterpillar like the one I saw this morning? No. A caterpillar doesn't feel right either. I may not be quite as resplendent as a peacock but I'm more than just a bug.

How about a cat? Maybe. Actually, yes. I like lounging around, making myself comfortable on sofas, sidling up to people, sleeping.

Yeah, a cat feels right. Okay, now I need to get into the mindset of a cat. I try to have cat-like thoughts when Jasper blows the whistle.

Christ, now I actually have to be a cat. I open my eyes and get onto all fours, glancing around the room at everyone else, coming out of their cross-legged positions and assuming the stance of their inner animal.

I crouch on all fours, feeling a pang of embarrassment. Am I really doing this? Am I really pretending to be a cat?

'Meow,' I utter, cringing.

I can't believe I'm doing this.

'Meow,' I try again.

I begin to prowl across the hall. A man who appears to be channeling his inner bunny rabbit hops across my path, but catching sight of me prowling, he hops away, alarmed, fully embodying his rabbit self. I want to laugh and yet I can't help admiring his commitment to the workshop. I consider chasing him. Do cats chase rabbits? I'm not sure. I decide to hiss and meow at him instead.

I saunter on but stop in my tracks when I spot a woman embodying her inner snake. She sits in the lotus position with her hands towering above her head, slithering around. She eyes me menacingly and I'm worried she's going to slither over. I scamper away.

On the opposite side of the hall is a man standing on all fours making intermittent 'baa' noises like a sheep. He eyes me boredly.

I meow at him. He baas back.

I decide to sit near him and pause for a moment, taking in the commotion in the hall. A grown man is walking around with his arm dangling by his nose, clearly getting in touch with his inner elephant. Another man barks at him. A petite girl flaps her arms about, pretending to fly around the hall while letting out chirping noises. I wish I had my phone with me. I'd love to furtively make a YouTube video of all of this. I don't think I've ever seen anything more ridiculous in my entire life.

The sheep baas at me again, snapping me out of my reverie. Thoughts about YouTube videos aren't very feline. I should at least try to stay in the zone. I prowl away.

I spot another woman who appears to be channeling her inner cat too and prowl towards her, when I feel a scratching sensation on my leg.

I turn around to see Blossom, on all fours, growling at me.

What the hell? I back away, but she suddenly roars and charges at me. She clearly identifies as some kind of wild cat or tiger.

I start scampering across the hall, but she's following me, scratching at my feet.

Oh my God. She is actually insane. She's trying to attack me, like a real tiger would! She wants to turn me into her personal prey.

I dash across the hall, trying to get away from her, but I can hear her growling and roaring behind me. I throw a few panicked imploring looks towards the other participants, but they just smile encouragingly, as though they're impressed at how well we're getting into character.

'GRRRRRR!!!' Blossom growls again.

I glance over my shoulder to see her frothing at the mouth, eyes manic.

I need the tutor. Where is the tutor?

I scan the hall and spot him in the corner, hopping around,

dancing like a monkey with another person who appears to be a monkey.

'Help!' I cry out as Blossom scratches my leg again, but he doesn't hear me.

He simply carries on jumping around like an excitable monkey.

Blossom grabs my leg. I try to free myself, but her grip is too tight. She roars and crawls on top of me, causing me to topple over. I land on my back and she pins me down, roaring in my face. Tiny globules of spit land on my cheeks.

This is actually terrifying. I truly do feel like a cat that's about to be mauled to death.

I look towards the teacher, but he's still pretending to be a monkey.

Blossom roars again, getting even closer to my face, as I struggle to free myself. Another globule of spit lands on my cheek. She looks ravenous, deranged, like she truly wants to tear a chunk off my flesh.

Suddenly, amid the cacophony of animal noises, I hear the high-pitched trill of a whistle.

Finally, Jasper is putting an end to all this.

'Time to return to your human state,' he shouts, above the din.

Blossom rolls her eyes. She was clearly enjoying mauling me, the psycho.

Reluctantly, she moves off me. I shoot her a look and prowl away, momentarily forgetting that I no longer need to be a cat. I stand up and hurry to the opposite side of the hall.

At a safe distance, I turn and look around at her. She's standing up now too and smiles at me as though nothing untoward just happened. I gawp back. She's clearly unhinged. She obviously hates me because I'm the ex of her new man, but to attack me while pretending to be a tiger is just next-level weird.

'Now, we're going to channel our inner *beasts*,' Jasper informs us, grinning enthusiastically.

Inner beasts? Some people just did! I feel like pointing this out to him, but it's not worth it. I need to get out of here before Blossom tears me apart.

The teacher launches into another meditation, and everyone sits down, closing their eyes. I seize the opportunity to slip out of the hall, dropping a few rupee notes in the donations bowl as I sneak away.

Closing the door gently behind me, I walk away, breathing in the fresh air and relishing the peace and calm. I hear the sound of a roar and look through a window to see Blossom, back to her tiger state, throwing herself at the glass, eyeing me maniacally while growling with frustration. I walk away as fast as I can.

15 CHAPTER FIFTEEN

I head back to the guesthouse, still reeling from the weirdness of the spirit animal workshop.

Did that really just happen? Did I really just get mauled by my ex's new girlfriend, pretending to be a tiger? I shake my head, astounded. This place never ceases to surprise me.

I still feel a little rattled, but I have to admit, I wanted a good story to make Priya laugh and I certainly got one. I decide to take a detour to the main hall to send her an email. It's been a few days now and I could really do with updating everybody back home on how I'm doing.

I head towards the main hall, passing the field where the buffalo grazes languidly in the sun. As I near the hall, I pray I won't run into Paul like last time. That really is the last thing I need today.

I walk inside and do a quick scan, but I can't see him, thankfully. I look around, trying to figure out where the computer room is when a poster catches my eye. It features Guru Hridaya's face, his eyes penetrating, as though they're trying to reach into the viewer's soul. Underneath is the slogan: 'Letting go of your ego is the first step towards finding your true purpose'.

Hmm…

I see what Meera means about him. He's basically telling his followers to relinquish their identities. And I suppose once they do, they become empty vessels, willingly servile. No wonder they end up doing free labor and devoting themselves entirely to the ashram. It's actually really sad. The people he's trying to brainwash are clearly lost and unhappy and in need of support and yet they're getting exploited and preyed upon instead. I feel sorry for them. It's probably the reason I'm not really that angry at Blossom, in spite of everything, because like quite a lot of people around here, she's no doubt really lost.

I walk away from the poster, still feeling slightly disturbed by it when I spot a woman striding purposefully towards the kitchen, looking like she works here. I ask her where the computer room is.

'Upstairs, first door on the left,' she tells me.

'Thanks,' I reply, but she's already marching away.

I head towards a spiral staircase in the corner of the hall and make my way up. I feel excited. I can't wait to get online. It's been ages since I had a proper internet session. I don't have a clue what hashtags are trending, I don't know what stories are in the headlines, I don't know if anyone has been cancelled, I don't even know if Paul has changed his relationship status on Facebook. There's so much I don't know that I'd normally be paying attention to every hour of the day.

I take the first door on the left and walk inside. There are half a dozen computers at numbered booths. I pay for half an hour and a woman sitting at a desk browsing Facebook hands me the login details for the computer in booth four.

I sit down and enter the details. Excellent. Internet, here I come.

I log into my emails. It feels like forever since I've been online, and yet really, it's only been four of five days. Nevertheless, my inbox is full of messages from family and friends asking how the trip's going. I reply to all of them, drafting a particularly long message to Priya telling her all about the spirit animal workshop. I know I shouldn't, but I can't resist logging into my work emails too. I'm still curious as to why Mr Pearson visited the office the other day, even though I know it's not that important and pretty much irrelevant to my time in the ashram. But there's nothing interesting in my work inbox so I log onto Twitter instead.

I check my notifications. A picture I posted at Heathrow of the departure screen with my flight details, adorned with the caption, 'Bye England!', has thirty-five likes and a ton of comments, which I reply to. I scroll for a while, liking and commenting on my friends' tweets and checking out the latest hashtags, but the kind of thing that tends to keep me entertained in London, feels sort of irrelevant here. I find I can't summon the energy to care about #ThrowbackThursday or #GetTheToriesOut.

I log on to Facebook and I know I shouldn't, but I can't help checking out Paul's profile. I'm only human after all. I click onto his page. He's changed his relationship status to 'Single'. Of course, he has. It was only a matter of time, but I still feel a cold shiver of unease as I take it in. *Single*.

Six years. We were together for six years and now it's well and truly over. And everyone knows it's over.

At least he hasn't unfriended me. I suppose that's something. Not that I should really care about Paul's friendship. I click through his pictures. He's uploaded a couple from the ashram – a shot of him meditating with garlands of flowers around his neck, and another of him standing in front of a temple doing a peace sign, but there are none featuring Blossom.

I look at his relationship status again. Single. Unbelievable.

I know I shouldn't care, but it feels so strange. Feeling deflated, I log out of my emails and head onto BBC News to see what's going on in the world. After all, there's more to life than relationship statuses.

And yet, the news is exactly as it always is. It's just warmongering, politics, and climate catastrophe stuff. I read a few articles, but since World War Three hasn't broken out, I give up. I don't need to know the ins and outs of what's going on in Westminster or Donald Trump's latest gaffe while I'm over here.

I pay for my internet session and head back downstairs. The canteen has been set up for lunch and the spread of dishes looks just as delicious as it did the other day.

I grab some lunch, opting for a takeaway box. I decide I'll get some for Meera too as a thank you for taking me and Seb to the paratha place last night. That evening, eating parathas, chatting to Seb, with the sound of the waves crashing in the distance, isn't one I'll forget in a hurry. I pick up some lunch for Seb too and head back to the guesthouse.

Meera is sitting at the picnic table in the sunshine working on her laptop, a steaming cup of chai next to her.

'Hey!' I say, as I approach.

'Hey!' she looks up from her screen and smiles.

I spot a spreadsheet on her monitor.

'Just doing accounts,' she tells me.

'Oh right,' I reply, feeling a twinge of envy for her lifestyle.

Even doing accounts looks relaxing. Getting to work in the

sunshine, surrounded by nature, sipping chai, must be heavenly.

'I got you some lunch,' I tell her, taking one of the boxes out of the bag I'm carrying.

I hand it to her. I look around for Seb, but I can't see him. I'll leave his box in the kitchen for later.

'Oh Rachel, thanks so much!' Meera gushes, looking genuinely touched.

'That's so kind,' she adds. 'I'll get us some cutlery.'

She heads into the kitchen to collect some knives and forks.

I open my box of food, feeling eager to tuck in.

Meera comes back and hands me a fork.

We tuck in. The flavors are so rich and captivating that we eat in complete silence, for a few moments, wrapped up in how tasty our meals are.

Eventually, once we're nearly done eating, I mention the poster I saw in the hall, describing it to Meera.

'It kind of gave me the creeps,' I comment.

'Yeah, he's creepy,' Meera replies, taking a sip of chai before tucking in again.

'He does seem controlling. I feel sorry for the people that get swept up in it,' I say.

'Same,' Meera sighs, digging her fork back into her food, before suddenly wincing.

'Ouch!' she gasps, clutching her stomach.

'What's up?' I ask, alarmed, wondering if there's something

wrong with the food.

'Period pain,' Meera groans. 'I'm having cramps.'

'Oh no,' I comment sympathetically.

'I went to the chemist to get some paracetamol, but they'd run out,' Meera says.

She eyes me hopefully. 'Do you have any?'

I think through the things I packed. I have malaria tablets, tablets for diarrhea and sleeping pills that I thought might help with jetlag, but I don't have any paracetamol, which is probably quite foolish given that both malaria and diarrhea can be pretty uncomfortable. I explain that I don't have any, apologizing.

'Don't worry about it,' Meera insists with a smile, although I can tell from the way she's clutching her stomach, with her brow knotted, that she's in a lot of pain.

I'm trying to think of how to help when a couple of women wander into the guesthouse. One of them has henna tattoos all over her arms and the other is Madeleine – the quiet French girl from Spiritual Ascension Snakes and Ladders. She smiles at me.

Meera gets up to greet them.

'Hi, can I help you?' she asks.

'Hi, is the asana yoga class happening here?' Madeleine's friend asks in a loud brash American accent.

'No, sorry. It's in the guesthouse next door. The next one to the left,' Meera tells them, pointing in the direction of the guesthouse they need to go to.

'Oh right,' the girl replies.

They turn away. Neither of them thanks Meera, and I find myself feeling irritated at how rude they're being and how they don't seem to be at all bothered about having interrupted our lunch.

'Hey,' I call after them. 'You don't have any paracetamol, do you?'

They turn back.

'What for?' Madeleine asks.

'Women's troubles,' Meera replies, smiling awkwardly.

'Oh,' Madeleine says. She roots around in her bag and I feel momentarily hopeful.

'No, sorry,' she sighs, looking up.

'You know, when I have period pain, I just meditate through it,' Madeleine's friend pipes up, with a smug smile. 'I just rise above the pain,' she adds.

I glare at her. Even Meera glares at her. She meditates through period pain?! What is up with these people? I've truly had enough of these sanctimonious spiritual types.

Meera and I exchange a look.

'Whatever!' I scoff, turning back to my food.

Meera laughs.

'Yeah, whatever!' she echoes, rolling her eyes.

'It works!' The girl insists, but Madeleine has the good sense to lead her friend back out of the guesthouse.

Meera and I finish our lunch while mocking the idea of meditating your way through period pain.

Once we've finished our meals, I ask if I can borrow one of the rental scooters on offer at the guesthouse.

'Sure,' Meera replies.

I hop on the scooter and head off towards the nearest town, feeling the breeze in my hair as I whizz through the streets. The first chemist I come across must have been the one Meera stopped in at earlier, as the man working there tells me, in broken English, that they don't have any paracetamol. I jump back on my scooter and ride through the town, looking out for another place. I check in vain at a supermarket, before finding another chemist. The man working there doesn't speak English and I have to mime writhing around in agony, but I get my hands on a pack of paracetamol eventually. Then I hop back on my bike and take them back to Meera.

16 CHAPTER SIXTEEN

Five Rhythms Dance Meditation

Moon worship and chanting

Tribal forest dance workshop

    I leaf listlessly through the ashram brochure over breakfast, but I can't quite bring myself to take part in any weird activities today. Two days in a row of having endured Spiritual Ascension Snakes and Ladders and having channeled my inner cat is enough enlightenment for me. I want to do something real, something practical. I gaze out over the garden. I guess I could see if Meera needs a hand with the gardening. I finish off my coffee and have a look around the guesthouse for her, but I can't seem to find her anywhere.

    I'm not really sure what to do with my day. I decide I'll grab my bag and hop back on the scooter I borrowed yesterday to do a bit of exploring. I rev up my scooter and whizz out of the guesthouse. It's another beautiful day and it feels good to ride along the dusty path, gravelly stones rumbling under my tires. I scoot past palm trees, the buffalo and the main hall. I'm not really sure where I'm heading. I figure I'll stop when I feel like stopping.

    I pass other guesthouses. Some of them are housed in the

prettiest, quirky buildings, like hobbit hovels with tinted glass windows and winding chimneys. They're so adorable and fantastical-looking. I slow down in front of a couple of them to take pictures on my phone.

In the distance, I spot the temple. Technically, the temple is the epicenter of the ashram and yet I haven't been yet. It doesn't particularly interest me, but I should probably check it out. I get back on my scooter and head that way, going down the path at a slow speed. As I approach the temple, I spot a swimming pool. My heart leaps. I had no idea the ashram had a pool! I can pass the days swimming now.

I park my scooter outside the temple and walk up to the entrance. As I approach, I hear chanting from within. There are rows of shoes by the front door. I kick mine off and take a few steps closer, peering inside. There are rows and rows of people, sitting cross-legged, chanting mantras from small booklets adorned with the guru's face. What the hell? I spot a stack of the booklets by the entrance and pick one up.

I creep into the hall and sit down at the back, opening the booklet. It's full of chants. They're in Hindi but the English translation has been included. I flick through them, reading passages here and there.

I let go of my desires, my wants, my ego,

And embrace the spirit,

The one true leader: Guru Hridaya,

Heart of the world, conscious being.

I flick through, but all the chants are similar. There's nothing about spirituality in general, it's all about worshiping the guru and negating the self. I look around the room at the people chanting this stuff. Why are they willfully brainwashing themselves? My gaze wanders over to one woman who looks exhausted, a lost searching look in her eyes. She looks like she needs a good hug, and yet she's half-heartedly chanting instead.

I decide to attempt to join in with a chant just to see how it feels. I glance at the booklet of the man sitting next to me and turn to the page he's on, but I can't get through one whole verse without feeling strange. I give up and just sit there, letting the chanting wash over me. I get bored after a while and sneak back out of the hall, placing my booklet back on the stack. I retrieve my shoes and head back to my scooter.

I'm about to hop back on my bike and get away from the weirdness of the temple, when I spot Guru Hridaya hanging around by the back of the temple twenty or thirty feet away.

I feel starstruck. I can't believe I'm looking at the actual guru! He's almost started to feel like a celebrity to me. He's wearing bright orange robes with a matching turban and tons of gold necklaces. He's plump and would be pretty non-descript were it not for all his eye-catching glimmering jewelry. He even has a shiny gold bhindi and a nose ring with a chain attached that dangles across his cheek towards a hoop in his ear. I stare at him, almost starstruck. I've seen his face on websites and posters, heard chants about him, and picked up on so much gossip, that it feels odd to finally lay eyes on him.

One of his assistants approaches him, ushering him into a waiting car.

He gets inside and his assistant closes the car door. The driver starts the vehicle and the car begins to pull away. I find myself wondering where Guru Hridaya is heading. What do gurus do all day?

I reach into my bag and root around for my sunglasses. I don them, and without really knowing what I'm doing, I hop on board my scooter, twist my key in the ignition and begin following the car.

It heads out of the ashram, weaving through the streets. I follow at a slow pace, keeping a certain amount of distance. I'm not sure why I'm following a guru. But I did decide to explore today, didn't I? And what better way to explore than stalking the ashram's guru. No, not stalking. Familiarizing.

The car retreats further and further out of the ashram until it arrives at the main road along the coastline. It takes a left, heading in the opposite direction to Meera's uncle's restaurant. I have no idea what lies left, but I follow.

The car picks up pace, pelting down the road. I rev my accelerator, determined to keep up. The ocean stretches into the distance to the left of me, the waves crashing against the shore. Unlike the last time I saw the ocean, at night with Seb and Meera, I can see it clearly now. The sea glitters into the distance – a vast, shimmering expanse – but the sandy shore is littered with plastic bottles, cans, and trash. It's sad that it's so dirty as it could be such a beautiful beach were it not for all the rubbish. The wind rushes through my hair. I should be wearing a helmet, but I didn't feel I needed one as I cruised leisurely around the ashram. I'm beginning to wonder if I should turn around and head back. The guru's car is going fast, very fast. Who knows where they're going? They might be driving for miles. I might not even have enough fuel. I have half a tank, but I have no idea how far that will get me. And anyway, I don't even know why I'm really doing this.

We must be three or four miles away from the ashram and I'm about to turn around, when the guru's car begins to slow down. I spot a building that looks like an LA mansion. It's unlike anything I've seen in the area. I brake and draw to a halt, stopping far enough away from the guru's car that he shouldn't be able to spot me.

I watch as he gets out of the car and waves to his driver, before dialing a code into a security system at the gates of the mansion. They open and he walks through, wandering down a pathway towards the front door. The mansion is enormous. Spectacular. It must have half a dozen bedrooms. It even has a pool at the back.

I wait for a moment. The driver of the guru's car starts turning the car around. I start up my scooter and try to look inconspicuous, continuing along the road.

The driver passes me but doesn't pay me much attention.

I wait until he's out of sight and draw to a halt not far from the mansion. I park my scooter and creep furtively towards it. I reach the gates and peer down the path. I spot the guru in his front room, visible through the plate glass windows. He reclines on a large, plush-looking sofa, clearly perfectly at home in his surroundings.

Meera told me he lived at the ashram in a modest hut, like he was a self-sacrificing modern-day Buddha. And yet here he is, looking completely at home! Has he been leading a double life? Is this where the donations from his devotees get spent? Does he even do charity work? I feel outraged, frustrated. Something's definitely not right. I reach into my bag and take some pictures of the mansion with my phone, but it's so far along the path that they're grainy and indistinct and you can't see the guru inside, even when I try to use the zoom function.

I want evidence. I look around, wondering what to do, when I spot a letterbox. Ha! I can just check the guru's mail and find a letter addressed to him. I try to pull the mailbox open, but it's locked. I should have realized it would be. Yet I peer in and spot a few letters inside. Fortunately, I have quite slender fingers and I reach into the letterbox to grab the corner of one of the letters. I try a few times to grasp it, feeling anxious. What if Guru Hridaya has CCTV and he's watching me? What if he comes out to see me rooting through his mail?

I'm sweating, stressed, and I'm about to give up when I manage to get hold of one of the letters. Slowly but surely, I pull it gently out of the letterbox, until I'm holding it in my hands. Excellent! I look at the address but of course, it's in Hindi and indecipherable to me. I take a picture of it to show Meera later and then post the letter back into the box.

I look back down the driveway at the guru in his mansion. He's still lying on the sofa, relaxing. Someone – a woman – walks over to him and hands him a drink. It's hard to make out, but it looks like a beer.

I shake my head. So much for relinquishing your vices and material desires. The guru couldn't be any more ostentatious, with his palatial beachside mansion and booze-drinking. Unbelievable.

Feeling disgusted yet pumped full of indignation, I jump back on my scooter and speed off towards the ashram. I barely register the sea this time. I don't feel relaxed or soothed by the sound of the rolling waves. I'm simply too shocked. Too angry. The cheek of the guru! The audacity! The hypocrisy. I can't wait to tell Meera about this. The wind blows through my hair as I speed back.

I reach the ashram, slowing down as I take the turn inside. As I pass the main hall, I spot Paul wandering along the path with Blossom. They both look my way, but I ignore them. I don't care about either of them right now. I just rev my scooter and speed off towards the guesthouse.

I spot Meera sitting at the picnic table with her laptop, like she was yesterday.

I park my scooter and dash over to her.

'Hey!' I say, feeling a little breathless.

'Are you okay?' she asks, looking a little taken aback. 'Your hair's all over the place!'

'Oh!' I laugh, patting my hair down, realizing how frazzled I must look from my chase. 'I'm fine!'

I sit down at the picnic table.

'I just saw Guru Hridaya. I was at the temple and he was outside, at the back. He got into this car and I followed him. Anyway, they drove out of the ashram, like three or four miles away, to this mansion,' I babble, pulling my phone out of my pocket.

'This enormous mansion! I swear it's where he lives, Meera,' I tell her, retrieving the picture.

I show her the shots I took.

'I found his mail, look!' I hand her my phone with the picture of the guru's letter on screen.

'Oh yeah.' Meera nods, taking in the pictures. 'That's his place,' she remarks casually.

'What?' I balk. 'I thought he lived here. I thought he had a humble life?!'

'No, not really!' Meera laughs. 'He stays here a few days a week, but he doesn't really live here. It's just part of his image, you know?'

'But…' I utter. 'All that money he takes in donations, does it just go on his mansion?'

Meera shrugs. 'I don't know. Like I said, we stay out of his way and he stays out of ours.'

Meera hands me back my phone.

'I can't believe it…' I take my phone. 'Doesn't it bother you?'

'Yeah,' Meera sighs. 'But we can't do much about it. Some residents tried to lobby him to be more ethical a while back, but it didn't achieve anything. I just wish he'd pay tax on all the money he makes from this place, then at least locals would benefit too.'

'He doesn't pay tax?' I query.

'No. He claims the money he receives counts as donations and therefore isn't taxable by law, but not all the money the ashram makes is from donations. He's tax dodging, but no one really says anything,' Meera tells me.

'It would make a huge difference to the area if he did pay,' she continues. 'We'd have better roads, better policing, better schools, the ocean wouldn't be as dirty, but he doesn't pay anything. It makes me sad. It's a shame, especially for when I have kids, you know? But no one challenges him,' Meera notes ruefully.

'Why?' I ask, feeling unsettled.

'He's rich. We can't go up against him.' Meera shrugs.

I nod, understandingly, although I'm completely taken aback. Guru Hridaya must be making millions from this place with all the visitors and workshops and donations, and yet he doesn't give a penny back to the local community? It's terrible. I can't believe he could have the audacity to live tax-free here when so many local people, like Meera, are helping to prop his ashram up. No wonder the roads are pitted with potholes and the beach is scattered with litter.

'What's up?' Meera asks.

I realize I've gone silent, lost in thought. Meera doesn't know I'm a tax lawyer. I simply told her I had a City job in London, and she didn't ask any questions. I have an overwhelming urge to read up on Indian tax law and understand this situation. I need to figure out whether what Guru Hridaya is allegedly doing is legal.

'Nothing, I'm fine,' I insist. 'Is there a library here?'

'Err, yeah,' Meera replies.

She reaches for a pamphlet on the table and opens it up, showing me a map. She points to where the library is.

'Cool!' I reply. 'Thanks. I'm just going to go there for a bit.'

'Okay…' Meera shrugs. 'See you later.'

'See you!'

I hop back on my scooter and head to the library for an afternoon spent reading about Indian tax law.

17 CHAPTER SEVENTEEN

A couple of days have passed and I've managed to get my head around the basics of Indian tax law, having spent hours researching in the library.

It turns out you can use Wi-Fi in the library for as long as you want as long as it's for educational purposes so I've scrolled endlessly, reading articles on Indian case law, while catching up with people back home on Facebook in the background. The library is the quietest place in the ashram that I've found so far, even quieter than the meditation spots. Hardly anyone goes there. There are just a couple of regulars, who seem to be dedicating their time at the ashram to reading, but it's mostly empty and very peaceful. The building the library is housed in is striking, with a tall domed ceiling and towering shelves.

As well as reading up on Indian case law, I've been researching the guru thoroughly and I'm pretty sure he's breaking the law by not paying tax. I'm confident he could be prosecuted but I'm not entirely sure what to do with the information. Yes, my company could technically take action against him, but is a London law firm really going to file a lawsuit against a guru in India? Hardly. Who would pay them? If the locals were going to pay a firm to sue Guru Hridaya, they would have done it by now. It seems that, like Meera said, there really is a dynamic of 'you mind your business and I'll mind mine' between the local people and Guru Hridaya and his followers. The attitude they adopt is almost like an Indian head wobble - they don't really approve but they don't disapprove strongly enough to do anything about it, they just let it go. Also, suing a multimillionaire con artist of a guru would no doubt be an expensive and stressful endeavor and I doubt many of the locals around here, who are mostly small business owners, have the resources or time to take that on.

I sent my boss an email yesterday explaining everything, just in case Pearson & Co is interested. I know my firm is probably going to think I'm a bit sad, unable to stop focusing on tax law for more than a week but this case is about more than me being a workaholic, it's about helping the local community. I may not have gelled particularly well with the hippyish side of ashram life, but I've found a way to connect with this place in my own right, and I want to help if I can.

I wasn't sure how Nigel would respond to my email. Would he write it off as nonsense? After all, suing a guru does sound out-there, but he replied this afternoon suggesting we catch up. He said he wanted to 'discuss my email', but left it at that. For all I know, he's going to give me stern orders to stop reading about tax law while on holiday or perhaps, just perhaps, he is interested in the case.

I borrowed a spare mobile from Meera for the call. She's been totally excited about the case, ever since I told her that I specialize in tax. I check the bars of reception as I pace back and forth in front of the library, my palms clammy with sweat. Nigel's meant to call any minute now. I stare at the screen and when it finally starts ringing, I feel a jolt of alarm and excitement. I'm nervous. As I answer, I realize I haven't been this invested in a case for a long time.

'Hello,' I say, picking up.

'Rachel, hi,' Nigel answers. 'Are you there? How are you?'

'Yes, I'm here. I'm good!' I reply. 'How are you?'

'Oh, I'm well. All's good over here. How's the ashram then?' Nigel asks, sounding tickled.

Ever since I told him that I was going to stay in an ashram in India, he's found the idea hilarious, and his amusement clearly hasn't waned.

'It's good, actually!' I tell him. 'I like it more than I thought I would, although I haven't really got on board with the spiritual stuff.'.

'No, it sounds like you've been more interested in the local tax litigation,' Nigel laughs.

'Haha, yes!' I admit, feeling a little embarrassed.

I can't tell if Nigel thinks I'm a ridiculous workaholic loser who needs to learn to take a day off or if he finds my interest in foreign tax law somewhat admirable.

'Well you know, you can take the girl out of the legal world, but you can't take the legal world out of the girl!' I babble, laughing nervously.

'Ha! Have you been enjoying yourself though aside from reading up on case law?' Nigel asks.

I think about the spirit animal workshop and Spiritual Ascension Snakes and Ladders. Nigel already finds the concept of the ashram ridiculous enough, I'm definitely not going to be mentioning those things. They'd blow his mind.

'Yeah, it's lovely! The weather is beautiful, the scenery is stunning, the people are interesting,' I tell him, gazing down the path towards lush palm trees as I speak, thinking of Meera and Seb.

'Wonderful!' Nigel comments. 'I can't wait to see your pictures.'

'Oh yeah, I'll show you when I'm back at work. Or I'll add some to Facebook soon,' I insist, remembering that Nigel and I are technically Facebook friends after he added me following a team-bonding trip to Center Parcs.

'Great! I'll keep an eye out. So…' Nigel draws in a deep breath and I can tell that the small talk part of our conversation is over. 'I've been looking into what you sent me.'

He pauses.

'Yes,' I gulp.

'It's an interesting case,' Nigel says. 'Very interesting.'

Interesting? Very interesting?

I grin. This is good. This is very good! I've worked with Nigel for long enough to know that he doesn't describe a case as "interesting" if he's not interested in pursuing it.

'I'm not going to lie, Rachel, your email certainly took me by surprise, but funnily enough I think this case could be quite a good thing for the firm,' Nigel continues

A good thing? Not just interesting but a good thing! Wow.

'Right, okay, great!' I reply, eager to hear more.

'You may have noticed that a few weeks ago, Mr Pearson visited the company,' Nigel says.

I cringe, remembering the incident in the hall with Mr Pearson commenting that my jacket was on inside out.

'Yes, I remember,' I reply.

'He came in to discuss the image of the company. As you know, we've been focusing on corporate cases in recent years, pursuing the highest paying wins over supporting clients who may not have such deep pockets,' Nigel says, lowering his voice a little, as though his admission is a shameful secret he doesn't really want to acknowledge.

'We've needed to focus on money for the sake of the firm and all its employees, times have been tough and in a difficult economic climate, you have to follow your business interests,' Nigel says.

I get the feeling he's rehearsed this defense. Perhaps he's said the same thing at some point to Mr Pearson.

'But while protecting the interests of the firm is of course important, it's also important to give back. Not just to make a positive contribution, but for the sake of our public image,' Nigel continues.

I picture him sitting at his desk, winding the cord of his phone between his fingers the way he does when he's taking an important call, concentrating, and choosing his words wisely. Nigel's a pretty suave person. He wears custom-designed bespoke suits that cost thousands of pounds. He goes skiing twice a year and has a VIP membership to the Royal Opera House. I've never once heard him talk about 'making a positive contribution' or helping people in need. He's a great lawyer, but Nigel is all about pursuing the maximum amount of profit possible. He's part of the reason I've put in such long hours over the past few years. He creates a working environment that's all about making the maximum return, and if I'm reading this right, it sounds like maybe he's taken the pursuit of profit too far. Perhaps Mr Pearson has put his foot down.

'Our competitors have been engaging in quite a lot of pro bono work, whereas, as you'll know, we haven't been focusing on that side of the business for a while,' Nigel comments.

I can't help smiling as I imagine him squirming, twisting his phone cord, hating to admit how corporate and money-hungry he is.

'Yes…' I reply, wondering where exactly he's going with this.

'It's not like neglecting pro bono work was a deliberate move or anything like that, we've just had so much demand from our corporate clients and unfortunately pro bono cases weren't top priority,' Nigel says, clearly feeling a little defensive.

'No, I understand,' I insist.

'Anyway, unfortunately, Mr Pearson believes it's beginning to affect our public image. He came to see me to discuss the issue, stressing that we needed to take on a more diverse range of cases in order to show that the firm cares about people and real life issues as well as its commercial interests,' Nigel explains.

'Oh right,' I reply, relieved that I finally know what Mr Pearson's visit was about.

'He asked me to look into pro bono cases and get back to him with a few proposals, and then I got your email and I thought it seemed like the perfect opportunity!' Nigel enthuses.

My ears prick up. Oh my God! Nigel wants to take on my case! It makes total sense that he'd be at a complete loss when it comes to finding clients that aren't deep-pocketed multi-national corporations. Supporting a community in southern India to uphold its local tax laws must have struck Nigel as an ideal way to reshape the firm's public image.

'Mr Pearson and I have discussed it, and we think your case could make a real splash in the press. It could inject a bit of life into our brand,' Nigel says.

I feel my heart swelling with triumph. Of course, Nigel isn't particularly bothered about the plight of the local people over here and is more interested in the firm's image, but who cares? What matters is that he sounds like he wants to take on the case! That's the most important thing.

'We think it would be a good idea if you partner with a local firm over there in India. Find the evidence you need and build your case. You can come back here and work remotely or, and I don't know if this is something you're considering, but perhaps you could extend your trip and stay for a while, build your case on the ground?' Nigel suggests.

Stay? I've been investigating this case for hours on end and yet weirdly, I haven't given much thought to potentially staying here to fight it. I didn't want to get carried away. Could it take a few more weeks to build the case? Probably not. I'd probably be looking at a few months at least. Maybe even longer. I gulp. I kind of knew, deep down, that staying her for a while was what I was potentially signing up for, but I didn't let myself consider it, as I assumed Nigel would laugh at my email and hit 'delete'. I hadn't dared contemplate sticking around.

'I'll have to think about it,' I tell Nigel. 'Are you really serious about this? The firm definitely wants me to take on this case?' I ask, still unable to quite wrap my head around it.

'Yes, we do,' Nigel insists. 'Obviously, there are still some areas to explore – which firm you'll be working with locally, whether you'll be needing support from a paralegal here, contracts, that kind of thing, but we're serious about this.'

'Wow, this is great!' I enthuse.

'The PR team won't stop talking about it! They're keen to make a big splash!' Nigel laughs.

'I bet!' I reply, thinking of the PR team, several of whom are frustrated aspiring novelists, who would no doubt love to get their teeth stuck into a story about a corrupt guru in southern India. It would definitely make a welcome change to all the dry press releases we put out about corporate cases.

'Look, why don't you give it some thought over the weekend and get back to me on Monday?' Nigel proposes.

'Sounds good,' I reply, as I spot Paul, walking towards me.

He stops and lingers outside the library, peering at an information stand.

'Okay, well let's catch up on Monday. Same time?' Nigel suggests.

'Yep, same time. That would be great,' I enthuse, although I still feel distracted by Paul.

I can feel him listening in on my call.

'Excellent, speak soon,' Nigel says. 'And good work!'

'Thanks Nigel!' I reply. 'Speak to you on Monday.

I say goodbye and hang up.

'Seriously?' Paul balks as I take a deep breath, still reeling from the call.

'Sorry, what?' I look over at him, properly taking him in.

He's still wearing the white ashram robes, with his hair bound into those awful stubby dreadlocks. A few of his dreadlocks have even been adorned with ribbons and beads. Blossom probably threaded them on. He looks ridiculous and for the first time in years, I feel no desire whatsoever when I look at him. In fact, I feel a slight sense of revulsion. Despite being in India, Paul looks pasty and puffy-faced and totally unattractive.

'You're here in India and you're still talking to Nigel?' Paul scoffs.

I roll my eyes. 'Why don't you just mind your own business?'

'You can't stop working for five minutes, can you?' Paul sneers.

I look him up and down and feel a surge of anger. I step towards him and look him straight in the eye.

'Do you know what, Paul? I really, genuinely, don't care what you think of me anymore. You broke up with me. You made your point. So why the hell do you feel the need to put me down? Get over yourself,' I spit.

I don't bother waiting for a reaction. I turn around and march back to the library.

I have a case to prepare.

18 CHAPTER EIGHTEEN

I know it's Saturday and I should probably take a day off from reading about tax law but I get a notification on the phone I borrowed from Meera that a book I ordered from the library has arrived and I can't resist going to collect it.

I take it out and bring it back to the guesthouse, with the intention of lying in a hammock and leafing through it, but when I get back, I see Seb, skipping with a rope on the lawn.

'Hey stranger!' he says, grinning as he spots me.

'Hey!' I reply, feeling secretly very pleased to see him.

I've been so busy burrowing away in the library for the past few days that mine and Seb's paths have barely crossed. I wanted to give him space as well. After our talk the other day, I figured time for reflection was probably what he needed, rather than having me around, flirting with him.

'How's it going!?' Seb asks.

I sit down on the lawn next to him and place my library book by my side.

'Not bad,' I reply. 'Really good, actually. I've been doing a lot of reading.'

'Yeah,' Seb lets his skipping rope drop and glances towards my book. 'I noticed!'

I laugh, feeling a little embarrassed at the title of my book: *The Tax System in India: Evolution and Present Structure*.

'Just can't help myself!' I joke.

Seb laughs and sits down on the grass next to me, wiping the sweat from his forehead with the back of his hand. Even sweaty and panting slightly, he looks hot.

'Meera told me about the case. I think what you're doing is really cool,' he comments, smiling at me.

I feel a swell of pride in spite of myself. I know that tax law isn't cool, but I can tell Seb's compliment is sincere and it's nice that, unlike Paul, he doesn't think I'm a total drag who can't stop working. It's nice that he gets it.

'Thanks, Seb,' I reply.

'I knew there was something sparky about you,' Seb muses, as though he's almost making the observation to himself.

'What do you mean?' I ask.

Seb turns to me. 'Well you know how some people get when they come here. They just get swept along with the herd, following the guru, getting competitive over yoga and all that rubbish.'

I think of Paul and Blossom and nod. 'Yeah, I know what you mean.'

'As much as I love meditating, you haven't really done that either,' Seb comments.

I smile awkwardly.

'I don't mean that in a bad way. I mean it in a good way. You've found your own way to grow and contribute to this place. I don't know many people who come to an ashram and become experts in Indian tax law! You're unique. You're special,' Seb remarks, meeting my gaze.

His eyes are shimmering blue as ever and I feel a jolt of electricity. His words are so kind, so sweet and so complimentary, that I feel myself blushing ever-so-slightly.

'Wow, thanks Seb!' I gush, still looking into his eyes.

I should look away, but he's not and I can feel a pull between us. There's such a connection, it's so obvious. And yet, his vow… I can't forget that. I look away.

'That's really sweet of you,' I add, feeling genuinely touched.

There's something so effortlessly honest and real about Seb. He doesn't bother with small talk and doesn't care about trying to say the right thing or trying to impress. That's why his compliments are so moving and mean something. That, and the fact that I find him irresistibly appealing.

'You're welcome!' Seb says, flopping back on the grass.

He gazes up at the cloudless sky.

I lie back on the grass next to him, admiring the endless sky, although despite its bright beauty, my thoughts wander to Paul. The stark difference between Seb's encouragement and Paul's mean bullying comments yesterday is hard to ignore.

'You know, not everyone has your opinion. I know I shouldn't care but I ran into Paul yesterday and he was being so rude, saying how I can't leave work alone. He was really sneering,' I admit.

'Ignore him,' Seb scoffs. 'He's probably just bitter that Blossom dumped him. He's probably lashing out.'

'Blossom dumped him?' I balk, feeling a jolt inside.

I prop myself up on my elbow, turning to Seb.

Seb's eyes widen. 'Didn't you know?'

'What? No. I've been in the library for the past three days,' I remind him.

'Oh right, yeah, sorry. I thought you might have heard from Meera or something,' Seb comments.

'What happened?' I ask, leaning closer, eager to hear the full story.

I know it's wrong, but I can't help feeling ever so slightly smug. Paul has been such an arse to me ever since I arrived in this place that it's quite satisfying to hear that he's been knocked off his perch.

'Blossom dumped him. In the middle of a meditation session the other day. They had this big fight and she stormed off, telling him she found him "capitalistic and uninspiring".'

I snort with laughter.

Seb smirks.

'It was really dramatic. Paul looked like he might cry,' Seb tells me.

'Oh God, that's brilliant!' I laugh wickedly. 'I can't believe he looked like he was going to cry.'

'His face went all red and blotchy,' Seb recalls.

I picture Paul with a red and blotchy face. That's exactly the look he gets whenever he's about to burst into tears.

Seb grins. 'Rumor has it that Blossom got back with her ex that evening. Paul had been staying with her, but she just kicked him out and left his bags on the porch. She won't even acknowledge him now.'

'Oh my God! How come you know all this?' I ask.

'I heard from a guy I know at the gym. He runs one of the other guesthouses. Paul came round looking for a place to stay. Apparently, he was really cut up. He even inquired with Meera to see if there was a room here,' Seb says.

'Here?' I echo, in horror.

'Yeah, that's why I assumed you'd have heard, I thought Meera would have said something, but maybe she was trying to be tactful and didn't want to mention Paul to you,' Seb suggests.

'Maybe,' I comment. 'Or maybe she didn't want to distract me from the case.'

'Yeah, possibly,' Seb replies, shrugging.

I think back to yesterday and seeing Paul looking so pale and puffy-faced. It makes sense now. He was clearly feeling down on his luck because he'd just been dumped. And yet, I feel no sympathy. It's so typical of him that the first thing he'd do after being dumped is take shots at me. I realize, finally, that I really am over him. I feel nothing for him. Nothing but pity.

'So where's Paul now?' I ask.

'I'm not sure, but someone said he's staying in a hotel in town. The Marriott,' Seb tells me.

I snort with laughter again. So much for his spiritual quest! He's been booted out by a hippy girl and ended up at an international chain hotel.

'Oh my God!' I chuckle. 'I know I shouldn't laugh, but I can't help it!'

Seb laughs with me, although, despite how amusing I'm finding this whole thing, I'm slightly worried that Seb might think I'm cruel, relishing so much in the suffering of my downtrodden ex.

'Sorry, it's just Paul was so rude to me yesterday. I'm just glad he's got his karma after being such a...' I pause, searching for the right word, something that isn't an expletive.

'A dick. Paul's a massive dick,' Seb proffers.

I grin, wickedly. 'Exactly. He's a dick!'

I lie back down on the grass, gazing ruminatively up at the blue sky. To think, I wanted to marry somebody like Paul – someone so mean, with such terrible communication skills. It may have been on my Life List to get married by thirty but what's marriage worth anyway if it's to somebody like that? Getting married at thirty isn't an achievement if you end up stuck with the wrong person for the rest of your life. It's worth waiting around for another couple of years, or however long it takes, to find the right guy.

'So, do you want to go for dinner?' Seb asks.

'Sure,' I reply, the thought of crashing waves and roadside parathas springing to mind.

Seb goes to have a shower and to kill time while he's getting ready, I decide to make a bit of an effort. I wash my face and plait my hair. Priya was right, bringing hair straighteners to an ashram was a ridiculous idea. As if I could use them in my treehouse! I put some make-up on. It's been over a week since I've worn make-up. I never thought I'd go without make-up either, but Priya was right about that too. And yet, tonight, I feel like wearing it. I'm not going all out like I did the first night I got here when I saw Paul in the main hall. I must have been nervous that evening. The blue eyeshadow and bright pink lipstick probably were a bit much. I feel more like my usual self now and apply my everyday make-up – a bit of foundation, eyeliner flicks, mascara, a hint of blusher and tinted lip balm.

I root around in my suitcase and find a flowing, floral chiffon top that I haven't got around to wearing yet. I bought it because I thought it was suitably boho for an ashram, and yet it's a bit too dressy for standard ashram life. It's a bit too dressy for roadside parathas too, but I feel like wearing it, nonetheless. I take off my t-shirt and put it on. It looks a bit odd with the leggings I've got on so I pull on a pair of jeans instead that I also haven't got around to wearing since I got here. I feel almost like my London self, in the dressy top and jeans, with my usual make-up on. The only differences are my hair being in a loose wispy plait over my shoulder and my boho bag full of rupees. I put on my Prada wedges, which contrary to Priya's opinions, have served me well so far, despite growing a little dusty.

I climb down from my treehouse, feeling a lightness inside and a sense of excitement and adventure that's been missing from my life for ages. I find Meera sitting at the picnic table, flicking through a magazine. We have a chat, catching up on the case as we've been doing most evenings since I began looking into things. I consider mentioning Paul and I'm just about to say something, when Seb walks over, looking fresh and totally gorgeous. He's clearly made an effort too, swapping his usual loose vests and shorts for a shirt and trousers.

Meera's eyes light up.

'Are you two going out?' she asks, with a mischievous smile.

'Just to your uncle's place,' I reply, trying to act casual, as though this isn't a date.

I mean, of course it isn't a date. We're just going to a casual place for a casual meal. Seb's taken a vow of celibacy. It's definitely not a date. And yet, he's dressed up and I've dressed up…

'Do you want to come?' I ask Meera.

'Oh no, no, I'm busy,' Meera insists, smiling conspiratorially at me.

I try to ignore her suggestiveness, but I can't help smiling back at her, feeling quite grateful that she declined my invitation. As much as I like Meera, and I really do, I want to be alone with Seb tonight. I want to talk to him, one to one, like we did last time we were at the paratha place.

'I was just about to head in for the night anyway. You guys have fun,' Meera says, folding her magazine and getting up.

'Have a good night, Meera,' Seb says.

'And you guys,' Meera replies, giving us both a cheeky smile, which we awkwardly pretend not to acknowledge.

I pick up my bag from the picnic table and sling it over my shoulder.

'You look great, by the way,' Seb tells me, once Meera is out of earshot.

I realize he's looking at me in an almost enamored way, as though he's genuinely impressed. He's clearly gotten used to seeing me looking super casual and make-up free.

'Thanks!' I reply. 'You look pretty good yourself.'

'Thank you!' Seb smiles.

'Let's go,' I say as I get up from the picnic table.

We head out of the guesthouse. The sky has a burnt coppery tinge to it as the sun sets and the air is pleasantly cool and breezy.

We catch up properly on the past few days as we walk out of the ashram. Seb tells me how he's been busy meditating and working out and admits that he gave in to using the internet and caught up with family and friends back home, draining the data on his dongle. I recount the spirit animal workshop and he howls with laughter, especially when I fill him in on Blossom mauling me while getting in touch with her inner tiger.

Seb describes a book he's reading about the power of our subconscious mind as we walk along the seaside road. The sound of the waves is hypnotic, and I feel totally relaxed and content as we reach the paratha place. I've barely eaten today, aside from a quick sandwich I made in the guesthouse and gobbled outside the library earlier, and the smell of the freshly-cooked parathas, the chopped coriander and fragrant spices of the curries, combined with the salty sea air, is delicious, making my stomach rumble.

Meera's uncle, Ishaan, greets us like old friends, showing us to a table. Within minutes, he brings over bowls of curry and paratha. The curries cost less than a pound and yet they're so incredibly tasty, the flavors fresh and fragrant. Both Seb and I relish each bite, so distracted by the food that we barely speak apart from to compliment it.

'God, I love this place,' I say at one point, taking in the ambient vibes around us.

The restaurant has the same relaxed convivial atmosphere it had when Seb and I first came here. Everyone seems so relaxed and content. I think it's partly down to the amazing food and the gentle sea breeze, but it's also thanks to Ishaan, who clearly loves cooking and creating a sense of community for the people who come to his restaurant. He reminds me slightly of the guy who once ran La Dolce Vita – he has the same love of food and of making people feel happy and at home.

The sun sets and the sky takes on a velvety darkness. The moon is full, making the ocean glow silver. Occasionally, the sea breeze blows tendrils of my hair across my face. I tuck them behind my ear, while continuing to enjoy my meal.

'I love it here too,' Seb comments, looking across from the sea to me, holding my gaze.

His eyelashes cast spidery shadows across his cheeks, illuminated from above by a lamp.

I realize his knee is brushing against mine again. The electricity and connection between us is so unsettling, so tempting, and so undeniable. I smile shyly at him, feeling a blush creeping onto my cheeks, painfully aware of his skin against mine. I'm a thirty-year-old woman, I should be able to handle having someone's knee touch mine, and yet it's making me all kinds of flustered and awkward and uncomfortable. I edge my knee away and look back down at my curry.

'This is so good!' I enthuse, taking another bite.

A smile twitches at the corner of Seb's lips. He's clearly aware of the effect he has on me.

We finish our curries and stay for a cup of chai, continuing the conversation we were having before about Seb's book. Ishaan comes over and we chat to him for a bit, before heading back to the ashram. We walk back, the waves crashing, and it hits me that I feel perfectly content. Perfectly, perfectly content. I want to reach across to Seb and take his hand, but I can't quite bring myself to. I don't want to disrespect his vow. If anyone makes the first move between us, it should be him.

By the time we get back to the ashram, it's gone 10pm and the sky is pitch black. Normally, the ashram would be deadly still at this time, with everyone heading to bed, but as we pass the temple, I hear a peal of laughter and the sound of people splashing around in the nearby pool.

'What's going on?' I ask, my ears pricking up as I hear voices.

I can hear people talking, loud laughter, more splashing. It sounds like some kind of pool party.

'What's going on?' I ask Seb once more.

'Oh God,' he groans, lowering his head into his hands and drawing to a halt along the path.

'What is it?' I turn to him, confused.

We're just around the corner from the pool and I'm dying to have a look to see what all the commotion is about. Are people having a late-night swimming session? Is there some sort of workshop taking place? But if that's the case, why's Seb cringing? What's up with him?

'Come on!' I urge him. 'I've been meaning to check out the pool. Is there a workshop on or something?'

I walk further along the path.

'No, Rachel!' Seb rushes after me.

He grabs my arm.

'It's not a workshop,' he says.

His cheeks look a little flushed. He looks desperately uncomfortable, squirming almost.

'What is it then? It can't be that bad!' I point out.

'It's…' Seb ventures, before trailing off.

I carry on heading towards the pool and Seb's grasp falls away.

As I approach, the laughter grows louder. There are other sounds too, almost like moaning or groaning. I raise an eyebrow at Seb, to see him grimacing.

As we reach the entrance and I peer towards the pool, I freeze, in shock, unable to believe what I'm seeing: dozens upon dozens of writhing naked hippies in all kinds of contortions. Girls kissing girls on sun loungers. Couples fornicating in corners by the pool. A group engaging in all kinds of sexual and penetrative acts on a picnic blanket on the grass. Threesomes and foursomes and fivesomes and even a couple of solitary masturbators hanging out at the sidelines just enjoying the view. *What is this?*

I turn to Seb, eyes wide, speechless.

'I told you it wasn't a swimming event,' he comments, pulling a face.

'You didn't tell me it was an ORGY!' I point out, shielding my face with my hands, cowering.

'Sorry,' Seb replies.

I peer through my fingers at the fornication in front of me, unable to quite believe how full-on this group sex session is. There must be fifty to sixty people taking part, from all ages, from lithe twenty-year-olds to wrinkly grey men of sixty years old. Clearly anything goes here. A woman who looks about twenty-five is gyrating in the corner of the pool with an older guy who looks mid-fifties. Two middle-aged women are engaged in a threesome with an athletic young guy with dreadlocks. And two pretty women, who look around my age are kissing and frolicking in the pool, which accounts for the splashing noises I heard on the way here.

There are so many people kissing and caressing and writhing and touching and cuddling. And even though it's a shocking sight to take in, it's also weirdly erotic. It's making me reassess the ashram. I thought this place was just full of sanctimonious hippies - weirdos who go around channeling their inner sparrows. I didn't realize people here were into late night orgies. I didn't realize they actually had fun. I thought they were all uptight and boring but now I feel like the boring one. I can barely even look at what they're doing, let alone contemplate partaking.

'They hold these orgies once or twice a month,' Seb explains. 'I forgot all about it or otherwise I'd have suggested a different route home. Or suggested we stay at the guesthouse!'

I laugh. 'No, I'm kind of glad I got to see this!' I say, glancing away from the sight of one man's weirdly gigantic penis.

'They don't call them orgies though,' Seb muses, gazing unfazed at all the people having sex in front of us.

'What do they call them then?' I ask, genuinely curious, since I have absolutely no idea what this is if it isn't an orgy.

'I think they see the term "orgy" as a bit crude or too on the nose,' Seb comments, frowning slightly.

'So what do they call them?' I balk.

'They call them yoni yoga, since "yoni" is Sanskrit for vagina,' Seb tells me, his lips twitching. 'They sometimes call it priapic meditation, too.'

I snort with laughter. 'Are you actually kidding me?'

Seb laughs, shaking his head. 'No!'

'Oh my God!' I wheeze, unable to stop laughing.

I grab Seb's arm for support and flick tears from my eyes.

'I know!' Seb grins. 'I couldn't believe it either! When I first heard people talking about yoni yoga, I assumed it was some kind of pelvic floor exercise group. I didn't realize it was… *this*!'

He gestures towards the orgy.

'I would never have imagined this!' I insist, still laughing.

'It's crazy. I came to this ashram thinking it would be a place of purity and spirituality. I thought I'd be able to clear my mind and abstain from sex, but then a few weeks in, I discovered they have orgies and I realized that pretty much everyone here is horny and sex-obsessed,' Seb comments.

'Oh my God!' I utter, still in shock.

I look out over the sea of bodies again. Even though I can't quite get over the fact that these people refer to a mass orgy as yoni yoga and priapic meditation, I can't deny that there is something entrancing about what they're doing. Everyone is so unselfconscious and unapologetic. They're just enjoying each other, at the most primal and intimate level. Although it still feels a bit cringe-worthy to witness, like I'm watching a live porn show, there is something quite beautiful and almost joyful about it.

For the first time since I've been here, I feel uptight, disappointed in myself and unenlightened, because unlike all the people before me, I can't see myself ever partaking in something like this.

'So did you manage to resist?' I ask Seb.

'Resist?' he echoes.

'Did you manage to resist, or did you give in and try a bit of yoni yoga and priapic meditation?' I tease.

'Oh, I've tried yoni yoga, alright,' Seb remarks, giving me a wink.

Just the reality of him mentioning sex makes me feel a little hot and bothered, warm in my nether regions.

'Haha!' I laugh a little nervously.

'But not in this kind of situation,' Seb adds, nodding towards the orgy.

I look back at the sea of bodies. The man with the gigantic penis is now inserting it into a woman on a sun lounger. I flick my eyes away, feeling like a voyeur.

'Maybe we should go?' I suggest. 'I feel like a bit of a creep watching everyone!'

'Yeah, we probably should,' Seb agrees.

He places his hand on my lower back as we turn to walk away. The sensation of his touch is acute and momentarily drowns out all thoughts of the orgy, but as we walk back down the path, his hand drops away. Maybe he didn't mean to put it there? Maybe he placed it there almost involuntarily and then felt awkward?

I glance over at him, but he looks lost in thought, his expression unreadable.

'I can't believe I just witnessed an orgy!' I say, still in shock.

'Yep, anything goes around here!' Seb replies.

We chat about the orgy a little bit, cracking jokes, as we walk back to the guesthouse, and yet weirdly, underneath all the humor, I can't help feeling aroused. The hippies may not be the Brad Pitts or Kate Mosses of the world but there was something erotic about the sex scenes regardless.

Seb and I lapse into silence, the sounds of the orgy so far away now that it's inaudible. I find myself wondering if Seb's having similar thoughts. Was he turned on by the orgy too?

I want to say something – something – and yet my mind is blank. The only sound is the sound of the breeze rustling through the trees and our footsteps.

Suddenly, Seb stops in the middle of the path. He turns to me.

I stop and look at him, questioningly. His eyes have an intensity about them that I haven't seen before. He looks serious, a little awkward.

'What's up? I ask.

He takes a step closer and places his hand on my hip. He strokes the side of my face with his other hand and gazes into my eyes. I feel like everything's gone into slow motion. Is this really happening?

'I need to kiss you,' Seb insists, his eyes alight with passion.

We spring together like magnets, locking into one another, his soft lips on mine, mine on his. He kisses me softly, sensually. But as the shock of finally kissing passes, our embrace suddenly becomes hungry, ravenous, insatiable. We grasp at each other. It's like the build-up of weeks of tension has finally erupted and we can't get enough of one another. I let my hands roam over his back, pulling him close, feeling his warm body against mine. I feel dizzy with lust as he kisses me. He's the best kisser.

I want him. I want him right here, right now. I want him up against one of the trees. I don't even care. I want to feel him inside me.

'Oh my God,' I moan, melting under his touch.

'I've wanted this so much,' Seb gasps. 'So much.'

I can feel his desire, his eager kisses, his warm body, his searching hands.

He wants this as much as I do. He wants me. He wants me so badly and that makes me want him even more. I want to tear his clothes off. I want to break his vow. I want to have him.

'Me too,' I sigh, kissing him, slipping my hand under his shirt, feeling his silky soft skin.

He kisses me deeply, his tongue plunging into my mouth. He traces his fingers under my top.

'We should go back to the guesthouse,' I insist, feeling light-headed with desire.

As much as I want Seb, we're getting precariously close to having sex in the middle of a path, and even though this place is definitely more kinky than I thought, I still don't want to get kicked out for public indecency.

'Ok let's go,' Seb replies, while planting kisses on my neck.

It takes a lot of effort to pull apart, but we manage it, hurrying back to the guesthouse.

We clamber up to Seb's treehouse. I don't dare look around to see if Meera is still up. I can't face her 'I told you so' look right now.

We tumble into Seb's treehouse, and pull each other close, our bodies tangling. I start unbuttoning his shirt and he pulls my top off.

'Your body's incredible,' he murmurs.

He reaches behind my back to unfasten my bra and pulls it from my shoulders.

'Oh my God, you look amazing,' he sighs, as he kisses my neck, working down to my chest.

I haven't even managed to unbutton his shirt yet, but I lose my grip of his buttons as he plants kisses on my chest, working his way over my breasts. He takes one of my nipples into his mouth and sucks gently, flicking his tongue over it.

I moan, feeling light-headed, dizzy with pleasure.

'Oh God,' I groan.

I can barely believe this is happening. Seb and I are finally hooking up. My whole body feels tantalized, alive with longing and lust. I thought sex with Paul was good, but I already feel more pleasure from Seb touching and kissing my breasts than I've felt from entire sex sessions with Paul.

I want to feel Seb kissing me all over. I want to unbutton his shirt, do naughty things to him, and yet, something's holding me back. A nagging thought pulls me out of the moment: the girl, Vanessa. The abortion. Seb's vow. As much as I want to use Seb's body as a jungle gym, I don't want to sabotage his growth either. I don't want to be another mistake, like the fling he had in Thailand – an encounter he'll later regret.

'Seb,' I gasp, pulling him away from my chest.

'What?' he asks, gazing lustfully at me.

It takes every ounce of my self-control not to just kiss him.

'Are you sure about this? What about your pledge?' I say. 'I want you, so badly, but I don't want to mess things up for you.'

Seb smiles.

'It's fine,' he assures me. 'I've given up my pledge. It's over.'

'How come?' I ask, totally shocked.

'I spoke to Vanessa. We chatted on Facebook the other day. I was going to tell you. She's pregnant. She's found a new boyfriend. They've moved in together. She seems really happy, like she's ready to settle down,' Seb says. 'They've even started doing up the spare room for the kid. She said how the time feels right now and she's found the one. Everything's worked out for her. She doesn't have depression anymore.'

Seb smiles, and I can feel the relief radiating from him. He seems lighter, carefree.

'I'm ready to move on too. I don't care about my pledge anymore,' Seb insists.

I grin, feeling an immense wave of relief. We can have sex. Guilt-free, glorious sex, with nothing holding us back.

'I'm so glad!' I kiss him, pulling him close.

19 CHAPTER NINETEEN

I lie in Seb's arms as the birds chirp and the sun rises, rays of light filtering into his treehouse.

He kisses my forehead.

'Morning, you,' he says.

'Morning,' I reply, smiling and moving closer into his embrace.

It's been a couple of days now since we first got together, and they've been blissful. We've barely been out of each other's sight. We've meditated together (I did better this time), visited the beach and swum in the sea, and we've taken bike rides in the ashram's lush surroundings, cycling through forests and along the shore. And we've taken part in quite a few indoor activities too...

Meera is of course delighted to have been right about us, and for there to be another romance at the guesthouse. Seb and I have been in a loved-up bubble all weekend, unable to get enough of each other, but it's Monday now and I should really crack on with my case. I'm speaking to Nigel later and I know what I'm going to say. I'm staying! I'm going to stay in India and sue a guru! I might have to leave the ashram to avoid running into Guru Hridaya, but I won't go too far away. I'll still be near the same beach, near the same paratha place and not too far from Seb.

'I'm going to make some coffee,' I tell him, extricating myself from his embrace and throwing on a T-shirt and shorts.

Seb mumbles something sleepy and incoherent as I slip out of the treehouse and make my way down the ladder.

The morning air smells cool and fresh. I turn to head to the kitchen when I spot none other than Paul, sitting at one of the picnic tables, staring at his feet, a faraway expression on his face.

'Paul,' I utter.

He looks up, his face lighting up.

'Rachel!' He stands up. 'Hi! How are you doing?' he asks, a little breathlessly.

I eye him warily. He looks more like his old self. His dreadlocks are gone. In fact, he's had a haircut and his hair is neater and shorter than it's been in years. He's wearing jeans and his favorite bobbly navy shirt, the one he wore to La Dolce Vita all those weeks ago. No ashram robes in sight. He's clean-shaven now too, although he still looks a little tired and pasty. His eyes have a slightly manic, skittish look about them.

'What are you doing here?' I ask, instinctively backing away a few steps.

Only last week, Paul was getting at me for being a workaholic and now here he is.

'I need to talk to you,' he insists.

I eye him warily and wander into the kitchen. I don't really want to talk to him, but he follows me.

'What is it?' I grumble.

'I just… I wanted to say…' he stammers.

I grab a pan from the washing up rack and fill it with water from the tap.

'You wanted to say what?'

'I wanted to say I'm sorry,' Paul comments.

I glance over at him. He leans against the counter.

'I'm sorry I was a dick the other day. I'm sorry about Blossom, and coming here, and leaving you, and…' he sighs. 'I'm just sorry about everything.'

He fixes me with a contrite, imploring look.

I place my pan on the hob and light the ring. I turn to him as the flames lick the pan. I realize, looking at him, that I feel nothing anymore. For so long, I thought Paul was the one, but was he really the one, or was I just obsessed with sticking to my Life List?

'It's okay, Paul. You did what you had to do. Hopefully you feel better about everything now,' I comment as the water begins to boil.

'I was so lost,' Paul says.

I look through the kitchen window, glancing towards Seb's treehouse, wishing I was up there with him, but I turn to Paul and nod understandingly.

'I know. I'm sorry I came here, trying to win you back. I should have given you space,' I admit.

'No,' Paul protests. 'I'm glad you came. You were right. I don't know what I was thinking. We had a good life together and I ran from it. I panicked, but I know what I want now. I want to be together. I want to get things back on track.' Paul smiles tenderly.

I gawp at him. 'You want to get back together?'

'Yes! I'm sorry for everything, Rachel. I wish I'd never doubted us,' Paul insists, looking contrite.

'I can't believe this,' I scoff. 'You want to get back together! Two days ago, you were living with Blossom, and now she's dumped you and you want to be with me. Honestly, Paul, I don't think you know what you want.'

'I do. Blossom was a mistake. I want to be with you,' Paul insists.

He comes closer and places his hands on my hips, nuzzling the back of my neck as I watch my water boil, like he used to when I'd cook in our kitchen back home.

'Paul!' I shriek, recoiling. 'Get off me!'

I slap his hands away, feeing anger flood through me. The cheek of him, to assume he can just walk back into my life and decide he wants me, is galling.

'I'm not interested, Paul,' I spit. 'I'm not.'

Paul frowns, looking genuinely shocked.

'What? But you were so keen before. You wanted to get married?' he protests.

I laugh, finding him ridiculous.

'I did, but I don't anymore. Not to you,' I tell him.

'But you've always wanted to get married,' Paul reminds me. 'You've always wanted to settle down. That's what you've always wanted.'

His words sting a little. During all those years I was pining for him to propose, he clearly knew how much getting married and settling down meant to me, and yet he didn't take action. He had his chance, but the moment's gone. I may be falling way behind on my Life List, but the difference is, I don't care anymore.

'I've changed. I'm not desperate to get married anymore. If it happens, great, but I'm not going to pine for it,' I tell him. 'I'm just going to, you know, go with the flow.'

Paul raises an eyebrow.

'Go with the flow?' he echoes.

'Yes!' I insist.

'Okay…' Paul frowns, looking baffled.

I take my water off the boil and retrieve two mugs from the cupboard. I spoon coffee into them. All I want is to have my coffee and get on with my day. I don't want to be having this conversation, and yet I owe it to Paul, in spite of everything. We were together for six years, even if he has been pretty horrible to me lately.

I finish making the coffees and turn to him.

'Look Paul, a few days ago you were getting at me. You hate my obsession with home furnishings. I bore you. I made you really unhappy. Getting back together isn't the right thing to do.'

'But…' Paul mumbles.

'You can't just go from Blossom to me. You need to figure out who you are and what you want. That's why you came here to India after all,' I remind him.

'Blossom was a mistake. I know what I want now. I want you. I want our life back,' Paul claims.

I roll my eyes.

'It's over, Paul,' I tell him.

I explain how I've changed since I've been here and how I no longer want the things I thought I wanted. I tell him about my legal case and that I'm sticking around.

'Wow, okay…' Paul remarks, frowning at the floor as he takes it in. 'What about the house?'

'What about it?' I reply. 'You can stay there if you want for now. I suppose we'll have to sell.'

Paul shakes his head in disbelief.

'But you love the house. We've spent years on it,' he points out.

'I know, but there's more to life than interior décor,' I comment.

'I've been trying to tell you that for a while,' Paul teases.

We exchange a knowing smile that reminds me, fleetingly, of the closeness we used to have. Yet the closeness has gone now. It occurs to me that Paul still doesn't know the root of my obsession with home furnishings. He doesn't know about the lasting impacts of the homelessness I endured as a teenager and he probably never will. It's not worth going into it now. Paul and I are over. I never felt like I could share my feelings with him, and that's the point.

We touch on a few practicalities about the house and the future – a future in which we're no longer together.

'I still can't believe this. I can't believe you're staying here,' Paul remarks.

'I know. India's changed me,' I admit, looking out over the lush grass of the garden, the palm trees, hammocks slung between them.

Raja, the peacock, emerges from between the trees, striding proudly across the lawn, his feathers on full show. I can't help smiling.

'I guess it has,' Paul observes.

We say goodbye, and Paul tentatively offers a hug.

We embrace.

'See you, Paul. Have a safe trip home,' I say, as we pull apart.

'See you, Rachel,' Paul replies, still looking wide-eyed and taken aback.

I imagine it will take a while for everything to sink in.

He turns to leave, and I wave through the kitchen window, watching as he walks away. He turns out of the guesthouse and retreats from sight.

I take a sip of my coffee, feeling relieved. Paul wasn't the right one for me. He was the wrong guy at the right time, or what I thought was the right time. For so long, I've lived my life according to goals, ticking off objectives on a timeline. I've been so obsessed with keeping up with the people around me, settling down, getting married by a certain age, and achieving a fixed idea of success, that I didn't stop to consider whether I was truly happy. Or whether the person I was with was right for me.

The truth is that life is random, and the right people can come along in the most unexpected places at the most unanticipated times. I pick up the mugs of coffee and head out of the kitchen, back to Seb. I don't know what the future holds. I don't know if he's the one. I don't know if we'll be together this time next month, let alone long-term. I don't even know how long I'll be in India.

But what I do know is that I'm finding myself now, at my own pace, in a beautiful place. I'm taking each day as it comes and I'm smiling. And that's the most important thing.

Zoe May has written four other romantic comedies, published by HarperCollins, including *Perfect Match* (2018), *How (Not) To Date a Prince* (2018), *When Polly Met Olly* (2019), and *As Luck Would Have It* (2018). In her spare time, Zoe likes walking her dog, reading and painting.

Zoe's website is www.zoemayauthor.co.uk
To subscribe to Zoe's newsletter, visit www.zoemayauthor.co.uk/newsletter
You can follow her on Twitter and Instagram @zoe_writes

Printed in Great Britain
by Amazon